PAGEANT

PAGEANT DUET BOOK ONE

LILITH VINCENT

One woman. Three mafia men. A twisted marriage game...

The dangerous life I escaped has seized hold of me again. Three men have snatched my freedom and they're playing a twisted game of power, hearts, and blood.

My captors glitter like diamonds in the dark, each one more handsome and ruthless than the last. Konstantin, the scarred and heartless ringleader, and mastermind of my fate. Elyah, the demon from my past who once craved me and now covets my demise. Kirill, a bloodthirsty maniac with depraved needs who thrives on misery and mayhem.

Sixteen women are forced to compete in their twisted pageant, and one by one we're eliminated until there's only one jewel left. My captors' desire burns as hard as their cruelty, but the true torment only begins when the pageant ends.

Heavy is the crown that glitters on the winner's head.

Author's note: Pageant (Pageant, 1) is the first book in a mafia reverse harem duet and ends on a cliffhanger. The heroes only have hearts, eyes, and dicks for the heroine. It contains captive themes, violence, and a Why Choose romance with ruthlessly possessive men. The story is dark and potentially triggering, so please read responsibly.

PAGEANT: A MAFIA REVERSE HAREM ROMANCE (PAGEANT, 1) by LILITH VINCENT

Copyright © 2022 Lilith Vincent

| All Rights Reserved |

Cover design by Untold Designs
Editing by Fox Proof Editing
Proofreading by Rumi Khan

No part of this book may be used or reproduced in any manner whatsoever without written permission from the publisher, except brief quotations for reviews. Thank you for respecting the author's work.

This book is a work of fiction. All characters, places, incidents, and dialogue are drawn from the author's imagination and are not to be construed as real. Any similarities between persons living or dead are purely coincidental.

❦ Created with Vellum

A NOTE TO READERS

If you've read my previous series, *Promised in Blood*, please be aware that *Pageant* is darker and more violent. The men are crueler, and the light at the end of the tunnel is further away.

If you're new to the dark romance genre or certain dark themes or situations have a negative impact on your well-being, proceed with caution. This book contains scenes of a violent and sexual nature that some readers may find upsetting, disturbing, or triggering. Women are kept in cages and there's blood soaking many of the chapters. There's gun play, somnophilia, forced orgasms and mild torture. Additionally, the heroine suffers a miscarriage in Chapter Four.

This is a reverse harem romance. There are group scenes with the heroine and all the heroes, and she never has to choose just one. The heroes only have hearts, eyes, and dicks for the heroine. There is no cheating or sex outside the harem.

Still reading? Straighten your sash, put your lipstick on, and smile for the judges. The pageant is about to begin.

PLAYLIST

I needed sexy Russian voices in my ears while I was writing this book, and I love indie, electro, and hip hop. Here's a selection of my favorite tracks that I can imagine Elyah playing in his car and Kirill listening to through earbuds as he walks around town at night with his hood up. Konstantin doesn't listen to music. He prefers silence.

Link to playlist: https://spoti.fi/2ZSLeni

Пушка – 10AGE
Розовое вино – Eldzhey, FEDUK
ТАЙМАУТ – Nikitata
Я хочу – Grivina
Cocktails & Dreams – Otnicka
Не твой – Max Korzh
Положение – Scriptonite
Close Eyes – DVRST
Стеклянная – Guma
Без тебя я не я – HammAli & Navai, JONY

Сон – Ramil
Милая – 10AGE
No Cry – Luxor
Точка – Klava Koka
Капли – VERBEE
Просто открой – FEDUK
Нету интереса – 10AGE
SODA (RUDENNI Remix) – Eldzhey, RUDENNI, VACÍO
Антидепрессанты – Eldzhey
Bre Petrunko – FanEOne
Mango – Mr Lambo
Пополам – BRANYA, MACAN
Полет (Sowyol Remix) – Индия, SOWYOL
Зоопарк – 10AGE
Положение (Chicagoo Remix) – Dior, Chicagoo

1

Konstantin

Lake Como, Italy

A high-pitched scream shatters the afternoon serenity. It echoes up from the cellar, ricochets off the long, marble corridors, and pierces my skull. My head feels like it's about to explode.

Pinching my throbbing brow, I growl, "That fucking woman. I'll rip her to pieces before the pageant even begins."

The preparations for this event have taken me months, from finding the perfect place to the perfect women. The villa is private and secluded. The sixteen women locked in my cellar are glittering treasures. I won't allow one stupid little bitch to upset everything I've worked so hard to arrange.

The woman screams again, the sound filled with indignation and rage.

Kirill rolls his muscular shoulders and stands up. "Allow

me, Kostya. It will be a lesson for the others." His dark eyes gleam with perverse delight. He's as excited as a child at Christmas for the pageant to begin.

I glance at Elyah, the only one who hasn't heard the scream because he's staring out the window at the ornate Italian garden, sunk in blood-soaked fantasies. I can see them flickering behind his eyes like the koi fish in the lake beyond the window.

I slowly crack one knuckle after the next on my right hand. Among other things, this week is meant to bring Elyah peace and focus, but betrayal still burns too fiercely in his heart for anything to pierce it.

A moment later, Elyah rises to his feet smoothly. "I'll do it."

I smile to myself. Or maybe this is working.

The three of us stride down the long, marble corridors with their high ceilings and ornately carved columns. Outside, heavy golden sunlight beats down, causing heat to ripple above the winding garden paths. Swallows skim over the lawn. Below, the water of Lake Como laps against the verdant cliffs, the sound of the waves carry up to us on the afternoon breeze.

This place is paradise on earth, but for the sixteen young women locked in cages in the cellar, it's a living hell, and I am the gatekeeper.

We pass through a locked gate and head down a set of stone steps into chilly darkness. Down here, the air is damp and scented with fear. Through another locked gate, there's a cellar room containing a row of sixteen cells, six feet square with iron bars. Each one has a beauty huddled within, and all of them cringe away from us.

All but one.

She flings herself against the bars and screams, "*Let me out, let me out, let me out!*"

I unlock the cell, drag her from her cage by her hair, and twist her face savagely up to mine. "Little jewels are meant to be quiet."

"I'll fucking kill you, you Russian fuck! Don't you know who I am?"

"Who are you?"

"Asshole!" she shrieks. "I'm the daughter of—"

Pain stabs through my skull. I draw back my hand and slap her across the face. Hard. She sprawls across the damp concrete and comes to rest at Elyah's feet. He stares down at her, disgust etched into his chiseled, cold features.

"Does that feel like I care who you are, you *glupaya suka*?" I ask her. *Stupid bitch*. "Here, you don't have a family. You don't have a name. You are Number Eleven. You are obedient. Unless you are asked to speak, you are *silent*."

The woman's eyes nearly bug out of her head. "My father is going to kill you. He'll kill you all! He's in the Cosa Nostra. He eats assholes like you for breakfast."

Her whining, nasal voice goes right through me. Maybe she's a Sicilian mafia bitch, and maybe she's not. That threat might put the fear of God into Italians.

But we're not Italian.

We're Russian.

I don't care if her father is the president of Italy.

"Breakfast?" Kirill says in a soft hiss. "Tomorrow morning will be too late for you." He speaks as if to a child who has asked for a bedtime story. Hunkering down on his heels, he caresses her cheek. "Will Papa save you as you scream for mercy? Does Papa even know where you are? Does anyone?"

Hatred twists Elyah's mouth, and visions of this woman's demise dance in his eyes. *This pageant is for me, but it's for these men, too. I want a wife to take back to Russia with me, the most precious jewel I can find. She will be beautiful. Obedient. Self-possessed. She must have a heart as hard as titanium and nerves that can withstand the danger that perpetually circles me. My world is drenched in blood, violence, and money. Identifying the perfect woman from among these sixteen will be performed through a series of tests, just as a diamond or sapphire is tested to determine its value. Meanwhile, Kirill and Elyah, my two most trusted friends, are here to enjoy themselves. They're more than capable of testing women in the way I want them tested.*

Kirill glances at Elyah, a cruel smile curving his lips. "Let me teach this one."

Our friend shrugs and steps back. *Be my guest.*

I turn to the cages and address the women. "Are all of you paying attention? This is a lesson you will want to learn only once."

Kirill's expression suffuses with wicked malice, and the Italian's wails die in her throat. Before the pageant has even begun, she's failed. He grabs a chain that's dangling overhead, wrapping it around the woman's wrists and winching her up off her feet. Her legs kick back and forth as Kirill tears her dress apart down her back.

"No! Let me down." Her screams have increased to a fever pitch.

He picks up a leather switch from the far side of the room and tests it against his palm. "There can only be one winner," he explains to the women in the cages, "which means there will be fifteen losers. You can lose and keep your life, or you can lose like *this*."

He draws back his arm and cracks the switch viciously over the Italian's flesh. She screams in agony. It feels like someone is hammering red-hot nails into my skull. I want to reach up and rub the scar tissue at my temple, but I make myself stand as still as stone.

Kirill whips her again, putting the whole strength of his body into the stroke, his teeth grit, and eyes alight with manic pleasure.

And again.

And again.

Blood flows freely down the woman's back and spatters onto the floor. Half the women are watching the brutal spectacle with horrified, staring eyes. The other half have their faces buried in their thin bedclothes, fingers in their ears, and shoulders shaking with sobs.

Her screams ricochet off the walls and make my headache pound harder than ever. I need fucking *silence*. I pull out my gun, aim it at the Italian's head, and shoot. Her screams are abruptly curtailed.

I let out a slow breath. Peace reigns. The pressure in my skull ebbs away.

Kirill swipes at his blood-spattered face with his forearm. Then he yanks on the chains and the woman tumbles to the ground. "I don't think Papa's coming."

Elyah still seems on edge as I holster my gun. I wave my arm at the women. "We won't begin until tomorrow, but there's no reason you can't sample one of the contestants now. Choose one."

He walks down the room and stops in front of the cage that contains a woman with dark gold hair. His eyes narrow in hatred. She crushes herself into the corner of the cell, but it's too late.

He's seen her.

He unlocks her cage, points at the ground in front of his feet. Eyes dancing with visions of the Italian's death, she scrambles to do what he says, and then sits there, shaking.

Elyah snaps his fingers in her face. "Are you stupid? Are you just going to cry and scream like the other one?"

She jumps at the sound of his voice.

"Sniveling *suka*." *Bitch*. He grasps the waistband of his pants and savagely jerks down his fly. "Don't just sit there. Suck it."

The woman cringes away from him but reaches up with shaking hands to do as she's told. I lean back against the wall to watch. I doubt this woman is what I'm looking for, but perhaps she's tougher than she looks. I'm willing to give her a chance at being my wife.

Elyah doesn't want a wife. Elyah wants to torture an unsuspecting woman until she begs for mercy, which he'll deny over and over again. All the while despising her for her tears, her fear, her crying. The man doesn't know the meaning of mercy. Neither does Kirill, though he delights in the tears that Elyah loathes.

The women might not see it yet, but there's a purpose to all of this. I want a woman as flawless as a diamond, one forged in the crucible of searing heat and high pressure. A woman who will never crack or show signs of weakness. That's why I chose models for this game. Models are fiercely competitive, stunningly beautiful, and possess cutthroat ambition. Before the age of twenty, runway models learn to smile through the pain.

That's my theory, anyway. Maybe my plan won't work and all I'll have left at the end of the week is a pile of bleeding corpses. If that's the case, I can do this all over again with another group of women. And again, and again, until I find the one I want.

Impatience surges through Elyah's muscles. He grips the blonde's chin and forces her face toward his pants. "Fucking *do it*."

The woman fumbles with his clothing. Anger suddenly fills Elyah's expression as he fists the blonde's hair and inspects it closely. "Is this bleached?"

"Yes," she whispers.

"You fake, worthless whore." He plants a foot on her chest and shoves her back into her cage. She huddles in the corner as the door slams closed. Elyah turns the key in the lock and fastens his pants.

Kirill is hunkered down by the dead Italian, fascinated by her blood trickling over the concrete. "Now we're short by one woman."

Elyah strides past us to the door and takes the stairs two at a time. "Who cares? They are all the fucking same."

I care. Everything must be perfect. This villa, the execution of the tasks, the crowning of the ultimate winner. I want sixteen women. If it's not done right, then I don't want to do it at all.

Kirill and I exchange glances as Elyah's angry footsteps fade away.

"I'll go hunting," he offers, and gestures at the women in the cages. "There are plenty more where these came from."

Kirill has already snatched sixteen women from the streets of Milan. American women. Brazilian women. French women. British women. The friendless ones who wander the streets late at night, easy prey to a man who dwells in the shadows. Every September, beautiful women pour into Milan from all over the world. They walk the runways of fashion week by the hundreds, all with ambition burning in their hearts. Hungry to be looked at, desired, adored.

I'm giving them exactly what they want. "Do it."

We head back up into the fresh air and out through the front door of the villa. There's a circular gravel driveway around an enormous marble fountain. Beyond are the high gates to the villa, the only way in or out that's not over the cliffs.

"I'm worried about Elyah," I tell Kirill.

He glances at the house and then back at me. "Once we begin, he will forget about her. He will forget about everything that came before."

Perhaps Kirill is right. With sixteen playthings to torment and no one to interrupt us, what red-blooded man wouldn't enjoy himself?

I take an appreciative lungful of the evening air as Kirill gets into his black Ferrari. "Good hunting, my friend."

2

Lilia

In between swipes of the makeup artist's brush, I grab a can of sparkling water. There are about fifty people in the backstage area, and even this late at night, the Italian summer heat is stifling. Hairdryers are blowing, models pose for selfies, and assistants run to and fro with armloads of dresses. The show producer is shouting at the top of her lungs, and as we get closer to the top of the hour, her voice becomes shriller.

I pull the ring tab on the can, and my acrylic nail snaps.

"*Blyat*," I mutter. *Shit*. There's no time to get it fixed before heading down the catwalk. I'll just have to hope everyone's too captivated by the vivid crimson evening gown I'm wearing to notice my nail.

The brunette model next to me turns in my direction with

shining eyes and a delighted, incomprehensible sentence drops from her lips. I blink at her in confusion.

The woman's smile fades, and she asks in heavily accented English, "You don't speak Russian?" She has the high cheekbones and full lips of someone from Eastern or Central Europe. My own features are similar, though my hair is dark blonde.

I smile and shake my head. "Sorry, no. Just a few swear words I picked up from my father. Dad's Russian, but I was born in America. Are you Russian?"

She shakes her head. "Kazakh. This is my first big show. What is your name?"

"Li—" I start to say but stop myself. Even after eighteen months, calling myself Lilia is a lifetime habit I'm having trouble breaking. "Yulia."

"I am Ayna."

She can't be much more than seventeen. I've encountered dozens of women like her since I started modeling, village girls discovered by determined scouts, plucked from the Caucasus and Kazakhstan and sent down the catwalks of Paris, New York, and London.

Ayna reaches for a piece of sushi from a nearby platter and pops it into her mouth. "I love this," she says, grinning, pointing at her mouth as she chews.

All around us, the other women are ignoring the food like they exist on air alone. Our bodies are our livelihood, and we're constantly comparing ourselves to each other. Whose thighs are thinner? Whose breasts are perkier, skin more luminous, legs longer? Who will book the next show, and who is already getting past it at the ancient age of twenty-three?

Ayna seems oblivious to the unwritten rule, that even though we're surrounded by food and free champagne, none of it should pass our lips, at least not when anyone else is looking. I smile and take a piece of sushi for myself. She's right, it's delicious. The makeup artist powdering my cheeks shoots me a look of reproach. I'm twenty, not seventeen. I should know better.

While we wait for the call that the late-night show is about to begin, Ayna tells me about her village and how much she misses her parents, all the while nibbling on pieces of sushi. I listen and talk to her, struggling through my exhaustion. The designer thought it would add mystery and flair to host this show at midnight. Let us sleep, for God's sake.

Suddenly the show producer, a strident woman in her fifties with a lanyard around her neck, is standing in front of us, her nostrils flaring as she stares at Ayna.

"Are you *eating*?"

Ayna jumps guiltily, and sushi rice goes tumbling down the front of her evening gown. She shoves the rest of the piece back onto the platter and then stands there with her head down and fingers tangled together.

"Are you eating in your fucking dress for the show? That dress is worth more than you are," the producer snarls at her.

Every head backstage turns to stare at Ayna.

The woman jabs Ayna in the belly. "How much did you eat? Look at you, you fat cow. I can see your stomach. You think I can send you down the runway looking like that? Go and throw it all up." The producer points toward the bathroom.

Around us, several women laugh behind their hands and

exchange scandalized glances. It's not like I've never heard women throwing up in the bathrooms at shows, but it's obscene for a producer to actually tell a model to do it.

"Wh—what?" Ayna stammers.

The producer mimes shoving two fingers down her throat. "*Throw. Up.* Stupid fucking girl. Which inbred village were you dragged from?"

Ayna moves toward the bathrooms, her face flaming, but I grab her arm.

"Stay there." I turn to the producer. "Ayna's not going to make herself sick on purpose. She looks beautiful, and you're being a bully."

The producer scours me from the roots of my hair to the pointed stilettos on my feet. Her gaze fastens on my broken nail, and her face suffuses with savage delight. "You're even worse. How dare you come here with broken nails! Both of you, get out. You're fired, and I'll be telling your agencies about this."

"I broke my nail on your stupid cans of water," I tell her, pointing at the drink sitting in front of the mirror. "Why aren't there cups and glasses that we can actually use while wearing these ridiculous nails?"

"How dare you talk back to me!" She starts to shout for security, and half a dozen men in black T-shirts weave through the models to get to us.

I unzip the back of my dress and let it fall to the floor, kicking off my high heels as well. Standing in a nude thong and nothing else, I tell her, "I'm leaving. But let Ayna stay. She didn't do anything wrong."

Behind me, Ayna starts to sob as an assistant forcibly removes her from her dress. I can't bear the sight of her trying to cover her nakedness in front of dozens of hostile eyes, so I grab her T-shirt and jeans and help her into them.

"Your clothes," she whispers thickly, smearing makeup and tears across her cheeks.

I mutter that I don't care. After eighteen months of this, I'm used to standing around in nothing, or almost nothing.

You want strange men to stare at your body? Are you a slut who craves to be stared at? No daughter of mine is going to be a model. You're getting married, and I have already chosen your husband.

Dad's voice rings through my head, almost as brutal now as it was when I was seventeen. I pull on my shorts and an oversized T-shirt, slide into my sneakers, and grab my bag. Looping my arm through Ayna's, I whisper to her to hold her chin up, and march her out via the back entrance.

When we're standing on the street, I turn to her. "Don't be afraid to stand up for yourself. The producers will walk all over you if you let them. Remember that they need you, and if you're hungry, eat. There's nothing wrong with that."

"They did not think so," Ayna points out, wiping her eyes. "And they do not need us. They threw us out."

My mouth closes. She's not wrong there. "I guess we had bad luck. There'll be other shows."

Ayna pulls out of my grip, her eyes sparking with anger. "You should not have..." Words fail her and she gestures angrily around her head. *Butted in.* "I would have thrown up, and then I would have still been in the show."

She bursts into sobs, muttering words like "money," "mistake," and "my agent," punctuated by angry Russian. I can guess what she's upset about. Ayna's parents will be relying on the money she's sending them, and if she's fired, her failure will be her family's shame. At such a young, unproven age, she's worried her agency will drop her. Hell, even after dozens of shows I might be fired if that producer screams long and loud enough on the phone. I've already disappointed my family in every way possible, so I don't have to worry about that, but I desperately need this money, too.

Feeling hollow, I watch Ayna hurry away from me, still crying. This was my last show in Milan, and tomorrow I'm boarding a flight back to the United States. I'm booked for Paris Fashion Week next month, but nothing after that. At nearly twenty-one, I'm edging toward being over the hill, and I have no idea what comes next.

The alleyway I'm standing in is dark and smelly, so I head up the street toward the main road. What does a twenty-year-old Russian mafia widow do with her life when she has no education and her only skill is walking in heels? With the little money I've made, I suppose I could enroll in community college and get a part-time job. What would I be good at? Accountancy? Hospitality? Maybe I could work in hotels. I'm good at smiling and pretending that everything's fine. I've had so much practice.

The back of my neck prickles. It's a sensation I want to ignore, but my father taught me to pay attention to the cues my body gives me. *Trust your instincts*, he likes to say, tapping his nose, *and you won't end up with a knife in your back*.

I turn around and look down the alley. If there's someone skulking there, I want them to know I'm not the kind of woman to walk faster and pretend that everything's fine.

I'm not prey.

"Who's there?"

Nothing moves. Silence answers me.

"*Alo? Kto tam?*" I call in Russian. *Hello? Who is there?* None of my dead husband's friends have come after me so far, but that doesn't mean they won't.

"*Signore?*" I try, certain that there's masculine energy radiating out of the darkness. Perhaps a curious local has followed me. Or a dangerous one. Yesterday, I overheard two British models talking about their friend going missing, and that they knew of a German woman who never returned to her hotel. Women come and go during fashion week. Some meet husbands or sugar daddies, and others get fed up and go home. Some, like me and Ayna, are fired and slink away in shame. Probably no one's been abducted, but I still stare as hard as I can into the shadows, just in case.

Nothing moves. It must have been a cat slinking through the darkness. There's only a hundred feet between where I'm standing and a well-lit street. I turn and walk confidently with long strides, my ears pricked for any sound behind me. As I reach the main street and step into the light, I turn and take one last look down the alley.

No assassins. No Russian mafia. No lecherous locals. I guess I'm being paranoid. Is it paranoia, though, when there's a good chance that your dead husband's friends are waiting for the chance to slit your throat and silence you forever?

No one forgives. Especially not the Russian mafia.

But I'm in Milan, and both Russia and the Russian mafia in the United States are at a comfortable distance. I take a deep breath and let it out slowly.

"Lilia?" says a voice behind me.

I whirl around, panic spiking through me. I was so focused on the dark alley that I didn't check the main street. I turn and see, not a stalker or assassin, but a well-dressed, middle-aged couple. It's the woman who spoke, a chic dresser in her mid-forties with a dyed blonde bob, a short black dress, and heavy gold earrings. Her arm loops through her husband's, a graying man in a tuxedo.

The woman's eyes widen. "It *is* you. Lilia Kalashnik. What are you doing in Milan? Where have you been all this time?"

I recognize them. Alina and Leopold Lugovskaya, friends of my father's. They were at my wedding to Ivan Kalashnik, but so were five hundred other people. Blood thunders in my ears. I haven't come face to face with anyone from my old life since I fled my husband's home eighteen months ago.

My mind screams *danger*.

Run, and don't look back.

Pretend I don't know them.

Kill them.

I take a deep breath and smile brightly. "Mr. and Mrs. Lugovskaya. How are you? What a coincidence, running into you here. I'm working at Milan Fashion Week."

Mrs. Lugovskaya returns my smile, but it's hesitant. Mr. Lugovskaya is watching me with a heavy frown. These are my father's friends, so they have no reason to want me dead. All the same, they're Russian, so my nerves are screaming at me to run.

"Your father doesn't know where you are, Lilia," he tells me.

That's the idea. If he can't find me, he can't force me to marry anyone else.

"It was too hard to be in the States after what happened." I blink several times and let my eyes slide away from them, as if I'm overcome with sadness. The poor, grieving widow.

"It's wonderful to see you both." It's not. "I would love to stay and chat." I have nothing to say to either of you. "But I have a busy day tomorrow. Could I please ask you a favor before I say goodnight? Don't tell Dad you saw me. I need just a little more time to myself after what happened."

I don't have to spell it out to them. They will know about Ivan being gunned down in the street. I'm sure Dad gave them all the gory details.

The Lugovskayas exchange glances. Even though they feel for me, telling lies, even lies of omission, is lowly and dishonorable.

Mrs. Lugovskaya speaks first. "All right, Lilia, but first come have coffee with us. I feel responsible for you. If I left you here on the street and something happened to you, I'd never forgive myself."

I clench my fists. I'm a grown woman, not a child. "I don't—"

But Mr. Lugovskaya is already putting his hand on my back and propelling me forward. "Our apartment is just across the street."

I give in. If I don't go with them, within the hour they'll have called my father and told him where I am.

As we walk, a figure across the street catches my eye. A man is standing in an alcove, his hands deep in the pockets of his jacket with a hood over his head. Such a heavy jacket for a warm night like this. His attention flickers from me to the Lugovskayas and back again. Then he turns and walks away.

I feel cold all over. Someone *was* following me. Italian or Russian? Curious, or malevolent? I can't tell, but I'll book a cab to take me back to my hotel as soon as I've finished having coffee with the Lugovskayas.

We take the elevator upstairs. They've rented the entire

fourth floor of a majestic old building with soaring ceilings, cavernous rooms, and chic gold décor.

"How have you been, Lilia?" Mrs. Lugovskaya asks, setting down a tray on the low wooden table and pouring steaming coffee into tiny cups.

I perch on the leather sofa and drink my cup as fast as I can. "Fine, thank you. Work is keeping me busy."

"It was just terrible, the way your husband was killed," Mrs. Lugovskaya says. She trails off and glances at me expectantly. She wants the inside story about Ivan. I barely knew him, and he never felt like my husband. We were only married for eight months and then he was gone. There were two men I lost that day, and the one who causes me the most pain to remember isn't my husband.

"How is Yelena?" I ask. I seem to remember that they have a daughter called Yelena.

"*Da.* How is Yelena?" a rumbling, richly accented voice speaks behind me.

I whirl around. Out of the shadows steps a tall figure, dressed in black. Leather jacket. Black hoodie up over his head. I recognize him with a thump of fear as the man watching me in the street.

Slowly, he reaches up and draws back his hood. There are tattoos on his wrists and fingers, and for a moment I think it's—

Then he reveals his face. The man's eyes are dark and thickly outlined with lashes, in stark contrast to his pale skin and rosy lips. His jaw is smooth, and he has brown, almost black, curls falling over his forehead, the sides tightly shaved. He's young, just a few years older than me, but there's so much darkness in his eyes, as if he's lived through a hundred hellish lifetimes.

Mrs. Lugovskaya gasps and grabs her husband's arm. "Call the police."

Mr. Lugovskaya takes out his phone, but the stranger draws a gun from his pocket and fires. There's a muted *phht*, and the phone flies out of Mr. Lugovskaya's hand.

The man points the gun at him. Then at Mrs. Lugovskaya. Then at me. He's going to shoot us all. He's just trying to decide the order.

But then the man lowers the gun and squeezes the magazine release button, and the bullets tumble to the floor. He tosses the gun to the other side of the room and it goes skittering across the parquet floor. An assassin, and he's disarming himself.

Then he does something even more bizarre. He starts to undress.

He shrugs out of his jacket and tosses it over the sofa. Then he reaches behind his head and pulls off his T-shirt in one smooth motion, revealing a muscular torso covered in tattoos. Each one is inked in black and given space to breathe, and no two tattoos are touching one another.

A coiled snake.

The Virgin Mary cradling empty air.

A double-headed eagle with its wings spread.

A leaping tiger.

A skull with roses.

Barbed wire.

I suck in a shaky breath. I've seen tattoos just like them on the body of another Russian man. I've touched them, traced them in secret moments as if they were the keys to freedom. Keys to his heart.

Prison tattoos. Inked in despair. Inked in defiance. Inked with pride. He's showing them to the Lugovskayas because they mean something to them. The three of them know each other.

Even before I see the knife in his hand, I know we're all dead. He wasn't following me, after all. He was following the Lugovskayas, and I'm collateral damage.

He flashes a smile at me, a smile so cold that it turns the blood in my veins to ice. A smile that says he should be sorry that I've been caught up in this, but he's not. Then he turns away and advances on the Lugovskayas.

Mrs. Lugovskaya screams at the top of her lungs, a blood-curdling sound that shatters the night. The two of them are backing away, their mouths stretched wide in horror. The man follows them, taking slow, inexorable steps, the knife brandished in his fist. Inked across his muscular back, a Russian palace floats in the clouds, each tower topped with a decorative cupola.

Run. While he's not looking.

But the Lugovskayas. They don't deserve to die like this.

Panicking, I look around for a weapon. The magazine of bullets is lying on the floor. I edge closer to it around the sofa as quietly as I can, reaching down and snatching it up. They don't do me a lot of good. The gun is on the far side of the room behind the Lugovskayas, where I can't reach it.

Mr. Lugovskaya has his arms spread wide, protecting his wife. He glances over his shoulder toward the door into the master bedroom, and in that moment the assassin strikes. A vicious, downward stab that punches through flesh and bone. The man gasps in shock.

He's stabbed Mr. Lugovskaya six times before he's even fallen to the ground. He goes on stabbing him in the chest, throat, and face. Frenzied stabbing, full of hate. Blood gouts all over the place. I stand with my mouth open, sick, crunching noises filling my ears.

Mrs. Lugovskaya screams again and runs for the bedroom. The man gets up and goes after her, and I see the gun. I run over and snatch it up. It's a Makarov semi-automatic with a suppressor fixed to the barrel. A Russian handgun.

I've used this kind before.

Hope bursts through me. I can load the gun and shoot the assassin in the back before he can kill Mrs. Lugovskaya as well.

But as I fumble with the magazine, I realize I'm too late. The man has reached her. She screams, but the sound is cut short, and she makes a hideous gurgling noise, followed by the repeated *schhk, schhk* of his stabs.

Then silence.

I look up. The man stands framed in the doorway, blood dripping down his chest and face. Looking me dead in the eyes, he grasps the blade at the hilt and slowly draws it through his fingers, wiping off blood, and revealing clean, shining steel.

Then he points the blade at me.

Now you.

I stand up and back away, fumbling with the magazine with sweat-slicked fingers. Turning it around and around. If I could only stop for a moment and look at it, I could load the gun.

"Can you even use that, *neordinarnaya*?" The man's Russian accent is thick. He speaks in the same cold, gloating tone the assassins use in my nightmares. Then he laughs.

My terror is funny to him, and his ridicule sharpens my focus. I squeeze the magazine and realize by feel that it's the right way around and slam it into the gun.

Then I aim it at his head.

Two-handed grip.

Breathe out.

A split second before I fire, his eyes widen. It's the tiniest fraction of a moment, but I can see his surprise—*shock*—that I know what I'm doing, and I'm not going to hesitate, plead, question.

As if I want to ask this asshole any questions.

I pull the trigger, and he dives to the side. The gun kicks in my hand and the bullet pierces the plaster wall. Dismay plummets over me as I realize I've missed. The man is suddenly close enough to reach out and grab my ankle. His hand is closing in on me, quick as a snake. There's no time to re-aim and fire again.

I pivot on my heel and run.

When I reach the door I glance back, just in time to see him disappearing out the window.

Shit.

He wouldn't have jumped. We're four floors up and the fall would have gravely injured him. There must be a parapet, or he's clinging onto the carved stone and edging his way to another window. If I didn't know better, I'd hope that he was fleeing from the double murder, but there's no chance of that.

I've seen his face. Worse, I've seen his tattoos. You can read Russian prison tattoos like a book if you know what you're looking at. They identify him better than a set of fingerprints. He won't stop until I'm dead.

I walk quickly and quietly through the apartment, holding the gun at eye level and checking every corner before I proceed, ready to shoot anything that moves. I keep searching until I find the back stairs.

I pull the stairwell door open and listen. No voices. No footsteps. Didn't anyone hear Mrs. Lugovskaya screaming?

The stairs descend into deep shadows. I fumble for a switch, reluctant to plunge into darkness while there's a knife-wielding murderer on the loose.

A figure rushes out of the stairwell, both arms spread, and tackles me to the ground. I don't even have time to scream as I'm forced back into the apartment. I hit the wooden floor, and the gun flies out of my hand. I smell blood, and the stranger's skin is wet and slick. I hit and kick as hard as I can, but he's on top of me. I brace for the vicious stab of his knife, but it doesn't come.

Something slips around my neck and pulls tight.

My eyes bulge. I can't breathe. *I can't fucking breathe.*

The man pants in my ear. He holds the garrote with one hand while he searches his pocket for something else. I scrabble at the cord with my nails. Something sharp stabs me in the side of the neck.

The man lets go of the garrote. I sit up and half-turn toward him, my hand clamped to the side of my neck and my mouth open in horror. There's an injector pen in his hand. Light-headedness washes over me.

"What did you stick me with?" My tongue feels thick in

my mouth. My eyelids are heavy and there's a buzzing in the base of my skull. I try to gather my legs under me but they're weighted down and useless.

The man gathers me gently against his blood-streaked chest. He cradles me in his arms and presses his lips against my ear, and in his heavy accent, he says, "That was unexpected, *neordinarnaya*. None of the others put up such a fight."

My head spins and my whole body goes limp against his. What others?

Just before everything goes black, he whispers, "Welcome to the pageant."

3

Kirill

I went hunting for a dove, and I found two worms.

Leaving the blonde woman passed out on the floor, I go back to my two victims and survey their bodies. I shove Alina Lugovskaya's shoulder with my foot and she flops onto her back, her dead eyes staring at the ceiling.

I wish I could wake her up and kill her all over again. Her and her worthless fucking husband. The rage I held at bay while I was hunting the blonde woman through the apartment breaks over me. They should pay with more than death for what they did to me. I want their souls trapped forever so I can stab them, torture them, flay them into tiny pieces, burn them alive for all eternity.

I shove down the zipper on my jeans and take out my cock, pissing on the face of Alina Lugovskaya. A good long piss, all down her body to soak her clothes, and then up again.

I stare at the urine and blood dripping from her corpse, and then turn to her husband. His throat gapes in a crimson smile. I lift my foot and stomp on his neck, over and over again, until I hear the delightful crunch of his spine breaking.

It's something. But I'm still not satisfied. I'll never be satisfied.

I wander back to my little dove. There's a smear of blood on her pretty cheek and her T-shirt is daubed with more blood from struggling against me. Her legs are splayed, and my eyes drop to the apex of her thighs. Heat and desire roll through me, from the base of my cock up through my torso.

I glance around. There are no neighbors knocking on the front door. No sign of the police. The night is dark and the street outside is empty. I drop to my knees and reach for the waistband of her shorts.

"Let me look at you, pretty one," I breathe. "You just sleep."

I pull her zipper down and tug the shorts from her legs. Beneath them, all she's wearing is a nude thong. I can already tell that her pussy is shaved bare, and my mouth waters. Slowly, my thumb caresses her clit over her thong. Her breathing is soft and even, her lashes resting against her cheek. My fingers burrow a little and I grasp her clit and pinch it. I smile. Not even a flicker on her face.

In my pocket, my phone buzzes. I take it out and answer it, still staring at the woman. "What?"

"You've been gone for hours. Where are you?"

"Getting acquainted with our new Number Eleven."

Interest colors Konstantin's voice. "Oh? What is she like?"

I hang up, snap a photo of the woman's face, and send it to our group chat. A teaser of what I'm bringing for us. What a beauty she is, with her arched brows and slightly turned-up nose. I feel my way beneath her body and take a handful of her ass. Some of these models are all skin and bones down there, but Number Eleven is fleshy and warm, and I give her a squeeze.

The sight of her, unconscious and helpless, makes my dick hard. I groan at the thought of her waking up to discover me wedged tightly inside her. I reach for her thong, but before I can rip it off, my phone rings again.

Elyah. I cancel the call.

How long could I fuck her while she's like this before she woke up? What would she do if she opened her eyes and found me balls deep in her velvet pink pussy? I imagine her grabbing my shoulders in shock, and then I'd shoot my cum deep inside her before she could do anything to stop me.

Now I'm rock fucking hard. After three kills today, I need a release. My balls are aching, and Number Eleven is so perfect, warm, and helpless. I unzip, and my cock bursts out of my jeans, hard and eager.

I slide my hand around the woman's jaw and turn her face to mine. "Go on, fight me now. Try and shoot me in the head. You can't, can you?"

I pull her thong aside and spit on her pussy, letting it drop in a long, thin thread, and then rub it in with the tip of my cock. "Good girl," I purr, glancing up at her face. Her eyes are closed and her lips are parted. She has no idea what I'm about to do to her.

My phone rings again, and I cancel the call. "Fuck off, Elyah. I'll bring her when I'm ready to bring her."

I push Number Eleven's thighs open and wrap my hand around my length. My eyes are pinned to her face. Not a flicker. I've got hours before she starts to come out of it. Who'll discover me first, her or the cops? The apartment is full of death and blood, and I have the most beautiful doll at my mercy.

I play with her pussy, my swollen pink flesh rolling against hers. How good it would be to wait until she's almost coming around before I sink into her. There's a pinkish-brown birthmark on one of her outer lips, and I rub it with the head of my cock.

"*Neordinarnaya*, you won't let anyone take you away from me, will you?" *Extraordinary one. Not like the others.* How lucky she is. We don't want just any women. We only want the best. "Kostya will be so impressed when he hears how you fought me. He'll be aching to fuck you, but he'll want you with your eyes open and your—"

My phone rings again and I snatch it up with a growl. "Fucking *what*?"

"Where are you?" Elyah asks.

"About to get balls deep in Number Eleven."

"*Where the fuck are you?*"

"You can't come here. There are bodies everywhere."

"That woman. What's her name?"

I stick my hand up Number Eleven's T-shirt and palm her breast, rolling my thumb over her tight nipple. "You think I bothered to ask?"

Elyah snarls a string of expletives and I drop the phone from my ear. For fuck's sake. Resigning myself to whatever personal drama Elyah is going through, I zip up and get to my feet. The woman had a handbag, didn't she? I wander through the apartment until I find it next to the sofa. Inside is a passport.

Elyah is still swearing and ranting when I put the phone back to my ear. "Her name's Yulia Petrova."

"No, it is not."

"I'm looking at her passport right now."

"It is fake. It has to be."

I frown and tuck the phone against my shoulder. With both hands, I pass my fingers over the seams of the passport. Across the photograph of the blonde woman. Feels normal. Then I run my thumbnail along the edge of the front cover, and it slips between two pages. There's a page that shouldn't be there, and I peel it back to reveal an entirely different picture and name beneath Yulia Petrova's.

"Huh. It's fake. How did you know?"

"Bring her here."

"Who is she?"

"Bring. Her. Here." Elyah's voice is cold and menacing, and he hangs up.

My eyes narrow. Elyah never told me who the bitch was that betrayed him. It can't be this blonde, who I found talking to the Lugovskayas like they're old friends. His enemy and some of mine, together in Milan? It's too much of a coincidence.

I find my clothes and get dressed. The first Number Eleven was the Italian bitch who wouldn't stop screaming, and now Number Eleven is potentially Elyah's most hated enemy. I saunter back to the unconscious woman and gaze down at her. I thought I was hunting two worms and a dove. Perhaps it's two worms and a snake. If she is who Elyah thinks she is, I suppose I'll be out looking for a new Number

Eleven before the sun rises. Oh, well. Maybe he'll let me play with this one before he kills her. I pull her shorts back up her thighs and tug her T-shirt down. There's a black trench coat hanging in a closet by the front door, and I wrap her in it and haul her over my shoulder.

The back stairs are the quietest way out of the building. I pull up my hood and keep my head down as I carry her to my car. It's past one in the morning and I can hear distant traffic and voices as I buckle the woman into the passenger seat. With the coat wrapped around her and her cheek on the headrest, she looks like she's asleep.

It's a two-hour drive back to the villa at Lake Como. Number Eleven stirs only once as I take a sharp turn, her head rolling from the right side of the armrest to the left, her eyelashes fluttering.

As I roll through the gates of the villa, Elyah comes striding out the front door. Before I've even put the brakes on, he's torn open the passenger door, grabbed the black trench coat with both hands and pulled the woman's face into the light. She's pale, eyes closed, her beautiful neck arched and exposed.

Elyah steps back and pushes his hands through his hair. He groans and clenches his hands into fists. "It is her," he says in a voice raw with emotion. "It is fucking *her*."

Konstantin steps forward. "Are you sure?"

Elyah nods, his eyes wide, jaw tight. "I would know her anywhere."

"*Blyat*," I mutter. Of all the women here, I happened to snatch the one that Elyah hates most in the world. She walked into Milan, no doubt believing she was thousands of miles from danger. I get out of the car and walk around to stand with my two friends, all of us staring into the car at the unconscious woman.

I hold out my knife to Elyah. "I can get us another Number Eleven."

He looks at the weapon and then back at her. Her dark golden hair tumbles around her shoulders as she sleeps, no idea that we're discussing whether she goes on breathing.

Elyah takes a fistful of the woman's hair and wrenches her head back.

"You took me prisoner, Lilia Aranova," he seethes in her face. "Who is the prisoner now?"

4

Elyah

Two years earlier

Ivan Kalashnik puts a baseball bat in my hand and pats my cheek. "Welcome to America, kid."

I take a swing with the bat, propelling it hard through the air at an imaginary ball. It feels so good holding a weapon that I didn't fashion furtively from a toothbrush and conceal up my sleeve.

"Look at him, he's a natural," Ivan says, and the men around him laugh. Dima and Bogdan, his right-hand men. Vasily, a man my age who's as restless as a puppy. He bounces on his toes with excitement at what's to come.

I rest the bat on my shoulder, stick my other hand in my pocket, and reply in my thick accent, "Easy-peasy."

It's a phrase I picked up from the American flight attendant on the plane from Moscow. *Easy-peasy*. She smiled and said it every time I asked for a pillow or a cup of water. I think she sensed my nervousness asking for anything. It's been a long time since I've opened my mouth and wasn't immediately kicked in the teeth.

"We'll make an American of you yet."

"Not too American," I say, swinging the bat back and forth. "I do not like your fucking food." The men all laugh.

"After this, I'll take you home for dinner and you can try my wife's cooking. You won't taste as good in all of Moscow."

I can already picture Mrs. Kalashnik, a short, plump, bottle blonde with thick eyeliner and hot pink nails. She'll put plates of dumplings in front of me as she bemoans that I'm too skinny, all the while patting the muscles of my shoulders, my chest, and my back. I have aunts and second cousins just like her. They would pinch my cheeks and ask me how many hearts I have broken this week. Homesickness stabs through my chest.

"But first—work." Ivan nods to Vasily, who runs to fetch the prisoner.

Vasily drags a bound man out of the shadows of the cellar and throws him at my feet. He's been beaten and his nose and mouth are a mess of blood and pulpy flesh.

Ivan points a finger at the wretched figure cowering at our feet, his eyes gleaming with malice. "This man dared to make disgusting jokes about my wife. He dared to *touch* my wife."

"I didn't mean it, Ivan. I swear it," the man blubbers. He looks wildly around and his beseeching eyes land on me.

I don't care what he did. I'm not here to judge. I reach behind my head and pull my T-shirt and sweater off in one smooth motion and toss them aside. I don't want to arrive for dinner covered in blood. There's always a test when you join a new crew. Something you have to steal. Someone you have to kill. The men want to see how you operate. If you hesitate. If you hold back. I've never held back from anything in my life, and I never fucking hesitate.

The others stare at the tattoos covering my chest and arms. Figures and symbols inked into my flesh that tell the story of my life.

Thief. Killer. Prisoner. Too many years a prisoner.

The man at my feet sees the weapon in my hand and shakes in terror. I tap the bat under his chin. "Up."

I've never killed a man who's cowering at my feet and I'm not about to start now. He doesn't move, and so Vasily drags him up.

The man's terror spills into anger. "You bastard. You think this is a fair fight? You cock-sucking piece of—"

I grasp the baseball bat and swing it with full force at the man's head. His head snaps to one side. Teeth and blood explode from his mouth as he falls to his knees with a gurgling cry. I bring the bat down on his head again and again. Controlled swings, each one crushing a fresh piece of his skull.

After six blows, I stop and nudge the man with my shoe. He doesn't move.

The men are grinning at the mess I've made of their prisoner, and the blood spattering my chest and arms. Ivan picks up my T-shirt and sweater and throws them to me.

"Nice work. Hungry?"

"Starving," I reply with a grin.

Vasily tries to follow as we turn toward the door, but Ivan points at the body I just mangled. "Clean that up."

Vasily's face falls, but he doesn't complain as I pass the bloody bat to him with a shrug and pull my clothes on.

Out on the street, Ivan unlocks a big black SUV. He turns to us and holds up a finger. "Watch your mouths around my family, all of you. We were at the bar teaching Elyah about American football."

"Not baseball?" I ask.

Ivan chuckles and shakes his head like an affectionate uncle. He likes me, I can tell. I remind him of himself when he was young. "We've got a smartass here, everyone."

I roll my shoulders and get into his shiny black car. When we pull up to his house, I can't stop staring. We're in a leafy part of the city, and the houses are large and stand on spacious lots. Inside, the hall is huge and tiled with marble. Gilt mirrors hang on the walls and there's a chandelier overhead. A fucking chandelier, like this is the Kremlin.

Heels click over the tiles. I turn away from the décor and see the most beautiful woman I've ever laid eyes on walking toward me. She's tall for a woman, and slender, with a cascade of lustrous dark blonde hair over her shoulders. The clingy dress she's wearing shows off her incredible body. There's barely any makeup on her face, that I can see anyway. She must be Ivan's daughter. Who knew this ugly fucker could produce such a stunner.

"This is my wife, Lilia," Ivan says proudly, a possessive hand sliding around her waist.

That is his fucking *wife*?

"This is Elyah Morozov. He got into trouble back in the old country and he's starting fresh here. We've been teaching him about football. *Real* football, not that European shit."

I grit my teeth as a shadow passes over Lilia's expression. He could have stopped at *This is Elyah Morozov*.

"I am new driver," I say to her. Did I say that right? English is bloated with stupid, unnecessary words.

Her smile falters, and after saying an uncertain hello, she turns away from me to greet Dima and Bogdan and ask after their wives. I can't stop staring at her. Every new glance reveals more of her beauty, and my body, dead and boxed in for so long, suddenly feels alive.

You just killed a man for touching this woman. Lower your fucking eyes.

Ivan's children come downstairs, and I'm introduced to a bored twelve-year-old girl and a nine-year-old boy. Inessa and Alexei. I glance from the children to Lilia. Unless she started having children when she was six, they're definitely her stepchildren.

I follow everyone into the dining room, trying and failing not to stare at my boss's wife's ass in her tight dress. There's a sway to her hips that could make a grown man weep, especially a man who's spent the last four years in a Russian prison full of ugly, violent men.

At the dining table, the last place free is next to her. I sit down, hyperaware of my arm just an inch from hers. She's tanned golden and wears a diamond bracelet on her wrist, and there's an enormous diamond engagement ring next to her wedding band. Gone are my fantasies of motherly pats on the cheek as Mrs. Kalashnik insists that I have another helping of potato salad. In their place are visions of her slender fingers running along my jaw as I kiss her, then digging into my shoulders as I push her thighs wide with my knees, my cock jutting between us. The image of her naked body hits me with such force that I forget every word I know in English and mutter my thanks in Russian when she passes me the breadbasket.

Someone pours ice-cold vodka into a small glass in front of me and I knock it back. It burns my throat and tastes like home. All the food does, actually. Ivan wasn't wrong when he said his wife can cook. There's beetroot soup, pastries full of meat and potatoes, herring salad, and blinis with sour cream. It's warm in the house and I push up the sleeves of my black sweater and throw back another shot of vodka.

Lilia's gaze fastens on my forearm. There are drops of blood decorating the tattoos on my skin.

"How do you like American football?" she asks.

It's an innocent question, but there's a knowing expression in her sea-green eyes. I pull my sleeve down. "More violent than I thought."

"Is violence something you'll have to get used to here?"

If I pretend that I don't know what she's talking about and insist I am just a driver, she will not believe me. Ivan is fooling himself if he believes his beautiful young wife doesn't know exactly how he makes his money. I can't help the smile that spreads over my face. "Do not worry. I will be fine."

When the meal is over, Ivan and his wife escort me to the front door. Lilia is an inch taller than her heavyset, graying husband. He has his arm around her waist, and the sight of his fingers digging into her hip is getting on my nerves.

"Eight tomorrow morning, Elyah," Ivan tells me as we say goodbye.

"*Da, spasibo.*"

As I walk back to my car, I glance behind me at the house. A cozy setup he has here. Ivan seems fine, and while his men aren't the smartest I've worked with, they're all making plenty of money. I'm a free man; I have a job and a stomach full of good food and vodka. In the morning I might catch a glimpse of the delicious Mrs. Kalashnik, and perhaps I'll find a way to make her smile at me.

I already like America.

At five minutes to eight, I ring the Kalashniks' front doorbell. Today I've exchanged my sweater and jeans in favor of a black button-down shirt, black pants, and leather shoes. I was expecting one of the children to open the front door, but Lilia herself is standing on the other side, dressed in pale green pants and a white sleeveless blouse. There's a gold chain around her neck and her hair is pinned up with a few wispy tendrils around her face. She can't be much more than eighteen, but she dresses like she's trying to project an air of maturity. I suppose she has to when her husband's pushing fifty.

"*Dobroe utro*," I greet her, a smile tugging at the corner of my mouth. I can't help myself. The morning sun is burnishing her beautiful face, and suddenly I'm thrilled to be standing right where I am, on this doorstep.

Lilia looks at me blankly for a moment, and then understanding flickers in her eyes. "Oh, good morning. Sorry, your accent is thicker than what I'm used to."

"You speak *Russkiy*?" I ask, following her to the kitchen.

"No. My grandfather tried to teach me Russian when I was small, but I was more interested in my toys and helping my mother in the kitchen. Russia seemed very far away to me. I love the food, though."

A shame. I imagine her voice sounds beautiful when she's speaking Russian. "What is your father's name?"

Though she's Lilia Kalashnik in America, in Russia the only polite way to address this woman would be with her patronymic, a name derived from a feminine form of her father's name.

Besides, I dislike attaching her to her husband.

"Aran," she tells me.

"Lilia Aranova," I say softly. A pretty name that draws over the tongue like silk. Much prettier than her married name.

She turns to me in surprise, her chin tilting up to look me in the eyes. She might be tall, but at six-foot-three, I'm taller. "It sounds different when you say it. Americans rarely know to call me that and they give it so many hard edges."

That's because I'm saying it like it should be said.

"Ivan will be down in a minute. Coffee?" she asks.

I sit at the kitchen counter while she pours me a cup and hands it to me. I gaze at it with a smile. This time two weeks ago, I was standing in my cell while a buzzer sounded long and loud, wondering if this might be the day I'm shanked in the showers and left to bleed out on the wet tiles.

"What trouble did you get into in Russia that meant you had to come here?"

The smile dies on my lips.

"I'm sorry, that was rude of me. Forget I asked."

Lilia turns to sort through the refrigerator, but I can feel her cringing away from me. Her thoughts are as loud as if she were shouting them at the top of her lungs. Is there a murderer in her kitchen? A rapist? She saw the blood on my arm so she already knows I'm a murderer, and now she's wondering how safe she is, all alone in this kitchen with a strange man.

"I robbed banks."

Lilia turns to me, her eyebrows raised.

"And I stole from rival syndicate." I almost didn't survive in prison with so many inmates after me for revenge. The moment I was released, I skipped out of Russia with the help of a friend who knew Ivan Kalashnik, and then I came here. A fresh start where no one is baying for my blood.

"Did you hurt people?"

For the first time in a long time, I hesitate. "Sometimes. But not for fun. And only if they tried to hurt me first."

Her brow wrinkles in confusion. "Why would I think you hurt people for fun?"

I recall the glee on the faces of the men last night as I beat Ivan's prisoner to death, her husband included. Oh, *solnyshko*. You sweet, innocent child.

"What did you do before you were married?" I ask.

She gives me a faint smile. "I once stole a candy bar from the corner shop. I was seven."

I click my tongue and wag a finger at her. "You are very bad girl."

"*A* very bad girl," she corrects me. "You're dropping articles."

"Russian habit."

"I was getting into modeling," she says with a shrug of her shoulder. "I wanted to be a runway model. I liked the idea of travel and fashion shows, and the money is good." Her gaze drops to the ground and her cheeks burn. "Anyway, it's stupid to talk about that. Dad introduced me to Ivan, and now I don't need to work."

I watch her with my head tilted to one side. Someone has said bad words to her about that career. I wonder if her father slapped her face and told her she was cheap for wanting men to look at her. That's what my father would have done to my sisters if they said they wanted to be models.

Ivan clatters downstairs, and I force my gaze down to the counter as he gripes about something in the newspaper, gulping the coffee Lilia pours for him. A moment later, Ivan pats me on the back and tells me it's time to go. He gives his wife a peremptory kiss on the mouth and heads for the front door.

Lilia gives me a small smile as I stand up to go. It's faint, but it's there. "Have a lovely day, Elyah."

I follow Ivan to the front door, wishing I could reach back to my darkest moments in prison and share this morning with my former self.

Elyah, you are miserable and filthy, a piece of scum in a concrete cell, but one day soon, an angel in a faraway country will smile at you and wish that your day is lovely, and for a few minutes, it fucking will be.

Being Ivan's "driver" is simple and familiar work. Taxi him around in his sleek black car to his various businesses, legal and otherwise. Stand by the door and act like his bodyguard. Stand over people who don't want to do what he wants. Take people out back and soften them up when they *really* don't want to do what he wants. Eat with him. Talk to him. Visit strip clubs with him. It's just like home in many ways, only the pay is better and so is the weather, but it's harder to bribe the cops. Not impossible, though.

I start to long for mornings and dread the weekends when I'm not needed. Sundays are the worst. They are cold and lonely, even when the sun is beating down. I'm never happier than on Monday mornings when I'm on my way to Ivan

Kalashnik's home, humming under my breath. I ring the bell and wait for Lilia to open the door and smile at me.

She always smiles at me. Me. I'm fucking no one.

I've done things that would make her hide her face in horror. If she could see inside my head, all the lust-filled thoughts I've had about her, she'd turn away from me in disgust. In my head, I've fucked her forward, backward, sideways, and then all over again. I've shoved her to her knees and thrust my cock into her ass. She can't get enough of me. I sit at her kitchen counter and drink coffee with my face carefully blank while she tells me her plans for the day. All the while I'm devouring her with my eyes and trying to imagine how she tastes, how she sounds when she comes, the exact grip of her pussy on my cock. Her husband can't be screwing her. He just can't be. He's so old, and she's younger than I am. It would be criminal to force a beautiful woman like Lilia to suck Ivan Kalashnik's dick. Maybe Ivan can't even perform anymore. Yes, that's it. The only man screwing Lilia Aranova is me, in my head, morning and night.

Just over a month into my new job, Lilia opens the door and she doesn't smile. Her face is gray and she can't meet my eyes. She turns away without even saying hello, and suddenly my world crumbles to dust.

I follow her into the kitchen, wondering what I did to make her look at me like that. What someone else might have said about me. In the middle of pouring coffee, her hand shakes and she has to put the pot down and grab hold of the edge of the counter.

"Lilia?"

Suddenly, she bolts across the kitchen for the laundry room. I stare after her, wondering what the hell is going on. A retching sound reaches me, and I follow her and push the door open.

Lilia's leaning over with her head in the sink, and she's throwing up. Panic races through me. Has she been poisoned?

"You need doctor. I will get Ivan."

She waves a hand at me to stop, but she doesn't raise her head. "Elyah, no. I'm fine. I'm pregnant."

For a moment, I'm fucking confused. Then I swallow, hard. All this American food is softening my brain. I had myself convinced that Ivan wasn't having sex with his wife, that she's my angel who only exists for me in the few minutes I see her every morning. I picture my ugly boss with his hands on her perfect body. His tiny, limp dick is spent and shriveling as jealousy and disgust flash through me.

"*Pozdravl'ayu*," I mutter, and back away. *Congratulations.*

She turns the tap on and rinses her mouth, then straightens up. "Do you like children?"

I'll have to watch her stomach grow day after day with the baby inside her. She'll caress her belly and smile. The whole world will want to touch her because she's radiant and perfect, full of new life and hope. Ivan's fucking baby.

"*Net.*" *No.* I fling the word at her, stride out of the house, and slam the front door behind me. From now on, I'll wait for Ivan in the car so I don't have to look at her.

I stew on it all day, my boss in the back seat of his car while I drive him around. I hate this fucking country. I hate stupid American women who invite dangerous ex-cons into their homes instead of making them wait outside. Who talk to you and smile at you like they like you instead of treating you like the dirt that you are.

I shouldn't have to know that Lilia is fucking pregnant.

I don't fucking want to know that Lilia is pregnant.

I'm never looking at her again.

That resolution doesn't even last the day. The next morning, I'm ringing the front doorbell, my palms sweating.

Lilia opens it and she gives me an uncertain look when she sees it's me. I follow her into the kitchen and watch her pour me a cup of coffee.

"I am sorry for yesterday. I..." I trail off, wondering what the hell I can say. "I do like children. I miss my family."

Her face softens in sympathy, and she reaches out to touch my hand. "Of course you do. I'm sorry you can't see them, Elyah."

She turns away, and I stare at my hand. That's the first time she's ever touched me.

"Do you have brothers and sisters?" she asks.

"Three older sisters."

"Three! You must have been their pet and so spoiled."

I smile, because in a way she is right. When I was a boy, anyway. By the time I was a teenager, I was determined to protect them. I got into so many fights with their boyfriends.

"Any nephews and nieces?"

I nod, and my gaze drops to her belly. "I hear I have two nieces and a nephew."

"You hear? That's so sad you've never met them." Lilia notices me staring at her stomach and gives me a lopsided smile. "I guess I'll have to get used to this. Everyone loves to look at pregnant women and touch them."

I look away quickly. "I am sorry."

"No, it's all right. When I start to show, you can touch the bump if you like."

There's an ache in my chest. If I were her husband, I could palm her belly, and then slide my hand down and cup her pussy. Whisper in her ear how much I love her and our unborn child. Swear to protect them forever.

What is this stupid fucking feeling? I'm hard and horny and liquefying at the same time. Dissolving into a puddle of goddamn mush.

The following Saturday, I'm playing pool in a dive bar with Bogdan in the middle of the day when he gets a call. I lean on my cue, idly rubbing chalk on the tip.

Bogdan swears as he hangs up. "That was Ivan's lawyer. He's been arrested."

"What? Why?"

"Because the cops are cunts. They're searching his office. They'll be going to the house next."

Lilia. All alone while the cops turn over her home. I throw my pool cue on the table and hurry out, driving as fast as I can to Ivan's house.

When I burst through the front door, she's standing in the middle of the living room, her face chalk white as she stares at the cops crawling all over the place. The kitchen. The dining room. Walking up and down the stairs.

"I don't understand what they want," she says in a frightened whisper. Her teeth are chattering. I take off my leather jacket and wrap it around her shoulders. Her skin is ice cold.

"They are just being assholes," I tell her, chafing her upper arms with my hands, trying to rub warmth into her. Ivan is at the police station. I could pull her against my chest and wrap my arms around her. He'll never know if I hold Lilia close and pour my body heat into her.

And then what? I'll never be able to let go of her, my boss's beautiful, pregnant wife.

"Why has Ivan been arrested?"

"I do not know. Come sit down," I urge her, but she shakes her head when I try to tug her toward the sofa.

"I won't sit here like nothing's wrong with these people in my house." Every time a cop passes us, she glares at them.

For two hours, we stand there together. After pawing through every drawer and closet and confiscating every electronic device in the house, the police finally leave. Lilia pushes two shaking hands through her hair and moans. There are lines of pain etched into her brow.

"Lilia?"

Her legs buckle. I grab her as she collapses and my knee hits the floor. The back of her dress feels damp and sticky. When I draw my hand away, it's soaked with blood.

Oh, my fucking God.

"Elyah, my stomach hurts," Lilia whimpers. She opens her eyes and sees the blood all over my hand, and gasps. "The baby. Elyah, the baby."

I stare at the blood on the cream carpet, frightened buzzing filling my head. Why is there so much blood?

The baby.

It's killing her.

I scoop her up in my arms and carry her out to my car. She curls up in a ball in the passenger seat, gasping and shaking.

"You are going to be all right," I tell her, buckling her in and running around to the driver's seat. I pass my forearm over my sweating brow. I drive past a hospital every day, don't

I? A moment later, I remember where it is and gun the engine.

When we reach the hospital, I follow the red signs, hoping that they're directing me to the emergency doctors. I pull up to a set of double glass doors, scoop Lilia out of the car, and carry her into the waiting room.

Everyone ignores me. I can't read the signs. How the hell do American hospitals work? I can't find the English words to tell anyone what's wrong with her, so I simply shout at the top of my lungs, "She needs help."

I get a nurse's attention. Someone in a white coat appears with a gurney and wheels Lilia away.

There's so much blood on my hands. Blood on my shirt. How the fuck does this happen to a woman? It's like she's been attacked, only the enemy is inside her.

My jaw clenches. And Ivan fucking put it there.

I stand in the waiting room for an hour until a doctor comes and finds me. I think she assumes I'm Lilia's husband, and I don't correct her. She explains that they did all they could, but Lilia lost the baby.

"Is Lilia all right? Can I see her?"

The doctor takes me through the doors and down stark gray corridors to a room with a narrow metal bed. Lilia is laying on it, face washed out, eyes hollow.

I sit down on the chair next to the bed, hesitate, and then reach for her hand. There's a needle in the back and a plastic tube taped to her skin. I thread my tattooed fingers through hers and hold on.

For a long time, Lilia doesn't seem to know I'm there. Then she turns to me and whispers, "Maybe it's better this way. Look at what I was bringing a child into."

People have children in all kinds of shitty situations. Her husband is a criminal who's been arrested, but her life is protected and luxurious. And she already loved that baby. Lilia's love. What can a person need beyond that?

I shift to the edge of the bed and cup her face in my hands. "One day you will have beautiful child, and he will have everything because he will have you."

Lilia's face crumples and her eyes fill with tears. "Elyah, I want my baby back."

I draw her into my arms and hold her close. Am I the lowest creature in the world for taking pleasure from this moment as she's in the midst of pain? I don't care. I don't care. My arms wrap around her as she sobs into my chest, and I hold her tight.

I'll protect her. If Ivan goes to prison, I'll never leave her side.

Footsteps are coming down the hall. Heavy, familiar footsteps, and my heart sinks.

I stand up and wrench Lilia's hands from around my neck. When Ivan enters the room, I'm standing four feet away with my back against the wall, face impassive and arms folded.

Just a bodyguard. Just a driver.

There's barely controlled rage on Ivan's face. The police have wound him up all day and turned him into a snorting, furious bull, and now they've unleashed him on his wife. Without saying one word to Lilia, Ivan lifts his hand and backhands her across the face. Lilia's head snaps to one side and she cries out.

"You lost my child?" he bellows at her.

I step forward. "Hey!"

Ivan rounds on me, his eyes blazing with fury. "Have you got something to say?"

Over his shoulder, Lilia has one hand pressed over her cheek. Her eyes are huge and scared and she shakes her head at me.

Ivan plants his hands on my shoulders, turns me around, and shoves me out of the room. The door slams in my face. I grasp the door handle, ready to wrench it open and kill him with my bare hands. The only sound from the other side of the door is soft, broken weeping. I stand there listening to Lilia cry. Broken-hearted sobbing that claws at my guts.

Ivan doesn't say one fucking word.

He could come out at any moment and find me still standing there, but I can't walk away. I'm in prison again, only this prison has walls of pure torment, and there's no escape.

~

Lilia is discharged from the hospital a day later, and I buy a new shirt.

When she opens the door, I smile in greeting. Nothing's wrong. I'm not going to remind her of the worst day of her life. I never held her. I didn't see her husband hit her. I pretend not to notice that she's pale, her cheeks are thin, and her eyes are haunted. "*Dobroe utro*, Lilia."

"Good morning, Elyah." Her hand slides down the door and she turns away.

I follow her into the kitchen and take my usual spot at the counter. I've already heard from Dima and Vasily what happened with Ivan at the police station. They arrested him for money laundering, but his lawyer found a problem with the warrant, and he was let go on a technicality. I doubt they'll find any evidence on Ivan's devices. He's far too clever to leave anything incriminating on hard drives and phones that the police can find.

Lilia puts a mug of coffee in front of me. "You look different today. Is that a new shirt?"

I glance down at the soft, patterned shirt in shades of cream, gray, and sea green. It hugs my shoulders and biceps. The shop assistant couldn't stop touching me when I was trying it on. "I was on Vine Street yesterday, where the little shops are."

"Little, but expensive," she agrees with a smile.

I puff my cheeks out and widen my eyes. "I was not prepared. The shop assistant would not let me leave until I had bought this. I could rent an apartment in my town in Russia for the cost of this shirt."

Her gaze roams over me. "It suits you. I don't think I've ever seen you in anything but black."

Her hand is on the counter, and I reach out and cover it with my own. The last time I touched her, she was sobbing her heart out on my chest. Our gazes meet, and I can tell she's remembering that moment. Her eyes fill with tears, and I know.

I fucking *know*.

He's not letting her grieve the baby. She has to pretend everything's fine and nothing happened. Just like I do after seeing him hit her.

"I am sorry, Lilia," I whisper.

She pulls her hand from mine like I've given her an electric shock.

While her back is to me, I slop coffee down my front.

"Oh, clumsy," I tut, pulling my wet shirt away from my chest.

Lilia turns back and sees what I've done. "Oh, no! Go and rinse it off quickly in the laundry room under cold water."

I put my mug down and do what she says. The laundry room is just a short distance from the kitchen, a narrow, windowless room with a washer and dryer. I pull my shirt off, throw it in the sink and scatter it with a handful of detergent powder. Then I wait, counting slowly. When I reach forty-five, Lilia calls my name, and I hear her footsteps coming toward the utility room.

She comes in and sees me standing shirtless with my hands braced against the counter and glowering into the sink.

"Elyah, what are you..."

I turn to her, watching her face closely as her roaming eyes take in my tattooed chest and my muscled stomach.

That's right. Look at me.

Not a bit like your husband, am I?

I gesture vaguely at my shirt. "Was I supposed to add detergent?"

She gasps in dismay as she sees the mess I've made. "Elyah, what have you done? Don't worry, I can fix this."

I stand close to her as she turns the cold tap on and tries to rescue the garment. I run the tip of my forefinger along a lock of her hair. The faintest of touches, but her hands stop moving under the water.

"You look after everyone in this house so beautifully," I murmur. "Coming here every morning feels like coming home."

Lilia takes a shaky breath and resumes her scrubbing. She holds it up and it drips with water. "I think it's clean, but this is going to take hours to dry. I'll fetch you something of Ivan's."

"Do not bother. I have another shirt in my car."

Lilia tries to move past me, but I take her by the shoulders and slowly back her against the wall.

Don't look at my shirt.

Look at me.

Only at me.

I cup her jaw and say softly, "When I was sixteen, my eighteen-year-old sister was beaten by her boyfriend. She came home with black eye and bleeding lip. I was never angrier in my life."

Her eyes are huge as she gazes up at me. Soft, sea-green eyes, a shade I never saw until I met her. Beautiful eyes, wells of pure emotion.

I brace my hands on either side of her head and lean forward until my lips are close to hers. Does she remember what I said to her that first morning? I'm a killer, but I don't take pleasure from it. I'm not a psychopath.

But that wasn't the whole truth.

"I went out and found him and killed her boyfriend. I beat him to death. That kill? I enjoyed it." I take her hands and place them on my chest, pressing them over my thundering heart. "Every. Second."

"Elyah, don't."

I tuck my lips against her ear. For a moment, I close my eyes and savor the feel of my lips touching a part of her. Then I breathe, "I cannot stop thinking about you, Lilia Aranova."

She lets me hold her, her body against my bare skin. I haven't crossed the line. We're standing on it right now and we can both feel what's on the other side. I'm living in this moment with her, and she's going to imagine with me what it would be like if we were to cross it. When we cross it.

I let her go, leave by the back door, and walk around the house to my car. By the time Ivan comes out, I'm waiting by his car, dressed in my usual black shirt. He's reading something on his phone and barely gives me a glance as he greets me good morning. Lilia didn't tell him that one of his men stripped half naked and accosted her in the laundry room. I smile to myself as I get into the driver's seat.

Good girl.

The next day, I pretend like nothing happened. Lilia pretends, too, though her cheeks turn pink when she hands me back my shirt, washed and pressed and as pristine as the day I bought it.

"*Spacibo*," I say, taking it from her with a smile.

"*Pozhaluysta*," she says. *You're welcome.* Her accent is terrible and she puts emphasis on all the wrong syllables, but the word is music to my ears.

My smile widens. "You have never said anything to me in Russian before."

"Haven't I?" she says, shrugging as if it's nothing. But the red in her cheeks burns hotter.

All day, I can't stop fucking smiling.

Lilia is self-conscious and nervous around me for two weeks. I can feel that she's hyperaware of me as I sit in her kitchen, and maybe it's sadistic of me, but I love it. I drink my coffee and ask her bland, innocent questions, and my dick gets harder and harder the more she blushes and falters over her words.

On Friday, she opens the front door and she's wearing a short, sleeveless dress buttoned at the front, and my gaze travels down her body with naked lust. I don't try to hide the fact that I'm consumed with desire for my boss's wife.

Lilia's eyes dilate, partly in panic, partly because she can feel me undressing her with my eyes. She turns around and walks quickly into the kitchen, stares at the coffee maker, and then flees into the pantry.

I glance around the downstairs rooms and then follow her into the pantry, so quietly that she doesn't notice me until she turns to come out. I'm right there, inches from her body.

Her soft intake of breath parts her lips and she sucks in a piece of my soul. I take her face between my hands and slant my mouth over hers. She can have my entire soul. Every last drop of me. Her lips open beneath mine in surprise, and I don't hesitate. My tongue sweeps into her mouth and caresses hers.

A second later, her arms wrap around my neck and she's kissing me back with desperate hunger. I reach for the buttons on her dress and undo them, one after the other.

"Elyah." She grips my waist and follows the path of my fingers, like she wants to push me away but she needs me to keep going. I open the dress to her waist and pull it back.

"You want me to stop? You know how to stop me." I hook my finger in the lace cup of her bra and pull it down. Then the other one. The sight of her dark pink nipples and full breasts makes my mouth water. "Tell your husband what I'm doing to you. Go on, Lilia. Scream out for him."

If he discovers I've put my hands on his woman, he'll have me beaten to death, my dick sliced off and shoved down my throat.

I lower my head and take her nipple in my mouth, sucking her and rolling it against my tongue. I scoop her closer and press my hips into hers, the hard length of my cock tight against her belly.

"Feel how much I want you," I whisper along her throat. "I do not care you are married. I do not give a fuck that this could get me killed. I want you with every breath I take."

I reach between her legs and drag a finger up her pussy over her underwear. I find her clit and rub it quickly, and she moans in pleasure and arches into me.

I have to get out of here, now. Ivan will be coming downstairs at any moment, but now that I've got my hands on her, I can't stop fucking touching her.

I hook my finger into her panties and pull them aside. Her clit is swollen. Her lips are shiny. I run my finger down the seam of her sex and straight into her tight channel.

I groan softly and press my forehead against hers. She's wet. She's so fucking wet for me. In the final seconds before I have to tear myself away, I pulse my finger in and out of her, committing the grip of her slick flesh to memory.

"I am going to fuck you, Lilia Aranova. I am going to spread your legs and pound you with my cock until I burst inside you. I am going to own this pussy."

Lilia stares up at me, mouth open, nails digging into my shoulders.

I take my wet finger from her sex and press it against her lips. "My life is in your hands, *solnyshko*. If I wake up tomorrow, it is because you allow my heart to go on beating."

I step away from her, drinking in the sight of her flushed cheeks, her bare breasts, her spread legs. If we had more time, if her husband wasn't upstairs, I'd lift her up onto my cock and fuck her against these shelves. Her beautiful eyes fill with turmoil and need. That's the look I want when I'm balls deep inside her.

I go to the coffee maker and pour myself a cup and take my seat at the counter like usual. I'm drinking coffee when Ivan walks into the kitchen. Every time I lift the mug to my lips, I can smell Lilia's pussy.

"*Dobroe utro*, Elyah."

"Morning." I stare straight ahead. This is an ordinary morning. I'm just the driver.

Ivan looks around in confusion for his wife. She's always here when he comes downstairs, ready to pass him a cup of coffee. "Lilia? Where are you?"

I hold my breath, my coffee halfway to my lips. The seconds drag by. There's a gun holstered beneath my arm. If he finds his wife disheveled in the pantry, I'll have to kill him, and then I don't know what the fuck I'll do next. First, take Lilia. Everything else I'll figure out later.

Lilia steps out of the pantry, hair neat, dress buttoned, large cans of vegetables in each hand and not a trace of anything in her face. "Morning. I thought we had more butter beans."

Ivan gives a vague shrug. The contents of his pantry hold no interest to him.

I stare at Lilia as she places the cans on the counter, amends the shopping list, and pours her husband a cup of coffee.

I smile behind my mug. She's cooler than an assassin.

The following morning is Saturday. The weather turns bleak and chilly and rain lashes against my apartment windows. My mood sours. If it were a nice day, I might have driven by the park or down the street with the good cafés and watched people walking by, hoping to see Lilia out running errands or sitting in the sunshine. Instead, I do laundry and play the minutes with Lilia in the pantry over and over again in my mind.

Around three in the afternoon, the doorbell rings. When I open the front door, I'm shocked to see Lilia standing on the other side. Her hair is wet from the rain, a red purse hangs over her shoulder, and she's clutching something in her hands.

"I forgot I had this. I just found it at home."

She holds it out to me. My leather jacket that she was wearing when the police searched her house and she collapsed in my arms. I must have left it with her at the hospital. She could have given it back to me at any time. She could have waited until Monday.

"We can't do anything like that again," she whispers urgently. Her eyes are huge and scared. "From now on, when you come to collect Ivan, wait in the car."

Wait in the car.

Never talk to her.

Never touch her again.

I grab her by the wrist and haul her into my apartment, slamming the door behind us. I push her against it and my mouth descends on hers. Lilia whimpers in panic, even as she takes my shoulders and holds me fiercely.

"Elyah, we can't do this. He'll kill you."

"I do not care," I say huskily, kissing her again. All I care about is her. I'm not going to waste these precious minutes thinking about unimportant things like my life.

"He'll kill *me*."

"I will not let him." I lift her up and carry her to my

bedroom and lay her on the bed. I crush her mouth beneath mine and haul her thighs around my hips. Body to body. I reach for the button on her pants and yank them down her legs. I've been hard all day. I could thrust into her right now, but I make myself slow down. This is my apartment. My bed. I can take my time with her.

I sit up and pull my T-shirt up over my head. "Put your hands on me."

Hesitantly, Lilia reaches up and smooths her hands up my chest, drinking in the sight of the tattoos decorating my muscles. She touches a fist wrapped with barbed wire. A snake with fangs bared, ready to strike. A reaper with his cowl. There are words in Russian that she traces with the tips of her fingers.

"What do they all mean?"

She has Russian blood in her veins. Her father is in the Bratva, the Russian mafia, but she may as well have been born and raised on Mars for all she understands about my past. But she knows enough to realize that these tattoos have meaning.

"They mean I fight for what I want, and I never give up." As she strokes my flesh, I strip out of my jeans, unbutton her blouse, and then unfasten her bra. I'm fixated on her naked body. Her smooth skin. The way her chest lifts and falls as I tweak her nipples and take her hips in my hands.

I pull her underwear down her long, slender legs, and push them open. God, she's so fucking pretty. How can she be so perfect? The ruffles of her inner lips are pink and shiny, and I dip my head to savor her with my tongue. I groan and lick her again. "You taste so sweet, *solnyshko*."

Does she even know what that means? She's my sunshine.

She's my everything. I sit up and lean over her naked body, my cock in my hand, playing the swollen head over her clit. I savor the sight of the two of us, everything meaningless stripped away until we're just a man. Just a woman. Meant to be together.

"Elyah," she breathes.

My heart swells in answer. I have her now, always, no matter what comes next. "You want me? You need me?"

Her teeth sink into her lower lip and guilt flashes through her eyes, but she nods.

"You have to ask for it, Lilia. I want to hear you say the words. *Fuck me please, Elyah.* Say it in Russian. *Trakhni menya pozhaluysta.*"

"*Trakhni...*" she whispers in faltering Russian.

"*Trakhni menya pozhaluysta*, Elyah."

Lilia reaches out and wraps her hand around my length, slowly running her fingers up and down the veins, the swollen head of my cock. Squeezing me. Stroking me. "*Trakhni menya...*"

"*Pozhaluysta,*" I whisper, caught in the prison of her touch.

"*Pozhaluysta*, Elyah." She cups the nape of my neck and draws my face down to hers, kissing me with her lips open. Letting me devour her.

My woman.

Mine.

"I wanted you the first time I saw you," she confesses. "I tried not to look at you. Think about you. I could feel you before I ever touched you."

I grasp my cock and push it down her lips to her entrance. "I have not stopped thinking about you since the first night I saw you. I have ached for you, Lilia."

I'm on the cusp of thrusting into her when there's a knock on the front door.

No.

Not fucking now.

Lilia's hands freeze on my shoulders. I'm held on a knife's edge between desolation and utter bliss. She's spread open for me, panting for me, her pussy juices coating my cock. One thrust, and I'll be home.

"I know you're in there, Elyah," a loud, bored voice calls. Vasily, the only other one of Ivan's men who doesn't have a woman at home. "Stop playing with your dick and get out here. I want to get some food."

I grit my teeth and squeeze my eyes shut. The universe fucking hates me.

Vasily's knocking becomes an angry pounding. "Your car is out front. Open the door."

Lilia covers her face in horror and draws her knees together as she realizes who it is. With a groan, I wrench my body away from hers and sit up. She grabs her clothes and dives for the closet, closing the door behind her.

"Where is your car?" I ask softly through the wood.

"I parked two streets away."

Thank fuck for that.

"I'll get rid of him. Just stay there. Don't..." Don't go anywhere. Don't change your mind, *solnyshko*.

My hand slides down the wood, her silence piercing me with agony. No one will find out about us. I'll do whatever it takes to keep her safe.

"I am coming, *mudak*," I growl as I pull on my jeans and stalk toward the front door. *Asshole*.

I wrench it open and see Vasily's stupid fucking face staring back at me. "What? I was sleeping."

"I'm bored. Let's get some food."

"I said I was sleeping."

He peers past me. "Have you got a woman in here?"

I glance over my shoulder, and to my horror, I see that Lilia's red purse is lying on the carpet. "Give me two minutes." I slam the door in his face.

I snatch up the purse and stand outside my wardrobe. What the hell do I say? I want to beg her to stay right where she is and wait for me. I can get rid of Vasily in an hour, but it disgusts me even to consider asking a woman like her to sit in my shitty wardrobe longer than she has to, just to betray her husband with me.

Her husband.

My boss.

I pull on my discarded T-shirt and shoes. I put my hand against the wardrobe door and press my forehead against it. I can feel her heart beating just inches from my own.

"I am in love with you, Lilia Aranova," I whisper through the wood.

Silence fills the room. Maybe she hates me for pushing her to betray her wedding vows. I can feel the hate she has for herself.

"Hate me, please," I urge. "I am the one who is wrong, but I will not be sorry for wanting you. I will beg for forgiveness tomorrow, even though I will still want you then. I will always want you."

I leave her purse by the wardrobe and pull the front door closed without locking the deadbolt so she can let herself out.

Vasily drives us a mile down the road to a fried chicken

restaurant. I don't even know what I order, and I stare at my meal with a sour gut when it arrives at our table.

"You were there when the police turned Ivan's house over?" Vasily asks, pushing fries into his mouth.

I pick at my piece of chicken and mutter an assent.

"What were they looking for?" he asks.

"How should I know?"

Vasily chews noisily, the sound making me want to put a fist through his face. "What *do* you know?"

I glance up. "What?"

He shrugs. "You seem tense. You have been since the police showed up."

"I hate cops," I say, and then realize Vasily's gazing at me with a suspicious gleam in his eyes. Am I tense because I'm the one who ratted out Ivan to the cops?

Is there a rat in our midst?

I grab a paper napkin and wipe my fingers. "I'm not a fucking snitch. How fucking dare you?"

"Then why are you so jumpy lately?"

I need to get a grip. If Vasily has noticed I'm acting differently, then Ivan might, too, and that could be deadly. "Personal problems."

Vasily grins. "Woman problems? A handsome asshole like you can get another woman in a second. I'm the one who has woman problems."

I throw the napkin aside. I don't want another woman. I only want Lilia.

When I finally get home, my heart is pounding as I make my way to the bedroom. She won't still be in the wardrobe. It's stupid to hope. I pull the door open—and it's empty.

I sink to my knees and press my palm against the bare

spot on the floor, hoping to at least feel the warmth left by her body. But the carpet is cold.

When I ring the front doorbell the next morning, Ivan's son answers and lets me in. He doesn't say hello, just goes back to the cereal he's eating on the sofa. I stand in the silent kitchen, straining for the sound of Lilia's heels clicking on the tiles somewhere in the house.

I clear my throat and call to Alexei, "Where's Lilia?"

"She's going to the gym in the mornings now."

I turn away and clench my eyes shut. No, no, no. If I can't see her, then what's the point of being here? Being anywhere? I'll die if I have to stand in this kitchen every day with nothing but her memory and the scent of her in the air.

Ivan comes downstairs and I follow him out to the car, my eyes running over the side of his neck, the outline of his ribs beneath his shirt. All excellent places to slip a knife in while I have my hand clamped over his mouth.

Midway through the morning, Ivan says from the back seat, "You're quiet today. Did something happen?"

"I was stood up."

He chuckles. "By a woman? Don't let it get you down. I'll take you to Odyssey tonight and you can get as many lap dances as it takes to get the bitch off your mind."

Odyssey is a strip club. I won't be able to stop myself from committing murder if I have to watch Ivan throwing money at strippers while his wife waits at home. "I am busy tonight."

After lunch, we drive to Ivan's office, and I turn down the street and head for my usual parking spot. There are more cars than usual along the road. Shiny cars. Unfamiliar cars. I put my foot on the brakes and stop in the middle of the street.

"Why have you stopped, Elyah?"

I don't know. I grip the steering wheel, staring at the road ahead. All the hairs are standing up on the back of my neck. Something's off. Something's fucking wrong with this street.

I glance up at the buildings overlooking us, and a sniper pulls back out of sight.

I swear and slam the car into reverse. Ivan shouts from the back seat. There's a squeal of rubber, and a white van shoots across the road behind us. The back door opens and a SWAT team in full gear pours out.

They've come for Ivan, but they're going to take me, too. "Get out of the car. This side."

I open the door and roll out between the parked cars. Ivan follows me and we crouch behind a vehicle, guns drawn.

A loud, American voice calls across the street, "Ivan Kalashnik. Surrender yourself immediately. Throw your gun into the road and come out with your hands where we can see them."

I risk a glance around the car we're hiding behind and see a sandy-haired man in a blue shirt and a camel coat. There's a mole beneath his right eye. I don't recognize him, but if I were to guess, I'd say he's a federal agent.

I pull my head back and say to Ivan, "It is the feds. Keep your head down, there is—"

Ivan sits up and fires at the SWAT team. A split second later, his head explodes like a watermelon hit by a baseball bat.

"—sniper."

I stare as his body topples to the ground.

Now they can't take Ivan in. They can only take me. I dive beneath the parked car behind me and army crawl my way back down the street beneath the vehicles. The cops have lost sight of me for a moment. I reach a side street and someone is idling in their car and staring at the SWAT team. I yank the door open, drag the driver from the car and take off. His angry shout disappears behind me as I roar down the street. I don't slow down until I nearly run over an old woman at a crosswalk.

I slam on the brakes and take a deep breath.

Drive like a normal fucking person, Elyah.

Get Lilia.

And get out of the city.

I take the back streets and head for the woods above Lilia and Ivan's house, park among the trees, jog down and vault the fence. I can't see anyone through the kitchen windows and hurry around to the back door.

Without thinking, I pull back and ram my shoulder into it. Over and over again, until the wood splinters and breaks free under my force. "*Lilia!*"

The house is silent. I take the stairs two at a time and burst into the master bedroom. Where the fuck is she? The house doesn't just feel empty, it feels abandoned. All the hairs stand up on the back of my neck, and I don't understand why until I see that the wardrobe door is ajar. Only Ivan's clothes are hanging from the rail. I turn to her vanity and flip open the jewelry boxes. They're empty, too.

My phone rings, and I see it's Vasily and answer.

"Oh, thank fuck. You're alive." Vasily lets out a huge breath. "Where are you?"

"Looking for Lilia. I am at Ivan's house. Have you seen her? All her things are gone."

"Get out of there. Forget that bitch."

"What?"

Vasily suddenly explodes in anger. "She sold us out! She's been meeting with the fucking feds."

My blood turns cold. "Lilia would never do that."

"I have proof. She betrayed her husband. Maybe she hates him. Maybe she did it for her father. There was always something strange about Aran and Ivan getting involved. She killed her fucking baby from the stress. I doubt she even wanted that baby."

Vasily is raving like a madman and I shout over him, "What are you talking about? Do not say shit like that."

"Ivan suspected her! He was having me follow her."

Even though I saw Ivan die with my own two eyes, panic and guilt slices through me. "You have been following Lilia?"

Vasily takes a deep breath and says in a quieter tone, "I didn't tell Ivan about the two of you."

It's tempting to bluster and pretend I don't know what Vasily's talking about. *She was just dropping off my jacket. I would never lay a finger on the boss's wife.*

"You were not really hungry yesterday, were you?"

"No, brother," he replies.

I pinch my brow, trying to comprehend everything that Vasily has said. "You said you have proof she was speaking to the feds. What proof?"

"This morning Lilia went to a park and got into another man's car. They talked for twenty minutes. I took pictures. Hang on."

My phone buzzes. Vasily has sent me three photographs. Lilia, sitting in the passenger seat of a black SUV. She's talking with a sandy-haired man in his late forties with a mole beneath his right eye.

Recognition slams through me. It's the fed who tried to arrest Ivan.

I stare around the room, and my eyes land on a picture of Lilia in her wedding dress next to her husband, beaming at the camera. This is a dream. This is a fucking nightmare.

I hear Vasily's voice, tinny and distant, and I put my phone back to my ear. "Elyah, are you there?"

"Why did you not warn Ivan?"

"I tried to! I drove around all fucking morning. I went to the house. The gym. The restaurant. The office. Where the hell were you?"

"Ivan had a meeting downtown. You should have—"

"Called? I should have called Ivan while the feds were listening? I shouldn't even be talking to you right now, but they already got the man they wanted. Ivan's dead so we're all finished. I'm leaving and so should you. Lay low for a few months. And Elyah? Forget about that bitch."

The line goes dead.

This can't be happening. This can't be real.

I stare at the pictures of Lilia in the car with the federal agent, trying to find an innocent explanation.

No one in the mafia or married to the mafia has an innocent conversation with the feds. Lilia sold out her husband. She sold out all of us, and she didn't warn me. I laid my heart at my feet and she kicked dirt over it and turned away.

I'm nothing to her.

Less than fucking nothing. She sent me in there to die or to be arrested.

I wrench the clothing rail out of the wardrobe with a roar and swing it at her dressing table mirror. Glass explodes everywhere. I smash all the mirrors on the wardrobe doors and the framed photographs of Lilia and Ivan's wedding day. Every piece of her perfect life deserves to be destroyed.

I get into my car and drive blindly, taking turns without thinking until I realize that I'm on the freeway, heading out of the city. I keep driving, betrayal and hatred burning through me, every fresh wave stronger than the last.

As night falls, I snarl a promise to the empty road ahead. "Lilia Aranova. You are dead fucking woman."

5

Lilia

"Is she awake yet?"

"Shh. He's over there in the dark."

"I can't see him."

"He's right there, staring into her cell."

"Which one?"

"The scary one."

"They're all scary, Olivia!"

"The *cold* one. The one who wanted Celeste to suck his dick, but then he changed his mind."

"Do you think he knows this new woman? I think he knows her."

"Who cares? Just shut up. Do you want to end up like Valentina?"

"Poor Valentina."

"She should have kept her mouth shut. The scarred one, he hates screaming."

"He hates us all. We're all going to die."

The whispers fade away like a dissolving dream as I open my eyes. I must have been dreaming. My body feels heavy and there's a sick feeling in my stomach as I swallow. Just great. I'm overseas and I'm coming down with the flu. If I look really sick, they won't let me on my flight.

Adrenaline shoots through me. My flight. I don't remember setting my alarm before I went to sleep. I push myself up to sitting and the bed feels strange beneath me. My mattress at the hotel was thick and soft, but I can feel metal slats beneath an inch of foam, and a scratchy blanket drags across my legs. The air is clammy, and a light shines in my eyes through the darkness. Darkness glimpsed through the bars of a cage.

A jolt goes through me. I had a nightmare. A tattooed Russian with dark hair and dark eyes was pursuing me through a building. Blood dripped down his face and chest, and I knew that if he caught me, he'd stab me to death in a frenzy. It's not my usual Russian assassin dream in which I'm shot in the back of the head by a cold, taciturn killer, or thrown off a building to make my death look like a suicide. It was twice as terrifying.

My hands and T-shirt are smeared with blood. I let out a gasp and shoot to my feet. But it was a *dream*. What's the last thing I remember? What's the last thing I did?

I left the fashion show with a Kazakh girl, and she was mad at me for getting us fired. I ran into the Lugovskayas and drank coffee with them, and then—

Screaming.

Stabbing.

Blood.

I feel quickly beneath my T-shirt and run my hands up and down my arms and legs. No wounds. I'm not bleeding. It's not my blood, it's the Lugovskayas'. As I'm trying to come to terms with being covered in my father's friends' blood, my hand drifts slowly up to feel the side of my neck and I find a sore spot. Something…pierced me here?

Footsteps crunch beyond the bars. Fingers push into my cell and clench tight around the metal. Tattooed fingers marked with suns, moons, and crosses.

A deep voice whispers in the darkness, "Lilia Aranova."

My blood turns to ice in my veins. The figure beyond the bars is in deep shadow and I can't see his face. "My name's Yulia Petrova."

"You are liar, Lilia Aranova."

The bottom falls out of my stomach. My legs give out beneath me, and I sit down, hard, on the metal bed. Only one man calls me that. Speaks my name like that, like he's drawing his tongue across my flesh. Savoring every inch of me. Forbidden fruit.

"You are *a* liar," I whisper through numb lips.

He steps forward into the light. Two glacial blue eyes appear above his clenched fingers, burning with hatred. His proud cheekbones stand out in the stark light from above, and his fine, ashy hair is swept back. It's impossible.

It should be impossible.

He should be in America, or Russia, or in prison. Not here in Italy. Did he orchestrate this somehow? Did he send that other Russian man after me, the one with the knife and the dark hair and eyes?

"Elyah Morozov," I say in a shaky voice. "What the hell am I doing here?"

He takes a key from his pocket and unlocks my cell. His huge frame fills the doorway, and he grabs hold of the lintel above his head. Eyes narrowed. Biceps clenched. Body looming over me. Every line of his posture is to intimidate me.

How many times did I open the door to him in the brief months I was married? It must have been a hundred times. His chiseled jawline was always freshly shaved, his body scented with sharp, cold cologne that never failed to make my mouth water. A living weapon with a gentle smile touching his lips, speaking softly so I wouldn't be afraid of him. Sitting his huge body down at my kitchen counter. Asking me about my day. What I liked. What I hoped for. Covering up his tattoos beneath black shirts until the day came for him to bare them to me and reveal what he was capable of, what he wanted to do.

He never said out loud that he would kill my husband for me, but his tattoos said it. His eyes said it. His kisses said it.

Then he'd turn the killer inside off again like flipping a switch. I'd make him coffee, and he would sit at the kitchen counter and smile gently, and gaze at me like I was the most precious creature in the world. Elyah Morozov pretends to be a tame wolf, but he's a savage predator who'll pretend to be anything to get what he wants.

"You are the one in cage now, Lilia Aranova. You are the piece of scum who is nothing."

My chest heaves with despair. "You were never nothing to m—"

Elyah slams the wall over his head with the flat of his

hand and shouts, "Shut up! I do not want to listen to your lies."

He looms deeper into my cell, blocking out the light with his huge back until his features are cast in shadows so deep that I can't make out his eyes. His breath fans my face as he leans closer, and his voice is thick with hatred. "You will beg me for mercy before the week is out, and I will show you no mercy, just as you showed me none."

His hand slips around my throat and squeezes tight. I swallow hard against his fingers. When in hell did he ever need my mercy?

"I have waited two years to say this to your face. You are dead fucking woman, Lilia Aranova."

When a Bratva man vows to do something, he will never give it up while there is breath in his lungs. His honor as a man and to his code won't allow anything else. Elyah has spoken my death sentence, but he won't kill me right away. He wants to play with me first.

Elyah seethes fury into my face, and then he abruptly pulls back, slams the door of my cage, and locks it, then disappears into the darkness. I can hear him pounding upstairs, and then his footsteps fade away.

"Number Eleven?" whispers a voice to my left. "Did he kill you?"

It takes me a minute to realize that the voice might be addressing me. "Eleven? Do you mean me?"

"We all have numbers. They call me Number Ten."

"And I'm Number Twelve," says a voice to my right. "Did that man call you by your name? Do you know him?"

I'm still shaking from the shock of Elyah looming over me, pure venom in his eyes.

"My name's Lilia," I whisper back. Elyah and that unknown, dark-haired man seem to be working together. "Why have they taken the three of us prisoner?"

"Three of us?" says the woman on my left. "There are more than three of us. Everyone, say hi to Number Eleven."

Sad whispers fill the air. "Hello, Number Eleven."

"Hi, Number Eleven."

"I'm sorry, Number Eleven."

I push my cheek against my cage and peer left and right. I can make out a few hands holding bars just like the ones that lock me in. The row of cages stretch on and on. I wonder if we're being trafficked as sex slaves back to Russia. "How many of us are there?"

"Sixteen," replies Number Twelve. "They're obsessed with there being sixteen of us. They want to play a game."

Chills travel down my spine. "What sort of game?"

Number Ten sounds like she's shivering, too. "We don't know. Number Four overheard them talking about jewels. Maybe we're going to be smuggling jewels back to Russia?"

In my experience—which is limited because mafia wives and daughters are always kept in the dark about these things—illegal goods are smuggled out of big cities and ports. Maybe we are in Rome or Trieste. Smuggling doesn't sound like much of a game to me, though.

"Where were you all taken from? I was stolen from Milan. I was working as a model at fashion week."

"Me, too," whispers a voice from along the row of cages.

"And me."

"We all were," says Number Twelve.

Sixteen young models all stolen from fashion week. It should be impossible for our captors to get away with this unnoticed, but I heard about women disappearing and I shrugged it off. Even if we're reported to the authorities today or tomorrow, how long will it take for the search to begin? What if there are no clues?

I press my forehead against the bars and close my eyes, horror sweeping over me. This is sick. All those weeks I spent with Elyah, all those times he touched me, held me like I'd break, I never sensed the depraved monster inside him. The Hyde to his Jekyll. Being a hitman or enforcer for the mafia is one thing. Torturing women for fun, that's beyond what I've ever known from even the most depraved men in my life, and I've known some violent bastards. My father was one. My husband was another.

"Number Eleven, how do you know that man?" asks Number Ten. "What's he like? What do you think he wants?"

"Don't call me by that number. My name is Lilia. What are your names?"

Taut silence stretches.

"We're not allowed to say our names," answers Number Twelve.

"My name is Lilia," I call out in defiance. "They can keep us in cages, they can take everything else from us, but they can't take our names."

My voice fades away, and nothing but silence answers me.

Then someone speaks from Number Ten's cage. "My name is Olivia," she says, and then louder, "I'm Olivia."

Far down the row of cells, someone calls softly in a Hispanic accent, "I'm in cell one. My name's Alejandra."

Hesitantly, the women call out their cell numbers and their names. I grip the bars as I commit the names to memory, pride surging through me. These women are suffering a terrifying ordeal, but they haven't given up hope. No one's beaten yet.

"I'm so proud of you all. I promise that we're going to get out of this, alive and in one piece."

There are a few whispers of agreement. But only a few.

"She didn't see what happened to the last Number Eleven," someone mutters.

All the hairs stand up on the back of my neck. "There was another Number Eleven?"

"See that stain on the concrete over there?" Imani whispers. Imani is next to me in cell twelve.

I peer through the darkness to a spot on the floor that's stained a darker color than the surrounding concrete. A large stain, as if a great deal of fluid has been spilled, and my flesh ripples with goosepimples. There are chains hanging overhead the bloodstain on the floor, and I'm forcibly reminded of a carcass hanging from a butcher's hook.

I don't think I want to know. But I have to ask.

"What happened to her? Was it Elyah who killed her?"

"Don't say his name," someone hisses. "We're only allowed to call them *ser*." The Russian word for *sir*.

"He must love that," I say bitterly. An honorific means a lot to a proud man who was kept in a cell and told he was scum. When he worked for Ivan, he was nothing more than a tool. Treated like unthinking muscle, just as I was looked upon as a mechanical doll.

Cook. Smile. Suck. Fuck. Get pregnant. Never complain. Never cry or show weakness.

"It wasn't him. It was a dark-haired man."

"Russian, tattooed, dark hair and eyes, two sandwiches short of a picnic?" I ask, looking around my cage, searching for any sign of the woman who was in here before me. No words of comfort or despair are scratched into the bricks. There's not so much as a bobby pin to show another woman was ever locked in here. Just that awful stain on the floor outside.

Olivia shudders. "That's him. But who is..." she takes a breath "...Elyah?"

I am new driver.

I knew that was rubbish when he spoke the words two years ago. The first moment I laid eyes on him, I knew he was a violent criminal, but growing up like I did, coming face to face with violent criminals wasn't out of the ordinary.

I stare through the bars at the cellar beyond. This, whatever this is. It's sick.

"I used to know him. He worked for my husband who was in the Russian mafia in the United States. Elyah was in the mafia, too."

From the looks of it, he still is, and he's working for a new *Pakhan*. Once a man is in the mafia, he rarely gets out alive, nor does he want to. The Bratva is a brotherhood, one where members are linked by a code rather than blood.

That code is law to these men. It's life.

"Where's your husband now?" Imani asks.

"He's dead." I feel nothing when I remember Ivan. Not sadness. Not even hate. Just an empty, cold spot in my life, inhabited by a ghost. "Who else is keeping us locked up? Is it just two men in charge?"

"There's a third," someone whispers. "I've heard the dark-haired one call him Kostya."

Kostya, a diminutive of Konstantin. Probably another Russian as the Bratva prefer their own.

Before I can open my mouth to ask if this Kostya is in charge, I hear the sound of heavy footsteps coming downstairs. There are gasps from up and down the cages, and everyone falls into silence. Terrified silence.

A tall, muscular man in a black T-shirt crosses the threshold and looks up and down the row. His face is cast in shadows, but I can make out the tattoos inked into his biceps, forearms, and fingers.

Then he steps into the light.

It's him. The dark-haired man who killed the Lugovskayas.

His voice is a deep, accented purr. "Who is talking?"

A faint echo comes back to me, that same voice murmuring in my ear as he held me close, *"Welcome to the..."*

Welcome to the what?

The man pulls a telescoping baton from his belt and expands it with a vicious downward flick of his arm. "Someone is going to tell me who is talking, or I will drag you out of your cages by your hair and beat you, one by one, until you all confess. And then I will beat you all again." He disappears from view as he heads for the first cage.

I sit down on the edge of my bed. "It was me. I was asking for help."

A clattering sound fills the air as the baton drags along the bars of the cages. The sound gets louder and louder, closer and closer, until the man appears in front of my cage. The baton stops with a clang.

I keep my eyes low, my shoulders slumped. I'm so weak. So confused. Just a stupid little woman.

The man laughs, low and deep. "And did anyone help you?"

I shake my head.

"These women will not help you, Number Eleven. If one does, her death will be slow, and I will do it out of Kostya's hearing so she can scream and scream. I love to take my time, *neordinarnaya*." He says this with pride, like a man boasting about his stamina in bed. "Do not think that you're safe from me because Elyah has claimed you as his."

Elyah's to torment. Elyah's to kill.

"*Hey*." He slams his baton against the bars. "Look at me when I'm talking to you."

Slowly, I raise my eyes. It makes my heart pound to behold his sleek, handsome face. Every drop of blood has been washed from his jaw, his lips, his hands, but the frenzied killer who murdered the Lugovskayas still lurks behind his eyes.

A crazed smile tilts the corner of his mouth. "Elyah will choke the last breath from your lungs, but I will play with you first. We already had hours and hours alone together. Do you remember? Killing makes me so fucking horny."

He steps closer to my cage and presses his hips and the zipper of his black jeans against the bars. My blood runs cold in my veins as I realize what he's implying.

"Did I put your clothing back on you the right way around? I can be so careless sometimes."

Breathe in. Breathe out. Picture the garden at home. Your *real* home. The place that Dad left you year after year, where you were so, so lonely, before you understood that a lonely garden is really paradise on earth.

"What a tight snatch you've got."

The flowerbeds in summer. The bees on the lavender and the scarlet poppies nodding in the breeze.

"Tell me, *neordinarnaya*. Did Elyah ever kiss that sweet little birthmark you have on your pussy?"

The small, pale brown mark on one of my outer lips. He's not bluffing about undressing me. *What did he do to me?*

I leap to my feet and lunge through the bars with both hands at the Russian, while he steps back and laughs. He runs his tongue lasciviously over his top lip, so fucking delighted that he's managed to tear away my pretense of submission and fear.

"Spit in my face. You know you want to."

Lose control. Give him an excuse to lose his. I can hear what he'd say to Elyah as they stood over my mutilated corpse. *She insulted me. I had to teach her a lesson.*

I force my hands back through the bars and sit down onto my narrow bed, my burning face turned away from him. I can't take my revenge while I'm in a cage.

But I will. One day he'll pay for this.

I feel him standing at the bars to my cage. Gloating. Smirking. It takes him ten minutes to drink his fill of my humiliation and terror, and he breathes heavily the entire time.

Fucking creep.

Finally, the dark-haired man grows bored and heads back upstairs. As soon as I'm alone and the room falls silent, I stuff my hand down the waistband of my shorts and feel around. I'm not sore down there, or even chafed. I'd know, wouldn't I, if he'd screwed me while I was unconscious? I take a deep breath and slip two fingers inside my underwear. Not wet and sticky, but damper than normal, maybe? I don't know. I pull my hand out and take a tentative sniff of my fingers, hoping to hell I'm not going to smell semen, but there's just my scent.

I wipe my fingers on the rough blanket, shuddering at the gaping hole of time between falling unconscious in the Lugovskayas' apartment and waking up here. I was at that man's mercy for hours.

Trembling, I push myself into the corner of the cell and sit on the floor, my arms wrapped around my knees as I stare into the darkness beyond the bars. If anything happens, I'll be ready for Elyah and the dark-haired man, and the mysterious Konstantin.

I'll be ready for anything.

~

"Up, my little jewels. Get up."

The jangling of keys and scraping of locks fill the air. I inhale sharply and raise my head. I must have fallen asleep with my cheek on my knees. Panic slams through me as the door to my cage swings open—

But the armed guard doesn't even look at me before moving on. There's another guard dressed in a black uniform holding the chain of a mean-looking dog. These men are *shestyorka*, I presume. Low-ranking muscle to keep us in line.

I can see the dark-haired man lounging in the corner, one thumb thrust into the waistband of his jeans, the sole of one shoe propped against the wall. His hungry eyes scour the cages, and when they land on me, he winks.

I hold his gaze for three heartbeats and look away slowly. I wish I could ask Elyah how he survived the mind games and constant vigilance that captivity demands. We talked about so many things, but never that. Then with a jolt, I see him enter the cellar room. His powerful shoulders move under his black button-down shirt, and his blond hair is dark with water. He's just showered and looks exactly like he did when he worked for my husband.

For a moment, I forgot that he's not a memory anymore. He's here. He's my captor.

A man in a black suit with a black shirt and tie stands in the middle of the room. His tattooed hands are clasped in front of him. This, I presume, is the Konstantin one of the women mentioned. He has an expensive, authoritative air about him, from the cut of his suit to the arrogant way he holds himself. He's older than Elyah and the dark-haired man by about ten years, and he has the attitude of a *Pakhan*. The boss.

His left cheekbone and temple are a mass of scar tissue, and silvery scars disappear into his dark hair. As he turns his head, I see the edges of a tattoo on the side of his neck.

He makes a beckoning motion with his hands at us and speaks in a deep voice. "Come out, my jewels."

I can't hear anyone moving. No one wants to be the first. Swallowing my hatred of our captors and keeping my face carefully neutral, I step out of my cell and stand just beyond the door, staring straight ahead. One by one, I feel the other women emerge from their cages and line up beside me. Some are fidgeting. Others are shaking.

Elyah comes down the row with a box under one arm, passing out bottles of water and cereal bars. My mouth is parched and my stomach rumbles. When he reaches me, Elyah twists open the bottle of water and holds it up. "Would you like water, Lilia? Or would you prefer a cup of coffee?"

Him and me, sharing cups of coffee. I stare back, not saying anything.

Elyah tilts the bottle and pours the contents onto the ground, staring me right in the eyes. The water spatters at my feet. He drops a cereal bar and crushes it under his heel. Then he moves on.

I glance at the woman on my right. Olivia, the first one to tell me her name. She has tangled brown hair falling to her waist and she's wearing a wrinkled sundress. In her hands is an unwrapped cereal bar, and there's an anguished expression in her coppery eyes. She's a fraction of a second away from offering me some of her food, and I look away quickly and give a tiny shake of my head.

While the other women eat and drink, I watch Konstantin. His features are dramatic and handsome, but there's a sharklike expression in his crystalline, gray eyes. He stares at us like we're merchandise, his gaze not meeting ours but landing on our breasts, our hips, our legs. Even when he looks into our faces, he's searching for beauty. Perfection. Not humanity.

He called us little jewels. We're being appraised for our worth.

Konstantin waits for the rustling of cereal bar wrappers to die away, and then he lifts his chin and speaks. His velvety, accented voice fills the dank room.

"How beautiful you all are. What a pleasure it is to welcome you here."

Then he smiles, as if the irony of welcoming us to a place where we've been brought against our will has just occurred to him.

"My name is Konstantin, and we're going to play a game. Like all games, there are rules, and there's a winner. Only one winner." His gaze sweeps along the row of women. "You want to be that winner."

There's a box sitting at his feet, and he leans down, picking it up and opening it. Something inside glitters and we all strain to see what it is.

Konstantin draws the object out, holding it flat on his palm. It's a tiara, sparkling and pristine, set with pinkish, almond-shaped diamonds and clusters of hundreds more pale, precious stones.

"Fourteen million dollars' worth of pink diamonds. Fit for a queen." He lifts his gaze to us. "Or my wife. You will be judged on your beauty. Your poise. And above all, your strength. If you cry because we hurt you, we will hurt you more. Don't try and manipulate us with your emotions. I have no mercy. My friends have no mercy."

So that's what he has planned. A sick, twisted version of a beauty pageant, only it's our lives on the line, and I doubt these men care about our views on world peace.

Konstantin glances at Elyah and the other man, who have moved to flank him. "Do what I tell you to do, and what my friends Elyah and Kirill tell you to do, and you'll keep your fingers and toes and all the blood inside your veins. Maybe some of you knew each other before, but now you don't. You are not friends. You are competitors. If you try and help each other, you will be punished."

I put up my hand.

Konstantin's eyebrows creep up his forehead. With the air of a man humoring a child, he strolls over to me and looks me up and down. "Number Eleven. I've heard so much about you already."

I bet he has.

"You have a question?"

"What happens to the women who lose?" I ask.

He leans down closer to me and smiles a cold, vicious smile. "What do you think happens to useless whores?"

Despair washes over me, and I wonder if there are other women in this room like me. Women who have been treated like property all their lives. Women who have broken away and found a few scraps of independence through modeling work, only to end up here, locked in this desolate cellar, face to face with a smiling psychopath.

It feels dangerous to say anything else, so I glance at Elyah, and back at Konstantin.

"You're wondering when Elyah is going to kill you? He's generously allowed you to compete, but you won't win the pageant. I'm sorry."

Over Konstantin's shoulder, Elyah glares at me with pure venom. Watching me struggle without any hope of getting out of this is the first way he's going to torture me.

"The longer you stay in the game, the longer you will survive. As soon as you're out, I'll hand you over to him."

"And the other women?" I ask.

"What about them?"

"What's going to happen to them?"

Konstantin frowns. "Why do you care?"

The idea of one human caring about another is so alien to him. "Please don't hurt them. They're not from our world. It's not fair."

I didn't hear any Russian accents. None of their names are Russian. These women just want to go home to their families, whereas I've been living on borrowed time for two years. I knew it was going to end this way; perhaps not so elaborately, but death is death whether it's in pursuit of a hateful, glittering crown or being hunted by a hitman in a dark alleyway.

"Number Eleven, I have to recoup my losses. One woman will win, you will be killed, and the rest will be sent back to Russia and sold." He turns and speaks to the others. "Which is why you must all follow my rules. If we cut your faces, your price will be cheap. You will end up in a whorehouse gnawed by rats and used two dozen times a day. If you try your hardest, you may fare better. I'm not an unreasonable man. You may get a husband out of this."

On my left, Imani almost starts to sob, and Konstantin notices her stifled tears.

"Now, now. There's no need for that. We won't be monstrous unless you are bad girls." He spreads his hands and smiles. "Haven't I been nice to you so far? All models want rich husbands to take care of them, and I know many rich men back in Russia."

My teeth grind together but I swallow down my retort. A rich husband sounds great until he's beating his defective property while she lays in a hospital bed. But as I peer to my left and to my right, I wonder how many women here are being won over by what Konstantin is offering.

"As for me, I want a woman I can treat like a queen," Konstantin tells us. "She'll want for nothing. She'll know only power and riches by my side."

Several heads lift with interest. Konstantin can probably provide what he's offering, but the cost will be dearer than they can imagine. The life of a Bratva bride is full of danger and soaked with blood. All the jewels he gives you won't make up for being treated like a vessel and a whore.

He turns the crown in his hands, and all eyes are drawn to

it. Even mine. The glittering object seems to emit an alluring force. A prize fit for an underworld queen.

"The only way out of this to safety and happiness is to earn this crown." Konstantin smiles his cold smile, and gazes from one of us to the next. "May the best woman win."

It's a trick! I want to shout. *Don't believe a word he says. The only winner will be him.*

We all need to unite against these men. Together, we're smarter than the three of them. Men can be fooled. We have no choice but to play this *Pakhan's* sadistic game, but we must play to survive, not to win.

"You have twenty minutes," Konstantin announces, turning toward the door. "Anyone who is late will be punished."

After Konstantin, Elyah, and Kirill leave us, silence reigns. The armed men unlock a door at the side of the room and stare at us. We stare back at them and then at each other, wondering why we haven't been forced back into our cages.

"I think we're supposed to...get ready?" one of the women says, pointing at a rack of clothes against the wall. Then she shoots a fearful look at the guards, wondering if she's about to be beaten for speaking. The men stay where they are, faces impassive.

"Ready? What for?" Imani asks in horror.

Olivia walks over to the rack and begins sorting through the garments. "They're all swimsuits. And there are numbered sashes as well. Are we going swimming or something?"

When I was in high school, one of my friend's sisters was a beauty pageant hopeful, and we watched her on television as she competed for the Miss America title. She was cut during the first round when they all modeled swimsuits.

"Don't be dumb. It's a pageant, remember?" another woman says, striding forward and grabbing a red bikini and holding it up in front of herself. "These are for the first round of the competition."

She disappears through the unlocked door, and I see there's a dark sort of bathroom beyond. Some women head inside, and some go for the swimsuits and sashes. Others stay where they are, too frightened to move. One woman has a terrified expression on her face and stares straight ahead, hands clenched.

Olivia turns and looks over her shoulder at me. "Come on. You don't want to be left with the crummiest bikini."

I shake my head and stay where I am. Better that I wear the worst clothing when I'm going to die anyway.

Olivia peruses the rack, then comes over to me holding a green and gold bikini and whispers, "The longer you stay alive, the better chance you have of escaping."

I smile at her in relief. She understands what we have to do, and it gives me hope that the others do, too. "Don't worry about me. You go and get ready."

Olivia hesitates. "I don't know if you've noticed, but everyone here is terrified. I've been here two days and Imani is the only one I've been able to talk to. You were here two minutes and you got everyone saying their names. We need you."

"What we need is some way to escape," I counter.

"We'll find it, but don't die in the meantime."

"I don't plan on dying faster than I have to."

Olivia still seems worried, but she takes her bikini and disappears into the bathroom.

I glance around and see that there's one other woman who hasn't approached the rack, and I walk over to her. "I know we did introductions last night, but now we can put faces to names. I'm Lilia. What's your name?"

"Alejandra."

Alejandra is in cage one. No wonder she looks terrified. Whatever happens to us is probably going to happen to her first. "There's no need to hang back. You should go and get ready."

"No," she says through her teeth. "Screw them and their sick games."

A perfectly understandable reaction, but not one that's going to keep her alive.

I take my place at her side, and together we watch the other women pulling on their bikinis and sorting through boxes of makeup. Some seem dazed. Others have fallen into the zone, testing shades of foundation on their wrists and brushing their hair like we're backstage at a fashion show.

Alejandra glances at me uncertainly. "Aren't you going to get ready?"

I shake my head. "As long as they have me to punish, they won't hurt you, so I won't get ready, either."

Alejandra turns pale. "They really will punish us?"

"You saw what happened to the last Number Eleven. Men like this don't take no for an answer."

"I thought that was just because she was screaming," Alejandra mutters, twisting her fingers together. "They will cut me if I don't obey?"

"I'm sorry, yes. They meant every word."

Alejandra's face creases and she's on the verge of tears. "But I don't want to play this game. I just want to go home."

My heart twists painfully in my chest as I think of my *babulya's* home and her garden full of flowers. What I wouldn't give to be with my grandmother right now. "So do I. We all do. As long as you're alive, there's still hope of getting out of this. We'll find a way, together."

I speak as softly as I can so the guards don't overhear me, but most of their attention is on the long legs and bare skin that's suddenly on display.

Alejandra brushes the tears from her cheeks. "All right. I'll go and get ready. But what about you?"

I give her a quick smile. "I'll be fine. Go choose your swimsuit, and then I'll grab whatever's left."

She does, and when I go over to the rack a few minutes later, there's only one swimsuit remaining. It's a beige bikini two sizes too big for me. I put it on and tie knots in the briefs and the top to make it fit better, and then add the white satin Number Eleven sash over the top. I don't have the energy for makeup, but I pass a brush through my hair, use the bathroom, and drink water from the single cold tap, and then stand at the side of the room, trying to ignore my growling stomach.

Ten minutes later, the guards corral us all upstairs and along a marble corridor. Most of the curtains are drawn, but I get one quick glimpse out a window and see a beautiful garden and sunlight sparkling on blue water. The ocean? Or a lake? That's interesting. I wonder how many of these women are strong swimmers. Perhaps we could escape across the water.

The house itself has towering ceilings and expensive old-world décor. It feels hundreds of years old but kept in pristine condition. We pass a bookcase, and I recognize Italian words in gold on leather-bound books.

My heart leaps. Could we still be in Italy? If so, the families of the missing women won't have far to look for us. I'm not going to sit back and wait for a rescue, but it's a possibility that someone might come for us.

We're forced into a room and made to wait by an enormous carved wooden door. We all stare at it in trepidation, wondering what's on the other side. The three Russian men, I presume, waiting to stare at us, judge us, make us dance to their twisted tune. Will they call us in one at a time and enjoy us trembling in fear before them? Or will we all go in at once and be able to draw strength from each other? I have a horrible feeling it's going to be the former and we'll be made to face these men alone.

One of the guards patrols around us with his snarling, slavering dog. No one dares speak.

Mentally, I catalog all the terrible things that could happen to us on the other side of that door. I wonder if we'll be raped. Ivan was never gentle, and he never asked if I wanted to have sex with him. He was just on me suddenly, and I learned to switch off and think about something else. The fact that I never had an orgasm was beneath his notice.

I picture Elyah forcing me to have sex with him. Making me hurt one of the other women or have them hurt me, and cold sweat breaks over me. Who will we be once the sun sets tonight? Sixteen broken dolls, played with roughly and cast aside?

Bruised. Bleeding. Crying.

An accented voice over a loudspeaker calls, "Number One."

Suddenly, the door opens, revealing a dark room beyond and a guard standing in the doorway. My stomach feels like it's been sucked out of my abdomen. The guard searches the women for the one wearing the Number One sash. Alejandra shoots me a terrified glance over her shoulder as he grabs her and drags her through the door.

"No, please! *Meu Deus*," Alejandra wails. *My God.*

I feel like I'm watching her being led to her execution. All around me, fourteen women cover their faces and huddle together, some of them breaking into sobs. This is wrong. This is *obscene*. Maybe we shouldn't be playing along, biding our time until we find a means of escaping. Maybe we should rebel right this second and take our chances, guns and dogs be damned.

I dash forward and reach for Alejandra, my only thought to pull her back to us as I scream, "Let her go!"

The guard turns his rifle around and slams the butt into my ribs. All the wind is knocked out of me and I double over.

A door closes. When I look up, Alejandra is gone.

6

Konstantin

A woman enters the room, and behind her a scream of protest ends with a moan of pain.

The room is dim with a spotlight overhead, illuminating an empty space with a woven rug. Elyah, Kirill, and I sit behind a long table that's cast in shadows. There are no windows, but there are three doors. One for the guards, one to let the women in, and one to let the women out. If they behave, they'll pass through this room unscathed. If they don't...

I glance to my left where Kirill is sitting, hungry for these women's defiance.

After being pushed through the door, Number One stands with her back against it, her chest lifting and falling with panicked breaths. The guard departs and the four of us are left alone.

I lean forward into the light and beckon the woman toward us. "Come forward, Number One."

She doesn't seem to hear me. Her ankles tremble and both fists clench at her sides. I stare at her for a full minute, waiting for her to do something. Anything.

Kirill makes an impatient noise and folds his arms. I glance at Elyah and see that he's not even looking at Number One. He's staring at the door that Lilia Aranova will soon step through.

I stand up from behind the table and approach the shivering woman. She sucks in a frightened breath and huddles against the door as if it's going to protect her. What a beautiful body she has. Long legs and shapely hips and thighs. Warm, tanned skin. Dark hair tumbling over her breasts.

I crook a finger under her chin and tilt her face up to mine, but she refuses to look at me.

"Are you going to kill me?" she whimpers.

"It's understandable, your terror. I have to be frightening out there," I murmur, nodding to the door behind her, "but in here, I want you to relax. I want to get to know you."

Number One raises her sparkling, jewel-like eyes to mine. They drift to my temple, and the ugly scar left by the bullet that tore across my skull.

"Are you staring at my scar?"

She looks away quickly. "No."

Liar.

Women always stare at my scar, as if it's the most important thing about me. How I received this injury is a bitter memory, though my scar has its uses. It unsettles my enemies and distracts my business associates, and I wear it with pride. Between my scar and my presence, people understand what I am the moment they lay eyes on me. Strong. Rich.

Powerful.

These women need to learn that my scar is the least terrifying thing about me.

"Tell me about yourself, Number One."

"What?" Her bewildered gaze darts from me to the men behind me.

I step back and perch on the edge of the table. "It's a simple question. Tell me about yourself. What you do. What you like. What you don't like."

"I want to go home."

I rub my brow and sigh. This is Number One's chance to shine, but she refuses to sparkle.

"Would you like me to help you, Kostya?" enquires a deep, dark voice behind me.

I gaze at Number One. "What do you think? Should I ask Kirill for his help?"

"No, please," she begs, backing away, clearly more afraid of Kirill than she is of me. That's a lesson she'll learn soon enough. If she dies or is cut, it will be on my orders.

"Did you listen to a word I said downstairs? This is a competition. The only way out of this is to win, and I decide the winner." I lean forward, speaking slowly and clearly. "I want to be entertained, Number One. If I'm bored, that's hazardous to your health."

Something of that seems to penetrate her brain. "Um, I'm a model. I'm Brazilian, and I like...I like...anime."

Anime. She likes fucking anime. I hit a button on the intercom on the table. "Take her away and send in Number Two."

A guard comes into the room and drags Number One away. Then he goes to the first door, opens it, and collects Number Two for us. She's the same as Number One. So are the next three women. Muttered non-answers. Shaking. Staring at my scar.

Beside me, Kirill is shifting restlessly. "Kostya," he growls.

The women aren't behaving, and he craves violence. I put a placating hand on his shoulder. "Soon."

I call for Number Six. The door opens, and a platinum blonde beauty strides into the room, chin up, breasts thrust forward. She's wearing a sky-blue bikini with silver high heels and her lips are glossy.

Finally, a woman who is taking this seriously. "Number Six. Welcome."

"*Spacibo*," she replies with a smile, thanking me, though her accent tells me she's not Russian.

"You're...Romanian?" I guess.

"Croatian." Then she gives a little laugh. "I'm sorry. *Spacibo* is the only Russian I know."

"I'm sure you're a fast learner," I say, my eyes running over her body. Her smile widens, and I settle back to enjoy what this blonde has to offer. "Tell me about yourself, Number Six."

She places a hand on her hip and strikes a pose, her attention squarely on me. "I'm ambitious, and I'm tough. I've been a runway model for two years and it's taught me how to survive. Most people are too scared to do what needs to be done to get somewhere in life. Most people are weak."

I couldn't agree more. "And how do you feel about being here?"

She hesitates, and then plunges onward. "Truthfully? I'm

pissed off. I'm cold. I'm confused." Her expression softens and she meets my eyes again. "I like that tiara, though. I've never seen pink diamonds before."

Of course she hasn't. Pink diamonds are the rarest of the rare. "How pretty they would look crowning your head."

She tosses her hair and gives me a flirtatious look. "They would, wouldn't they?"

I mentally move her to the top of my list.

"Well done. You may leave by that door." I indicate off to one side and reach for the intercom.

She hesitates, still looking only at me. "The other women have been saying all sorts of things about you... Sorry, how do I address you?"

"*Ser.*"

"They've been saying all sorts of things about you, *ser*. I don't think they're taking this competition seriously at all."

I hesitate, my finger poised over the button. Sometimes the best thing you can say is nothing. I watch Number Six, and I wait.

"Maybe you'd find what I overhear interesting in exchange for one or two small favors," she suggests. "I miss having hot water and proper food. The blankets are thin and scratchy, and I hate being cold."

Kirill bursts out laughing.

Frowning, Number Six looks at him for the first time. "What's so funny?"

He points a tattooed finger at the other side of the room, still laughing. "You will see when you go through that door, you stupid bitch."

Number Six stares at the door, and the long mirror beside it, but she doesn't understand. I press the intercom and call for a change of woman. Number Six leaves with a guard gripping her upper arm, her expression troubled.

The next four women are all as scared as the first, and they have nothing to say for themselves except for mumbles and choked tears. My scar starts throbbing as my frustration rises.

As yet another woman trembles and stammers before us, I snap my head up and roar, "Get the fuck out!"

The woman panics and hurries back to the door she came through, but it's locked and she tugs uselessly on the handle. I stab the intercom with a finger as I rub the scar tissue on my forehead to tell the guards to get rid of her. The man grabs her, and the woman trips and falls on her ass.

I gaze at her dispassionately as she struggles to her feet and is escorted from the room. Not daring to hope that the next woman will be any different, I turn my attention to the one the guard is bringing in. Lilia Aranova is standing in the doorway.

Elyah has gone totally still at my side. Kirill is radiating interest, and I recall how he told us with shining eyes how she almost shot him.

Number Eleven is an untidy mess. Her bikini is in knots to hold it in place and her feet are bare and dusty. Dark blonde hair hangs in lank ribbons around her face and her fists are clenched like she's ready to drop into a fighting pose. Nothing about her says beauty queen.

And yet she is beautiful.

I tap my long fingers on the tabletop as I watch her walk slowly into the room, taking in the exits, the furniture, us. She doesn't flinch as the door is slammed and the guard disappears. Someone taught this woman about survival. Or she taught herself out of necessity.

Number Eleven turns her unwavering gaze on me. She's not looking at my scar. She's looking into my eyes, her gaze boring through my skull like a bullet. What beautiful eyes she has, a delicate shade of sea green, edged with dark blonde lashes. The bikini she's wearing is ill-fitting and an unpleasant color, but it can't hide the fact that her body is stunning. Long, slender legs, and she has feminine curves to her hips and breasts.

"Tell me about yourself, Number Eleven."

"Why?" she shoots back.

I give her a smile. "Because I'm asking you."

She shrugs. "Sorry, there isn't much to say. I'm a model. I walk up and down a catwalk. My life is very boring."

That's a lie already. "You can shoot a gun. You're hiding from the Bratva in America who want you dead because you informed on them to the feds. You're the daughter of a powerful *Pakhan*, and you were once married to Ivan Kalashnik. I'm sure you have dozens of tales you could entertain us with."

Elyah leans forward, clasping his hands together on the table as his gaze burns. If he's hoping she'll look at him, he'll be disappointed. Lilia stares at me, saying nothing.

"You know you're a dead woman. Why not use your family connections to bargain your way out of this?" I ask.

There's a slight curl to her lip. "My father probably likes you three more than he likes me. Besides, I heard what happened to the last Number Eleven when she tried to use her father to get out of here."

I can't help the smile that spreads over my face. Number

Eleven has her wits about her. "You will die as soon as you're eliminated from this contest. Do you have nothing to offer me to save your life?"

There's nothing she can offer that will make me go back on my word to Elyah, but I want to dangle the possibility in front of her and watch her dance for it.

Number Eleven refuses to play. "I have nothing and no one. Though I can offer you a piece of advice, for free."

My eyebrows creep upward, the muscles of my forehead tugging on the scar. "Oh?"

"Beware of Elyah Morozov. Whoever you take as a wife, the moment she's yours, he'll try and steal her from you. He won't be able to help himself."

Beside me, Elyah goes rigid with fury.

I check my watch. "Four minutes. Faster than I expected."

"What was faster than you expected?" she asks.

"How quickly you would try to drive a wedge between the three of us. Do you think that Elyah hasn't told me every detail of what went on between the two of you?"

Number Eleven's eyes widen.

"You supposed that Elyah would be too afraid to tell his *Pakhan* how he nearly screwed his old *Pakhan's* wife? Elyah told me everything right away. All the lurid details. You were as cool as an assassin the day he nearly fucked you in your kitchen. Facing your husband, you didn't betray a flicker of what a disloyal whore you are."

"I must have really got to you, *neordinarnaya*," Kirill tells her with a laugh. "You would have taken my head off yesterday if I'd let you near me."

She flicks an indifferent glance at Kirill, and then looks back at me. "The day in the pantry when Elyah stuck his tongue down my throat? It wasn't difficult to act like nothing happened. Elyah must have imagined that he got me more flustered than I really was."

Anger races through Elyah's muscles and he clenches his fists on the table.

Lilia notices and laughs. "What nonsense has Elyah been telling you? That there was some great forbidden love between us like *Romeo and Juliet*? Please."

"Then what's your side of the story?" Just as with all the other women, I'm giving Number Eleven the opportunity to show me what she's made of.

"Why do you care?"

"I like to be entertained."

"There's not much to say. Elyah tried to flirt with me a few times, but he was very clumsy. When he finally got me into bed, nothing even happened between us. Maybe he had a problem, you know, down there." Number Eleven gives a pointed glance toward my groin.

"I could kill you right now and no one would stop me," Elyah seethes.

Still looking at me, she replies, "And yet you're sitting there doing nothing. As usual."

In one swift movement, Elyah jumps over the table and grabs her by the throat. Number Eleven's eyelashes barely flutter as she glares up at him, fearless and proud.

"You lying fucking whore." He squeezes her throat tighter and gives her a shake.

"You don't scare me, Elyah Morozov," she wheezes, her expression burning with hatred. "My father is Aran Brazhensky. My husband was Ivan Kalashnik. Who are you? A little boy who likes to get his dirty hands on what's not his. You were sent to prison for stealing. You tried to steal me. You're nothing but a common thief."

"You will die like bitch," he roars.

"I'll die with dignity. You're the one who'll have to clean up the mess I leave on the floor, *podkhalim*. That's what Ivan called you behind your back, did you know?"

Bootlicker.

Her expression fills with goading. "You never figured it out, did you? God, you're stupid, Elyah. I was planning on manipulating you into killing my husband, but the feds got there first."

"Why?"

Number Eleven shrugs. "He was old and ugly. I didn't like him and I was bored with playing housewife."

His lip curls back in a snarl. "Everything is game to you."

She lifts her arms and gestures around the room, at the desk Kirill and I are sitting behind. "Well, what the fuck is this?"

Kirill lets out a shout of laughter and claps his hands, loud and slow. "Ten fucking points. Five stars. What's our scoring system? I don't know, but Number Eleven wins round one for me."

Elyah shoves her away from him and her back hits the wall. They glare at each other, mutual hated sparking between them. His cheeks are flushed red. Number Eleven has completely humiliated him.

"You will fucking pay for this," he growls.

I press the intercom on the desk. "Send in the next woman."

As she's being escorted from the room, Number Eleven

flashes me a challenging look over her shoulder, one eyebrow arched. *So, are you entertained?*

Kirill is still laughing. Elyah is pacing up and down the room like a caged tiger. Number Eleven just detonated a bomb in this room and now she's gone, leaving us with the shock waves.

7

Lilia

As soon as the door closes behind me, I allow myself to take a heaving, panicked breath. I'm in a stuffy narrow room, and I brace my palm against the wall with my head bowed. I can still feel Elyah's hand around my throat, squeezing so tight that my pulse was throbbing against his fingers.

When I finally look up, there are ten sets of frightened eyes staring back at me in the gloom. All the women who went before me. They've been sitting in a double row of folding chairs before a...window?

No. A two-way mirror. We can see into the room where the men are holding the pageant, but those inside can't see us.

Someone stands up. "Lilia, what the hell were you thinking?"

It's Olivia, and she's staring at me with wide, shocked eyes, and she's so terrified that my heart starts to pound. What did those bastards do to her? As I look closer, there are no marks on her face or neck. No blood running down her body. I hurry forward and examine each of the women closely, scouring their bodies and faces for blood and cuts.

"Are you all okay? Did they hurt any of you?"

"Us?" Alejandra exclaims. "Do you have a death wish? I can't believe the things you just said to those men. We thought you would be beaten to death for sure."

There's not a mark on any of the women, and I breathe a sigh of relief. After the performance I just gave in there, I hope I'm at the bottom of the rankings. If there are any punishments to be meted out for low scores, they'll be mine.

I don't like pain. I sweat at the thought of the dentist and even a bikini wax has me cringing, so being flogged, or punched, or tortured with knives will turn me into a screaming, sobbing mess. I only hope I'll be able to draw strength from the knowledge that death will soon release me.

Overhead, I can hear Konstantin's voice through a speaker. With one eye on Number Twelve through the glass as she stands trembling in front of the three Russian men, I sit down in an empty seat and whisper to the women around me, "What happened when you were all called into that room?"

They tell me about Konstantin's bland questions, Elyah's stony expression, Kirill's boredom. No one can fathom what the point of the last few hours has been. Konstantin was impatient with many of the women, even yelling at some, but no one laid a finger on them except the guards who pushed them into the room and out of it again. It's puzzling, but I start to breathe a little easier.

"Marija offered to sell us all out," sneers the woman wearing Number Three, jerking her head at the platinum blonde in a blue bikini, silver heels, and a Number Six sash. She's staring straight ahead with her arms folded and a sour expression on her face that tells me she's been waiting for someone to tell tales about her.

"Fuck you, Nicoletta," Number Six mutters, who I presume must be Marija.

Nicoletta recounts how Marija was all smiles for Konstantin and seemed to impress him, until she offered to reveal our secret conversations to our captors in exchange for better food and more comforts.

Olivia shakes her head, her expression furious. "How could you, Marija? The first opportunity you get, you turn on us?"

Number Nine, who I remember is called Klara, gives Marija a dirty look. "While we were crying and nearly wetting ourselves and just trying to survive, you were thinking about food."

Nicoletta's gaze fastens on my reddened throat. "That beast nearly killed you. What do you think of what Marija did?"

Everyone turns to look at me, their angry expressions telling me they're eager to hear me denounce Marija. What she did doesn't exactly endear her to me, but I'm not about to pass judgment, either. Who knows what we'll all be forced to stoop to by the time this pageant is over?

"Marija was doing what she thought she had to do in order to survive. We all need to make it out of here alive, though I hope that we don't have to trample on each other to earn our freedom."

"I wasn't going to tell those assholes anything important," Marija says. "I just wanted another blanket. Bite me."

The other women don't seem like they believe her, but at least some of the heat has gone out of their expressions.

"Who's the judges' favorite so far?" I ask, hoping to change the subject.

"Marija," says, Daiyu, Number Five, and they all nod in agreement.

"Or she was, until she offered to be Konstantin's mole and Kirill laughed her out of the room," Alejandra adds. "No one seemed to interest the men until you entered the room, Lilia."

Number Seven, who I remember is called Madison, tosses her curly brown hair over her shoulder. "I'm so pissed off at this whole situation. I don't deserve this. I have a *life*. Maybe I should try insulting Elyah or Kirill next time. No one did anything to stop Lilia from mouthing off. These men have no goddamn balls."

She seems to be forgetting that Elyah nearly choked me unconscious. I grab her hand. "No! That's suicide. If you start talking back, then you'll be punished. Just try to fly under the radar while I draw the heat."

Nicoletta leans forward and goggles at Madison. "Are you forgetting what happened to Valentina, the first Number Eleven? Listen to Lilia and keep your head down."

The door opens and Number Twelve staggers through. Alejandra stands up to meet her, and Imani throws her arms around the other woman, who strokes her hair while she sobs.

"I know. I know, Imani. It's over now."

"It's not over," Imani cries as she wipes tears from her cheeks. "It's only the beginning."

A glum silence settles over us as we watch the next contestants. Number Thirteen, Shanae. Number Fourteen, Celeste. Number Fifteen, Deja. My stomach is in knots as each woman enters the judging room, wondering if this is going to be the moment when the gathering storm breaks and one of the women is beaten or killed for speaking out of turn. The two-way mirror and the speakers overhead give the impression that we're watching a twisted reality TV show.

As Deja describes her career to Konstantin and I worry at my broken nail with my teeth, someone whispers, "I wonder what they'll make us do for round two."

That's anyone's guess. Konstantin wasn't taking notes and he doesn't seem to have a particular goal in mind for round one. I suppose he wants to throw each contestant into the competition and see who sinks and who swims. By being laid back and friendly with his smiles and saying things like, "I want to be entertained," I sense he's lulling us into a false sense of security that the competition won't be too much of an ordeal.

I don't believe that for a second. Every detail of this twisted competition has been scrupulously organized, and behind that smile is a man as cold and ruthless as a shark.

Whatever happens next, we're going to suffer.

Deja is escorted from the judging room and pushed into ours, and though she seems shaken, she smiles when she sees us all gathered together.

"Hey, it's the afterparty. I thought there'd be champagne."

A few of the women laugh, and I feel the first genuine smile in days—weeks?—touch my lips. There hasn't been much for me to smile about in a long time, but the sight of Deja hugging Klara and Shanae sends happiness bursting through me. We've almost made it through the first task. There's just one woman left.

I turn my attention back to the two-way mirror and watch as the door on the far side of the judging room opens. A statuesque blonde wearing a red bikini and a Number Sixteen sash is pushed inside.

"Who's this?" Olivia whispers, and Deja, the woman in the cage next to Number Sixteen's, is the one to reply.

"Hedda. I think she's Swedish. I've been trying to get to know her since she was put into her cell, but she doesn't want to talk."

I realize I've barely noticed this woman and I don't remember her from earlier when everyone was getting ready. My heart lightens. Maybe she's already mastered flying under the radar. We're so close to this task being over and then maybe, just maybe, we can go back to our cages for the rest of the day without any broken bones or spilled blood.

Konstantin stares at Hedda for several minutes while the blonde woman studies the floor. "Hello, Number Sixteen. Tell me about yourself."

Hedda lifts her chin and her eyes flash. "I'm not Number Sixteen. I'm Hedda."

The bottom falls out of my stomach.

"Oh?" Konstantin asks, a delicate inflection to his accented voice. Kirill shifts forward in his seat. Our mirror-window is positioned a little behind the judges to one side. I can see some of Kirill's profile and his bright, hungry expression makes my stomach knot even harder.

Hedda doesn't say anything more, and I cross my fingers and I hope that she had one thoughtless moment of defiance.

"I told you to tell me about yourself, Number Sixteen. I won't ask twice, but my friend here will be happy to take over for me." He nods at Kirill.

Please, Hedda, say something bland like, *I'm from Sweden and I like drawing birds.*

But it seems like fear, exhaustion, and hunger have drained Hedda's sense along with the color from her face. She swipes at her sweaty forehead with her wrist and snaps, "Tell you about myself? Like I care if I am the one to marry you? Go fuck yourself, you Russian pigs."

The women around me gasp in shock.

"No, no, no," I moan.

Kirill gets to his feet, rubbing his hands together in glee as Konstantin sits back. Konstantin has an air of resignation as if he doesn't want this, but there's a slight tilt to his mouth that tells me otherwise. He turns his head to the right and stares directly into my eyes through the glass. That's what it feels like, anyway. I almost jerk back from that glacial gaze before I remember that he can't see me.

I hope you're all watching this, his expression seems to say.

Kirill slowly approaches Hedda, his towering height and his huge, muscular back dwarfing the slender blonde woman. She darts a quick look up at him and swallows nervously.

"What did you call us, Number Sixteen?" Kirill asks in his accented voice.

Fear flickers in Hedda's eyes, but she replies in a defiant whisper, "Russian pigs. Where are the oth—"

The dark-haired man backhands Hedda, as fast and as

vicious as lightning. She staggers and cries out, and when she straightens up, her palm is pressed to her reddened cheek.

Kirill smiles even wider, takes the baton that's hanging from his belt, and gives it a flick. It lengthens with a deadly *shhck* sound.

I leap to my feet and press my hands against the glass. Kirill advances slowly on Hedda as she backs away, and I'm reminded of the way he stalked me through the Lugovskayas' apartment. He found that thrilling, and as he looms over Hedda, he seems to be inviting her to fight back.

Hedda glances past Kirill to where Konstantin lounges behind the desk. His amusement seems to stoke her fury. "You can't keep me here! I'm from—"

Kirill grabs a fistful of her hair on the top of her head and slams the baton across her face. Blood explodes from Hedda's nose.

"Stop that!" I scream, beating my fists on the glass. The thick material seems to absorb the sound no matter how hard I strike it. Even my screaming seems muffled, and I wonder if we're in a soundproof room. When I run to the door and try the handle, it's locked.

I don't want to watch, but I feel like I have to. This is my fault because I didn't draw enough of their fury down on me. I didn't make sure that Hedda knew that making them angry was the worst thing she could do.

Hedda has both hands over her face, sobbing and retching at the same time. She backs against the wall and slides to the floor, her knees buckling and eyes glazed.

Kirill turns and looks over his shoulder at his boss.

Konstantin is watching the scene dispassionately. "Break her arms."

"No!" I scream, but no one but the other contestants can hear me. It's not fair. They can't torture Hedda simply because she acted like any sane person might in this batshit crazy situation. I fly into a blind panic, grabbing a folding chair with both hands and slamming it against the glass again and again.

All around me, the other women whimper and beg me to stop, no doubt terrified that I'm going to draw these three men's wrath down on all our heads. The glass is insanely strong, and no matter how hard I batter it with my metal chair, it doesn't break. They must be able to hear something on the other side because Celeste suddenly gasps.

"He's looking at us."

I pause for breath and see that Konstantin has stood up and he's on the other side of the glass, his hands casually in his pants pockets. On his full lips is a smirk that tells me he's having the most wonderful time.

We hear the rumble of his voice through the speaker. "Is there someone in there who wishes to take Number Sixteen's place?"

I slowly lower the chair I'm holding. Kirill digs a key out of his pocket and unlocks the door to our room and stands on the other side, waiting.

All the women turn to stare at me. Deja edges away from the door, clearly afraid that Kirill is going to reach in and drag her out.

I look past Konstantin and see Hedda, shaking and crying on the floor. I gaze down at my own arms. Strong. Whole. Healthy. I need them to feed myself. Take care of myself. Fight back.

I did need them. My hours on this earth are numbered.

That will be a comfort, at least, as Kirill breaks my bones. The throbbing pain will only last for hours. Perhaps a few days. Then I'll be dead.

I step toward the open door.

Olivia moans, reaching for me. "You can't, Lilia. You *can't*."

I hold out a hand to fend her off. "I said I was going to draw their heat and I meant it."

The women all stare at me in shocked silence as I file past them, and step through the door into the light.

I move past Kirill without looking at him and turn to face Konstantin. He smiles in a way that says, *Of course it's you*.

"Are you their whipping girl, Number Eleven? Will you take all their beatings for them?"

My throat is locked up tight and my mind is screaming at me to run back through that door and hide in a corner. Not trusting my voice, I nod.

"There won't be much left of you by the time this pageant ends. These women are ungrateful and disobedient. You'll be left in tatters in a day or two." He runs a finger down my cheek, the same side of his face that's been ruined. "Such a shame to destroy a beauty like yours."

I lift my shoulder in what I hope is a casual shrug. "I don't really want it. My beauty has earned me a little money, but it's brought me a lot more trouble than it's worth." For the first time, I allow my gaze to rest on his scar. Only his scar. It's shiny in places, the flesh raised and knotted. The outer corner of his eyebrow has been totally obliterated. From the looks of it, I think he's lucky to still have both eyes. "Beauty can only get you so far. In fact, it barely matters."

"What does matter?" Konstantin asks as he gazes down at me.

As if he doesn't already know the answer when he's holding all of it. "Power."

"What would you do if you had all the power right now?"

I don't even have to think about it. "I would make sure these women got out of here safely, and then I'd pull the rug out from beneath you. I would win, and you would lose."

His eyes are bright in his handsome face. "A pity your life will be cut short. I would have liked to see you try."

He steps away and moves back to perch on the desk, revealing Kirill, who gives me an evil grin. The baton is clasped in his right hand and the muscles of his forearm bulge. He's strong enough to break my arms with one blow, but the sadistic glint in his dark eyes tells me he's not going to stop at one. He could have shot the Lugovskayas, a quick and clean execution, but he chose a terrifying and painful death for them instead, stabbing them over and over again in a frenzy.

"Hold out your arms, *neordinarnaya*," he says, lovingly caressing the words as he advances on me.

On the far side of the room, Hedda is huddled against the wall, tears and blood dripping down her face and her eyes hollow with despair. I'll drown in her misery and fear if I'm not careful, and I look away quickly.

I hold out my arms and Kirill grabs both my wrists in one of his huge hands. I turn my head to look at Konstantin. This was his order, and my eyes fasten on his cold gray ones as I await my punishment. Kirill raises his weapon high.

A deep, expressionless voice speaks from Konstantin's other side. "Stop."

Kirill freezes and looks around as Elyah gets to his feet. He stays where he is, baton raised. "*Shto?*" *What?*

Elyah is the tallest of the three men, and as muscular as Kirill. The dark tattoos on his throat and collarbone stand out on his taut flesh. His wintry blue eyes run over me; his expression is pitiless as he drinks in my vulnerability. It's the same expression that was on his face when he unlocked my cell and loomed over me. My helplessness is a three-course meal for him.

He turns his attention to Kirill. "I have prior claim on her."

Kirill holds out the baton. "Then be my fucking guest."

My heart smacks against my ribs as Elyah takes the baton. I fight the whimper that rises in my throat. Kirill is one thing. I don't know him. I have never put my life in his hands. Even though we never had sex, I gave my heart to Elyah. I was closer to him than I have been to any other man in my life.

I trusted him. I craved him.

I loved him.

Stupid Lilia. I knew that men couldn't be trusted. I learned that brutal lesson a long, long time ago.

Konstantin is watching us with his arms folded. Elyah runs his tongue over his teeth thoughtfully, and then he reaches out and takes hold of my wrists. Kirill releases me and steps back.

As Elyah raises the baton high, my heart shrivels at the pitiless expression on his face. He wants to see me beaten and bloodied just as much as these strangers he calls friends.

But Elyah hesitates, and his gaze flicks to mine. One eyebrow rises ever so slightly. A question.

Will you beg for mercy?

Me, the proud, cold daughter of Aran Brazhensky. The prized wife of Ivan Kalashnik. Until the age of eleven, I grew up with the best of everything and never knew a day of hunger or the cruel bite of winter. After I was thrown out of my home, *Babulya* and I worried about how to clothe and feed me, but we always managed. I was on the cusp of embarking on a glittering career before I was dragged back into my father's world.

Elyah never had a glittering anything. He became a killer and a thief out of desperation, and he was treated like an object. A living weapon who was used by my husband, and before that, he was wielded by other powerful men. In prison he must have fought tooth and nail for every breath he took. Elyah has never had one sliver of power, until now. Konstantin seems to have earned Elyah's loyalty by treating him like an equal, and how exhilarating that must feel after being under someone's boot his entire life.

His hand tightens ruthlessly on my wrists, grinding my bones together. It will be the icing on the cake for him to hear me beg and then break my arms anyway.

You are the one in cage now, Lilia Aranova. You are the piece of scum who is nothing.

It takes all my willpower, but I keep my lips tightly closed. I may have been born in America, but I have the pride of a Russian, just like him, and he will never.

Never.

Hear me beg him for anything.

Elyah realizes I'm not going to speak, and he suddenly yanks me toward him, his face alight with fury. "You proud fucking woman. Do you know what you have done?"

His face is just inches from mine, but I don't react. The baton is still held high in his right hand. He's a hairsbreadth away from beating me to death with it.

"If you had begged me, I might have stopped at breaking your arms and let you live."

Elyah throws the baton aside and it hits the wall with a clang and falls to the carpet. As he turns away from me, he says, louder for the others, "If I start now, I will not be able to stop. I want Lilia Aranova to suffer. She is too rotten for quick death."

Kirill gives his friend a baffled look. "Then let me make her suffer."

"She is to suffer at *my* hands," Elyah snarls, rounding on him.

Kirill glares from the baton to Konstantin to Elyah, and then shakes his head as he curses in Russian.

I dig my nails into my palms, focusing on the pain instead of the relief that is pouring through me. I won't be beaten, broken, and killed. Yet. It's only a matter of time. I don't believe for a second that Elyah would have shown me any mercy, even if I had begged him.

Konstantin turns his attention back to Hedda who's wiping the blood from her chin as tears run down her face. My relief evaporates as I wonder if he's going to order Kirill to break her arms, after all.

I step toward her but freeze as Konstantin starts to speak.

"Number Sixteen, you have been eliminated and you will be locked in your cell until your fate is decided at the end of this pageant. Pray that the pageant doesn't end soon, for your fate is an ugly one. Just like your face."

Hedda wraps her arms around her knees, whimpering. It's time for us to get the hell out of here. I hurry forward to help her to her feet and propel her toward the door and back to the other women.

We're a silent, sad group as we're escorted from the soundproof room by two guards back to our cellar. Deja and I are supporting Hedda, who's shaking uncontrollably and barely seems to be aware of her surroundings. Deja and I exchange worried glances.

"Are you okay? I thought they were going to..." Deja swallows, the words too horrible to speak aloud.

"I'm fine," I whisper, aware that one of the guards has his beady glare on us and there's an assault rifle slung from his shoulder. Two years ago, Elyah pursued me relentlessly once he made up his mind that I should be his. He will pursue my death with even more persistence. Two broken arms won't be enough to soothe his burning sense of betrayal.

The guards let us use the bathroom and I wait in line to use the single toilet, splash cold water over my face from the tap, and drink a few mouthfuls. Deja and I wash the blood from Hedda's nose and chin and help her back to her cage. I think her nose is broken. She sits on the edge of her bed, dazed and unresponsive.

Someone has put a bottle of water and a packet of instant ramen on the floor of every cell, including mine. I'm not going to be starved, after all. Not at every meal, anyway.

The guards lock us into our cells and then turn around and leave us, switching off the single bare lightbulb and leaving us in gloom. A few rays of late afternoon sunlight are filtering through a tiny grate high on the wall.

"How are we supposed to eat dry noodles?" grumbles one of the women.

Klara says from two cells down, "Break the noodles up before you open the packet, and then shake the flavoring over and eat the pieces like potato chips."

Rustling and crunching noises fill the air as everyone follows her instructions, including me.

Imani, in the cell on my left, says around a mouthful, "Hey, that's actually not bad."

"The things you learn as a broke student," Klara replies with a laugh.

I munch and swallow automatically, turning over the events of the past few hours. The layout of the judging room disturbs me. I wonder whose idea it was that we're kept in fear and suspense as we watch the guards drag each contestant away before they come for us, then force us to watch the women that follow. It's sick.

Along the row of cells, I can hear Deja whispering comforting words to Hedda, who's started to cry. Hedda doesn't seem to hear her.

A soft voice calls out to me. "Lilia, are you there?"

It's Olivia in the cell on my right. I take my half-eaten packet of noodles and sit down on the cold concrete floor by the bars, picturing the tanned woman with long brown hair and copper-colored eyes sitting against the wall that separates us. "I'm here. Are you okay?"

"Me?" she gives a hollow laugh. "I forgot, you didn't see what happened to me."

I clutch the bars. "What happened?"

"Absolutely nothing. Konstantin asked me a few questions. Kirill was drumming on his thighs. Elyah didn't even look at me. I think I bored them. I saw through the glass how they reacted to you. They were dying to get to you, like you were the main event."

I sigh in relief. "You played it perfectly. You didn't break down and you didn't become defiant. Keep doing that and you'll make it through."

"After seeing what happened to Hedda, I absolutely will not talk back to those psychos," Olivia says with a shudder. "But you, Lilia. You were this close to being maimed or killed. I'm begging you, never make those men angry again."

I wish I could see Olivia's face and she could see mine. There's so much I want to express to her. Gratitude. Friendship. It's been a long time since anyone but *Babulya* truly cared what happened to me. "I only did as I was asked. Konstantin wanted to be entertained, so I put on a show."

"Boy, did you," she says with a laugh.

Her accent is unusual and not one I've heard before. "Where are you from? Britain?"

"Yeah. Essex, not far from London. People laugh at me because of that."

"Why?"

"Because Essex women have a reputation for being stupid and tacky, not runway models. It's a horrible cliché. There are TV shows about it. I love where I'm from and I love my Essex friends. I've actually lost jobs after designers hear me speak, can you believe it? Like my accent is going to tarnish their dresses."

Olivia doesn't sound annoyed, but I'm indignant. "That's ridiculous!"

"Yeah. It would be a nice problem to have right now, wouldn't it?"

I glance at the bars of my cage and realize she's right.

"I'd tell you all about my home and my mum and my dog, but..." Her voice cracks. "I think I might cry if I do."

"Of course. I understand."

Olivia is silent, and we both munch on our dry noodles. Finally, she says, "The quiet one. Elyah. He didn't strangle you or break your arms despite all the things you said about him. You even mocked his manhood." She makes a sound like she's puffing her cheeks out in astonishment. "A proud man like that and you told his friends he can't get it up? I really thought you were dead."

I rub my forehead as I remember all the things I said. I was running on autopilot and desperately trying to cover my fear. Being the worst contestant was all that I could think about.

"Imani and I watched him stare at you for hours after they brought you in here unconscious. Does he...love you?"

"It's not love. It's obsession."

"But maybe he did truly love you once?"

My stomach swoops like I've crested a roller coaster and I'm plunging down the other side. I can't remember those final weeks as Mrs. Ivan Kalashnik without being eaten up with shame, anger, and fear. I never thought I'd see Elyah again unless he was putting a bullet in my head.

"I don't know. It doesn't matter anymore."

"Trying to screw his boss's wife. The man must be reckless, or very stupid."

I turn until my back is resting against the wall and I stare at the uneven bricks on the other side of my cell. "You know who's stupid? Eighteen-year-old me, because I thought that Elyah's forbidden love was the most romantic thing that had ever happened to me."

I should have never allowed Elyah to make me smile, let alone touch me. Attempting to seduce me while I was married to his boss should have been a massive red flag, but from the first moment I laid eyes on Elyah—handsome, vital, confident, more than a little dangerous, and *very* forbidden—red was my favorite color.

"Maybe it was romantic. Dangerous men can have this weird pull on you. Goddamn pussy whisperers, some of them," she mutters.

I laugh, but quickly cover my mouth in case the guards are standing at the top of the stairs.

"I'm guessing your husband awoke nothing in your pussy," Olivia says.

I shudder, remembering Ivan pawing at me while I gritted my teeth. "Oh, God. Less than nothing. I hated... Anyway. I don't know what it was about Elyah. He was different back then. Polite and sweet."

"Sweet?" Olivia's voice is filled with incredulity.

I struggle to find the words to explain. "He described his hometown and how desperate and poor he was as a boy. I knew he'd been to prison. I even knew he was a killer, but it was because he had to kill, not because he liked doing it."

"Right. Much sweeter," Olivia replies in a strangled voice.

Sometimes I forget that not everyone has a *Pakhan* for a father and that death hasn't always been a way of life. We'd need hard liquor, not water and dry ramen, if we were going to unpack my whole past.

"Elyah was always giving me these looks like he'd cross oceans and climb mountains just to see me smile. I was so lonely, and then..." My eyes prickle with tears and I have to take a few breaths before I can go on. "I fell pregnant, but I lost the baby."

Olivia's voice softens. "Oh, I'm so sorry."

I reach through the bars across to Olivia's cage, and she

takes my hand. How good it feels to hold on to her. A friend in this terrible place.

"Let's not talk about the past," I tell her. "I want to focus on the here and now. I'm going to get you all out of here, alive. I promise."

Olivia squeezes my hand. "Yeah. We're getting the fuck out of here. All of us."

We say goodnight, and I crawl into bed and draw the thin blanket over me, praying for the oblivion of sleep. All's not silent, though. Hedda is sobbing, and the pitiful sound wears on my already raw nerves.

Her crying goes on and on until Marija snaps, "Do you think you're the only one who has something to cry about? Shut the fuck up!"

Hedda hiccups and sniffles her way into silence, until we have nothing left but the cold and dark.

8

Kirill

From the top of the stairs, I can hear someone sobbing.

Which one of our pretty jewels is crying herself to sleep? I picture her in the dark, huddled on her bed, with tears running down her cheeks. She doesn't know suffering. These women got off lightly when you consider only one of them was beaten.

It's not like we haven't made our expectations crystal clear. They've heard the rules and we tell them what they have to do. There's even a prize—a good one—waiting for the winner, and it won't be so bad for the losers.

Some of them, anyway. The ones who do as they're told. The others...

Who cares? They're as good as dead.

Someone calls out angrily in the darkness, and the crying stops. I stay where I am for a long time, listening to the distant hum of cicadas as night falls. I picture the women drifting off to sleep, one by one, long eyelashes closing over tired eyes.

On silent feet, I creep down the stairs and feel the air change from crisp and dry to damp and cold. I count along the cages. Eight... Nine... Ten...

Eleven.

A pair of eyes shine in the darkness. Contestant Number Eleven is awake, and she's gazing back at me.

I push my fingers through the bars of her cell and smile. "I was hoping you'd be asleep."

"What do you want?" she asks.

"Just saying hello to the judges' favorite." My smile widens as she flings me a dirty look. "How long?"

Number Eleven's eyes narrow. "How long what?"

"How long until Elyah strangles the life out of you? I can't wait to watch."

She rolls onto her back and stares at the ceiling. "Kirill, wasn't it?" she asks, as if she hasn't committed my name to memory. "When I get out of this cage, I'm going to make your life a living hell."

She's still wearing the badly-fitting bikini and I can just make out the peaks of her nipples in the darkness. I bite my lip and tilt my head to one side, remembering what she looked like naked. "I love that you think you can."

As I walk slowly along the row of cages, I see that some of our beauties are asleep, and others are just pretending. It's easy to figure out the difference when you know what to look for, and I've had so much practice.

"All tucked in safe for the night," I say in a singsong voice. Number Eleven is watching me, her eyes full of hatred.

I blow her a kiss and head upstairs.

When I head into the villa's enormous kitchen, I find Kostya and Elyah sitting at one end of the long table. There's a pan of something hot and savory sitting on the stove and both of them are eating pasta off plates.

"The little jewels are sleeping soundly," I tell them, twisting the cap from a bottle of vodka and pouring some into a glass. I lift my drink and toast the others. "Well, some of them. To an excellent first day. *Za zdrorov'ye.*"

The other two stop eating and lift their glasses and tap them against mine.

"You think it was excellent?" Kostya asks me before swallowing down his vodka.

"*I* had fun," I tell him with a grin. "Even if Elyah ruined it at the end."

Elyah makes a dismissive noise and goes on eating. I serve myself from the pot on the stove. Someone has made an enormous quantity of *makarony po flotski*, pasta with ground beef, and not very well, either. It's greasy and stuck to the pot, and the beef looks dry. I'm assuming it was Elyah or one of the guards because this is the epitome of cheap bachelor food.

"We are in the most beautiful part of Italy in an enormous villa and we are eating this shit," I grumble, sitting down with my plate. "Where is the *borscht* and the *pirozhki?*" I could murder some fried pastry filled with potato and scallions. Better yet, we should be eating good Italian food. *Pollo al vino bianco con funghi. Penne all'arrabbiata.*

"You can have *borscht* and *pirozhki* when we are back in London," Kostya says.

I pick at the greasy mess on my plate. "I hope your future wife can cook. Actually, why don't we get one of our women to cook for us? Now."

Kostya laughs. "You want models to cook you food? Do you enjoy tofu and celery?"

"Lilia Aranova cooks better than my *babushka*," Elyah mutters, chasing a piece of onion around his plate with his fork. He's eating with enthusiasm, but then again, he endured prison food longer than I did. *Makarony po flotski* would seem like a czar's feast to a prisoner.

I push my plate away. "You hear that, Kostya? Let's get her up here!"

Elyah points his utensil at me. "Do not. That woman is fucking slippery and we will all be poisoned to death."

"What with, ground pepper?"

"She would find a way," he mutters, forking pasta into his mouth.

"Shut up about the food, Kirill. Who is your favorite so far?" Kostya asks.

"Are you kidding? Number Eleven, no contest," I tell him. "She's the only one who has a fucking personality, but I'm grading on a different scale to you."

"And she's not on my list," Kostya reminds me.

I shrug. "Number Ten might suit you for a wife. Not too skinny. Childbearing hips. I don't know. It's too soon to tell."

"I liked Number Six," Kostya muses. "At first."

"Number Six is a fucking idiot," Elyah mutters.

I have to agree with him. Number Six offered to betray the other women to ingratiate herself with us the first chance she got. "She would throw her own mother under a bus. She would do the same to you the first chance she got."

"Loyalty is fucking rare," Elyah says.

"That's why I'm happy I have you two," Konstantin replies.

Elyah stops eating and looks up at him. "We have your back, always. If none of these women are good enough for you, we'll do this all over again. And I promise you this." He looks hard at our *Pakhan*. "Kirill and I will make sure that what happened with that devious bitch never happens to you again."

Anger unfurls in my chest as I remember how everything blew up in all our faces just eight months ago. If it hadn't been for Elyah, things would have been so much worse. Kostya would be dead, and I would have no one. No purpose. No one who gave a shit whether I lived or died.

A sour taste fills my mouth as I recall the older sibling I once called brother. You can't choose the family you're born into, but when you find your true brothers you will know what it means to be alive. Mine are sitting beside me right at this moment.

I cup the napes of their necks and look between the two men, swearing, "That disaster? Never fucking again."

"I'll drink to that," Kostya says, holding up his glass, and we toast each other.

"What's next for our little jewels?" I ask.

Kostya settles back in his chair, rolling the vodka around in his glass. "We thin the herd."

A smile spreads over my face.

"How?" Elyah asks.

"I'm going to test their integrity."

Elyah gives a humorless bark of laughter and pours more vodka into all our glasses. "Here is to weeding out the liars."

As I pick up my glass, I accidentally knock it against the saltshaker. It topples over and the cap comes off, spilling salt onto the table.

Elyah hisses through his teeth and scoops the salt back into the shaker and screws the cap back on. There are some grains left on the table and he takes a pinch and throws it over his shoulder. Then he mutters the Rosary and makes the sign of the cross on his chest.

"What did you do that for?" I ask.

He throws me an angry look. "You want to invite the devil here? You think we are so blessed that bad luck cannot touch us?"

I shake my head and drink my vodka. "You're such an old woman sometimes, Elyah."

∽

"I'm telling the truth," Number Four sobs. She's strapped into a chair, her wrists bound to the armrests and electrodes stuck to her upper arms. A machine on the table next to her buzzes, and she's zapped with an electric shock.

Number Four's piercing scream rends the air. Sitting just a few feet away, Kostya grasps his head with both hands, his teeth clenched.

"I told you not to *fucking scream!*" he bellows at the top of his lungs. A vein is throbbing in his forehead. "Get her out of my sight."

Elyah strides forward and begins undoing the straps

holding Number Four to the chair before dragging her up by her hair. Angrily jabbing the intercom, he yells, "Guard!"

One of the guards enters to take her away, and Kostya snarls, "She's eliminated."

That's two women out already, Number Two and Number Four. If we continue at this rate, we'll have culled half the women by the end of the day. Kostya puts his head back in his hands and groans like it's splitting open, while I pace up and down, fuming.

I hate seeing him like this.

"This is fucking stupid. Kostya, why are we running a task that makes these bitches scream? I thought we were hunting down the liars."

"Konstantin is not just testing their integrity," Elyah replies, resetting the machine. It's a polygraph that's been modified to deliver an electric shock to the interviewee when it detects lies. "He's seeing who can follow orders and who has self-control."

I shrug angrily. "Fine. But he doesn't have to put himself through this when I could test them by myself."

"Have you two finished talking about me like I'm not here?" Kostya growls, raising his head.

He looks like shit. Ever since he was shot, he's suffered debilitating migraines brought on by high-pitched noises and stress. "Let's take a break."

"We're not even halfway through," Kostya replies. He jabs the intercom and calls for the next contestant.

Number Five is a raven-haired woman who swallows nervously as Elyah buckles her into the chair and sticks the electrodes to her bare flesh.

"This is a lie detector, with a twist," I tell her. "If it detects a falsehood, you will receive an electric shock. Whatever happens, don't fucking scream. My friend here is this close to committing murder." I put a heavy hand on Kostya's shoulder.

The woman seems to be paying attention to the rules, but if she's not, we'll find out soon enough.

Kostya straightens his tie and pushes his hands through his hair, taking several minutes to compose himself while watching the woman closely.

"You said yesterday that you are from Montreal," Kostya says. "I hear the winters are hard there. Do you like the cold, Number Five?"

"No."

"Do you trust the other women?"

"Yes."

The machine crackles and sparks as it detects a lie. Number Five's eyes fly open, her fists clench and she gives a strangled cry of pain in the back of her throat. A moment later, she falls forward, gasping.

"Why did you just lie?" he asks.

Number Five breathes hard through her nose as she sits up, and her voice is shaking. "I want to believe the sixteen of us are all on the same side."

Kostya glances at the machine, but it remains silent. "There is only one side. My side. They can't help you. Do you believe me?"

Number Five opens her mouth but stays silent. I kick her. "Answer the question, Number Five."

It seems to cost her a great deal to speak, and her voice comes out in a whisper. "Yes."

Kostya smiles and gets to his feet. "Well done. You can go."

"I hate you," she mutters before Elyah can switch the machine off. He hesitates, but there's no answering buzz from the machine.

"I didn't need a lie detector to tell me that," Kostya says, smiling as Elyah flicks the machine off while I undo the straps holding Number Five down.

Numbers Six and Seven make it through the test without telling any lies or screaming. Number Eight doesn't understand what we want from her, and the machine shocks her repeatedly as she lies in response to even the simplest questions, and she screams every single time. Kostya glares at her with bloodshot eyes, his face pale and sweaty, and I rip her out of the chair and drag her from the room. Another one eliminated.

Numbers Nine and Ten both lie once each, but they manage not to shriek, and they don't lie a second time.

As Number Ten leaves, Elyah, who's been standing over the women while they take their tests, suddenly moves back against the wall and folds his arms.

I stare at him, one eyebrow cocked. "Shall I take over for you? Getting bored?"

Elyah gives a nonchalant shrug. "Just having a break."

Bullshit. He wants to watch Number Eleven squirm and scream. Fine. Let's make this interesting for him.

Number Eleven turns pale with fury as I buckle her into the chair. She's already figured out that this is no ordinary polygraph and looks like she wants to spit in my face as I explain to her how it works.

When she's all hooked up, I step back and glance over my

shoulder at Kostya. He's watching Number Eleven appraisingly.

"Did you love your husband?" he asks.

"No." Number Eleven's voice is firm but quiet.

"Why did you marry him?"

"Because my father told me to."

"Are you a good and obedient daughter?"

"No."

Kostya laughs. "This is no fun if you don't tell me any lies."

"Maybe we should have Elyah question her," I say, slanting a sly glance at my friend.

Elyah stays as still as stone, his gaze fixed on Number Eleven.

She returns his cool look, one eyebrow raised. "Fine by me. I know you have questions to ask me, Elyah."

Nobody moves. Nobody speaks.

"Ask me," Number Eleven demands, louder now. "*Did you inform on your husband, Lilia?* Go on, ask me!"

"I do not need machine to answer that."

"You proud fucking idiot," she snarls.

Elyah turns his face away and glares at the other side of the room. I can read his mind through every line of his body and the self-righteous set of his jaw. *I have nothing to say to you. I will wait until Konstantin is done playing, and then I will kill you.*

Number Eleven turns to Kostya. "What about me?"

"What about you?"

She watches Elyah for a moment, and then me. Finally, she turns back to Kostya. "Can I ask a question?"

9

Lilia

Konstantin's eyebrows rise. So do Elyah's. Even the dark-haired psycho standing over me seems surprised.

"Who is your question for?" Konstantin rumbles in his deep voice. He's freshly shaved and wearing an expensive suit, and he projects an aura of dominance and control as he sits before me.

When you look closely, though, he's frayed at the edges. A muscle in his jaw tics. His eyes are bloodshot and there's a sheen of sweat on his brow. I wonder about the instruction not to scream, and I remember a snippet of conversation I overheard as I awoke in this place.

The scarred one, he hates screaming.

Wiring women up to a lie detector that zaps them with electric shocks must be causing an awful lot of screaming. I wonder how many women have already been eliminated today.

"I have a question for him," I say, turning to glare at the dark-haired, dark-eyed man wearing a tight black T-shirt.

Kirill flexes his head from side to side, a smile spreading over his face. He takes his time stretching his muscles before finally straightening up. "For you, Number Eleven? Anything."

I twist my arms in my restraints. "Why don't we make this fair? How about you get yourself into this chair instead of me so I know if you're lying?"

"Why would I do that?"

"I thought a weirdo like you would get off on electric shocks."

Kirill gives me a wicked smile, showing all his teeth. "Not one of my kinks. But good guess. What's your question?"

"What did you do to me while I was unconscious?"

"Ah, yes," he purrs. "I've been thinking about that, too. How much do you remember?"

I sigh and shake my head. "Really? Answering my question with a question? I'm strapped to this machine and I'm doing as I'm told. Can't you give me a proper answer?"

Kirill saunters toward me. Taking my jaw in his hand, he murmurs, "We didn't get far, but oh, the things I had planned for you, *neordinarnaya*. How beautiful you look when you're asleep. When I locked you in that cell, I stood there for an hour watching you while you were out cold. Fuck, I was so hard."

My brows draw together in confusion. "Me being unconscious...makes you hard?"

He lowers his head to mine and speaks lovingly, as if he's begging for a kiss. "Do you really want to know?"

Of course I don't, but I want to eat up as much time as possible. "Yes."

The machine buzzes and my eyes fly open. Shit, I forgot about the—

Kirill whips his hand away a split second before pain bursts through me. I groan and fall forward against my restraints, my blonde hair tumbling around my face.

You *idiot*, Lilia.

When I sit up, Kirill has his hand in the air and he's laughing like a madman. "Did you see that? She almost got me."

I shake my hair out of my eyes and give him a dirty look, like it was my intention all along to give him a second-hand electric shock.

Kirill walks over to the two-way mirror and stares into it like he can see the women on the other side. "You little liar, Number Eleven. But seeing as you ask so nicely about my dick, I'll tell you anyway."

I can feel the women's disdain from the other side of the mirror as he seems to stare straight through the reflective glass.

"You probably won't believe this, but when I was a boy, fifteen, sixteen, I didn't know how to talk to girls."

Oh, I can believe it. "Now you're a grown-up creep who still doesn't know how to talk to girls," I fling back, remembering how much he enjoyed my banter yesterday.

Kirill laughs and meets my gaze in the mirror's reflection. "How stupid you are to piss me off. You sleep in this place while I hold the key to your cage. Would you like to hear my story, or should we go back to interrogating you?"

I keep my mouth tightly closed and my mind blank. I don't trust the machine not to zap me.

When I don't reply, Kirill continues, "The girls at my school talked about me behind my back. Freak. Weirdo. Pervert. But I got my revenge. I walked the streets at night and peeked in all their windows. I watched them sleeping in their pretty nightgowns and they couldn't stop me. They didn't even know I was there. I could have touched them while they slept. Stuck my fingers in them. Screwed them. I imagined their faces as they woke up and saw me." He turns around and rests his back against the glass. "That's the best part, Number Eleven. The tension. Wondering when they're going to wake up and catch you."

A sick feeling spreads through my stomach. Did he actually do these things, or were they a fantasy?

He strolls back to me. "Everyone wants something that's a little strange, Number Eleven. What gets you off?" He glances at Elyah, and then back to me. "Sneaking around with someone who's beneath you? Pristine, perfect Mrs. Kalashnik in her luxurious house, getting railed by a tattooed ex-con. How many nights did you lay in bed next to your sleeping husband, fantasizing about his driver's cock?"

Shit. How did I let him turn the conversation back on me? I never laid next to my husband fantasizing about Elyah, that would have been—

A bolt of electricity shoots through me, and I gasp in pain. "What the hell! I didn't even say anything."

Kirill bursts out laughing. "You must have been thinking

about lying. Did you see that, Elyah? She got her pussy all wet and frustrated over you."

"It is what I already knew," Elyah replies with a careless shrug, but there's a hint of a proud smile on his lips. I must have really got to him yesterday with my comments about never being attracted to him. I hope he laid awake all night rerunning our handful of hot and heavy moments through his head, breaking out in a cold sweat as he wondered if I had faked my desire for him the whole time.

I glare up at Kirill. Well, now he has his answer, thanks to this asshole.

Konstantin has been following the conversation closely but seems content to sit and watch. What a strange relationship these three men have. Not like any *Pakhan* and his underlings I have ever seen before. My father or Ivan would never sit in silence for long stretches while letting their seconds-in-command take the reins.

Elyah crosses the room toward me and hunkers down on his heels so our eyes are on the same level. "Have you had enough, Lilia?"

I glance at the machine, not sure how to answer. I don't want another electric shock, but I also want to keep eating up their time and energy so they have less to spend on the other women.

The safest answer is another question. "Are you going to let me out of these cuffs?"

He draws a sensuous forefinger along my jaw. "If you beg me. I love hearing you beg, *solnyshko*."

My head rears back in indignation. "I've never begged you for anything."

Another shock of electricity fries my nerve endings.

Elyah jerks his hand back and a stream of Russian expletives spill from my lips. "*Yob vashu mat'!*" *Fuck your mother.* That particular epithet I learned from my father's bodyguards.

"I thought you said she couldn't speak Russian," Kirill says.

"Swearing does not count," Elyah replies, and I can hear the smothered laughter in his voice. "Lying again, Lilia? You are very bad girl."

I rack my brain, trying to remember when I ever begged Elyah for anything.

He grasps my arms over the wires as he murmurs, "*Trakhni menya pozhaluysta*, Elyah."

Please fuck me, Elyah.

I swallow, hard. The memory of being pinned beneath his heavy body in his bed is shockingly vivid, but I'd forgotten he'd coaxed me to say those particular words. I went to his apartment in a moment of soul-crushing loneliness and weakness, and I've regretted it ever since.

Elyah stands up, a triumphant expression on his face, and swaggers back to his seat.

Konstantin is gazing at me with sharp interest. "Why did you want to fuck him, Number Eleven?"

I inhale sharply, panic slamming through me. "I don't want to talk about this."

"You don't get to choose what we ask you. Why did you sneak around with Elyah behind your husband's back?"

"Please ask me something else. Anything else. It's too private. Too painful."

"Answer the question or I will unbuckle those cuffs and Kirill will beat you until you're unconscious."

I squeeze my eyes shut. It's so cruel of him to ask when he already knows. "I was grieving. I was confused."

"Grieving who?"

I open my eyes and stare at Elyah. He didn't tell them? I thought he'd told them everything. Elyah swallows hard, his expression suddenly troubled, and I'm thrown back to that day two years ago as he stood by my side in Ivan's house while the police swarmed everywhere. Elyah's warm hand on my shoulder as he urged me again and again to sit down. The shock on his face as I collapsed, and his horror as he realized I was bleeding.

Elyah carrying me out to the car, his face white with panic as if it were his baby I was losing.

Elyah's arms tight around me as I sobbed in the hospital bed. His lips against the top of my head as he spoke gentle, heartfelt words to me. I would have a beautiful child one day, and the child would have everything because they had me.

When my husband backhanded me across the face for committing the sin of being an imperfect vessel, Elyah looked angry enough to murder him with his bare hands.

"Why didn't you tell them that part of the story?" I whisper.

He opens his mouth and starts to speak, but then he looks away again. There was no reason for him to conceal that part. It wasn't his baby, and he didn't even like that I was pregnant. I knew he was jealous as soon as I told him I was expecting.

"I had a miscarriage," I say, turning back to the other two, and before Kirill can mock me by asking if it was Elyah's, I snap, "Yes, it was my husband's."

But Kirill's expression is totally blank.

Konstantin studies me with his bright, shrewd gaze. "You lost your baby?"

Even now, the memory is sharp and painful. I can't speak and so I nod, blinking rapidly. It's lonely, losing a baby. There's a wretched, empty loneliness inside you where there used to be love. Nothing made me happy in the months after I'd married Ivan, but the realization that I was carrying something made of love, even if the way it was conceived was wretched and loveless, warmed me from the inside out.

Elyah, I want my baby back.

The man I said those words to as I sobbed my grief out on his chest is sitting just feet away, sunk in silence, unable to look at me.

"It wasn't there for very long. Just a few weeks, and then it was gone."

Kirill gets to his feet and saunters over. He stands before me, and his brown eyes are deep and fathomless.

"I'll give you a baby, Lilia Aranova."

His words are so unexpected and preposterous that my mouth falls open. "What?"

He takes my face between his hands. "A child with my strength and your beauty. Can't you just picture them?"

Of course that's what he'd see me as, an empty vessel waiting to be filled. Even if I wanted a child, which I absolutely don't, I wouldn't want one with him.

"When your friend is going to kill me? Even a mouth-breather like you should realize that throws a wrench in you plan. And I'm not having sex with you."

Kirill laughs softly. "Are you sure about that?"

"I've never been surer of anything in my life."

"Are you a deep sleeper?"

I jerk my face out of his grip. "You monster."

"You're perfect when you're fast asleep, those dark gold lashes against your cheeks. Every time I picture your eyes flying open and catching me balls deep in your pussy..." He sinks his teeth into his lower lip and moans. "I get hard."

There's a thick, twisting sensation low in my belly. What is *wrong* with this man? Is he some kind of sleep demon who feeds off you when you're at your most vulnerable? Slowly, his head dips toward mine, and those dark eyes flash with desire.

I turn my face away, my heart beating wildly.

Elyah is glowering at us from the far side of the room, his arms and jaw bunched in fury and his pale eyes filled with wrath. Kirill follows the direction of my gaze, and he runs his tongue over his top lip as he feels the tension crackling in the room.

Kirill's mouth is just an inch from mine, and he whispers, "How angry with him are you? Angry enough to take a little...revenge?"

"I was never angry with Elyah. Just disappointed."

"He was going to break your arms yesterday."

"So were you. I hate you all equally. I was happily going about my life before you brought me here."

"Happily?"

It's not Kirill who has spoken, or Elyah. Kirill steps back and I can see Konstantin, relaxed in his chair like a king on his throne. His expression is unreadable but his eyes are alight with interest.

"Say it, Number Eleven. I was happy before Kirill snatched me from the street."

I glare back at him, my lips tightly closed. Of course I

wasn't happy. A man like him knows that a woman in hiding from the Russian mafia lives in nothing but fear.

When I don't respond, Kirill grasps a fistful of my hair and gives me a shake.

"*Ow*. At least I was free before. I'm definitely not happy now."

"Of course you're not," Konstantin murmurs. The light is hitting the scars on his temple and cheekbone, making them stand out against his smooth skin. "It's hard for our kind to be happy. You should have taken what happiness there was within reach when you had the chance."

I thought about leaving my husband and running away with Elyah. I thought about it way too much because I was a romantic idiot consumed by daydreams, but it never would have worked. Ivan would have come after us in a murderous rage. My father would have, too, filled with fury over the daughter who dishonored him. Bratva men do not let betrayal and infidelity go. They would have hunted us down like animals. Elyah would have been tortured and killed and I would have been forced to give up any child I bore for adoption before I was even able to hold it in my arms.

Elyah and I would have had a few moments of happiness in exchange for a lifetime of pain. I know that as surely as I know night follows day. Even when I was a romantic idiot, I wasn't a fool, and I could never have done that to the man I loved.

"Like you are right now?" I say, turning the conversation back on Konstantin. I look around the judging room and the cruel machine he has set up to torture us. "This is what makes you happy?"

Konstantin smiles and spreads his hands. "Exactly." He

turns to Elyah. "Do you have any last questions for Number Eleven?"

My former lover stalks toward me, his fists clenched at his sides. His voice is a growl as he asks, "The day your husband was killed, you ran. You disappeared. Why?"

"I had no choice."

"Because you're a fucking snitch who needed the feds' protection?"

"No."

Elyah stares at the machine, waiting for the telltale buzz of electricity to burst through me. Nothing happens.

With a snarl of rage, he stabs the intercom on the table with his forefinger. "Get her out of my fucking sight."

Kirill unbuckles my restraints and removes the electrodes. I don't need his help getting to my feet, but he puts his hands around my waist and pulls me up.

I stumble against Kirill and his arms wrap around me. He buries his face in my neck, murmuring low so only I can hear, "Your silky pussy is going to feel so good against my tongue."

"If you touch me, I'll fucking kill you." I shove him away, and though he lets me push his muscular body back, his eyes are glittering with a dark promise.

One of the guards takes hold of my shoulder and propels me out of the room.

As the door swings closed behind me, Elyah seethes, "That machine is broken."

10

Kirill

The mountains have swallowed the sun and night has fallen, inky black and encrusted with stars. A cool breeze blows off the lake and ruffles my hair. The stone paths are still warm from the sunshine and perfumed flowers waft their scent into the sky. There's no moon tonight, and I can barely see my hand in front of my face, but I'm at home in the dark.

I love the dark. It keeps all my secrets.

I'm consumed with one thought and one thought only. Contestant Number Eleven's beautiful, defiant face as she swore, *I'm never having sex with you.* Of all the questions she could have asked today, she wanted to know what I did to her while she was unconscious.

"That's for me to know, *neordinarnaya*," I murmur with a smile as I carry on through the silent garden.

After Number Eleven left the room, we questioned the final four women. Numbers Twelve, Fourteen, and Fifteen passed the test, but Number Thirteen screamed once too loudly and was eliminated.

Eleven women left.

I wonder how they're holding up.

I step through a side door and enter the corridor that leads down to where the women are being held. There are two guards standing by the door, and I jerk my head at them to leave. "Take a break. One hour."

Wordlessly, they walk down the corridor and back toward the kitchen. I watch them for a moment, my heart pounding, and then slip down the stairs and into the darkness.

Before I leave the cellar, I cast a glance over my shoulder and see two eyes shining in the darkness. One of Kostya's little jewels is awake. I change direction and stroll toward her. When I reach the bars, I press my finger to my lips. "Shh. You won't tell, will you?"

She shakes her head rapidly, eyes wide.

"Good girl," I purr. "Because if you breathe a word to Number Eleven, I'll cut your face off and feed it to the dogs."

I give the terrified woman a final warning look and head out, a lazy smile playing on my lips.

I haven't felt this good in years. Kostya, I fucking love your pageant.

11

Lilia

I wake up in a cold sweat, the blanket laying over me like a hot slab of lead. I throw it off and sit up, fanning yesterday's dress against my sweaty body. Am I getting sick? I certainly had a night full of fever dreams. The confused hallucinations went on and on, sometimes fuzzy, and other times scarily vivid.

All of Kirill. Kirill in this bed, touching me. His fingers in my mouth. His mouth on my nipples. My clit. Spitting on my pussy. The slow, intense invasion of his cock.

I push my damp hair off my face. Holy shit. I'm having sex dreams about a murderous, knife-wielding madman. Being locked in a cage is sending me cuckoo.

Before I can pull myself together, a guard unlocks my cage and tells me to get ready. I stumble through the door and head straight for the bathroom, dying for a cool drink of water and to scrub myself all over.

There's no shower, only a cold tap and buckets. I wait my turn and then strip off in the small, tiled room with three other women. There's more space and less chaos today, and I realize with a hollow feeling that it's because so many of us were eliminated from the competition yesterday.

I wash my body down with a sponge and scrub my thong under running water, as I've been doing every day. I have to put it back on soaking wet, but at least it's clean and it's small enough that it dries quickly.

When I turn around to leave the bathroom, wearing only my thong, I notice that Marija is staring at me, a strange expression on her face.

"What? Have I got a rash or something?" I ask, checking my body for marks. Maybe I was bitten by a spider that gives you horny dreams. That would explain a lot.

Marija presses her lips together and shakes her head, pushing past me to the taps without a word.

That was weird. I haven't been able to figure Marija out yet. I stood up for her the day the others were angry that she'd tried to rat on us to our captors, but she hasn't said thank you. I didn't like what she offered, but I understand the instinct to survive at any cost. I've never given her any reason to dislike me, as far as I know, and yet she's always distant. The others tell me that Konstantin seems to favor her, and she was interested in his pink diamonds on that first day.

Well, I'm not her competition. If she keeps it up, she'll become Konstantin's bride and bring up his children in luxury. Good luck to her.

She'll need it.

There's a rack of clothing outside the cells, and I select a dress without looking very hard at it. It's turquoise and has long sleeves. I choose it mostly because I think it will be comfortable when I sleep in it tonight.

Numbers Two, Four, Eight, Thirteen, and Sixteen all sit miserably in their cells, watching the rest of us get ready. They won't be tormented today, but they'll have all the time in the world to wonder what terrible fate Konstantin has planned for them.

He's tested our nerve and our integrity. Our ability to follow instructions to the letter. If I break the rules and I'm eliminated, will Elyah kill me straight away, or will he want to torture me? I gaze down at the dress I'm wearing, wondering if I'll be alive for it to keep me warm tonight. He was furious when I left the judging room yesterday, and he spent the rest of the session sunk in furious silence, letting Kirill and Konstantin question the remaining women.

Everyone's nerves seem frayed and brittle as the guards walk us up to the corridor and along to the judging room. Terrifying days, wretched nights, and little food all take a toll on us, and I see more than one woman trembling as we're shepherded into the room outside the judging room door.

A few minutes later, the door opens, and Alejandra is dragged inside.

Celeste dissolves into shaking sobs. "When will this end? I feel like an animal in a slaughterhouse, counting down the moments until I'm killed."

I grasp her hand and squeeze it. "We're human beings, even when they force us to do things we don't want to do. We have to remember who we are even though they call us by numbers and treat us like cattle."

Marija is standing on Celeste's other side. She doesn't say anything, but she shifts on her feet and rolls her eyes.

"Have you got something to say?" I ask her.

Her lip curls. "Who put you in charge? Why are you even trying to be their favorite when they're going to kill you anyway?"

I give a barking laugh. "Me? Trying to be their favorite? I assure you, that's the last thing I'm doing."

"Not from what I heard last night."

"What?"

Marija shakes her head and turns away, but I'm not satisfied.

"I'd like you to explain what you mean. Do you think I'm working against you all somehow?"

Marija's lips tighten and she won't look at me, but Madison suddenly jumps in. "Why should we listen to you when you do exactly what they want you to do? At least Marija was open about what she wanted from these pigs. I'm starting to think you're hiding something, Number Eleven."

Marija folds her arms and nods, agreeing with Madison. Her words sting. I want to point out that Marija wasn't open, she just didn't know we'd all hear about her traitorous offer.

"Don't call me by that number. My name is Lilia, and I'm not hiding anything."

I gaze around at the other women who are looking back at me with troubled expressions. No one is more aware that she's disappointing these women than I am. I said I would help them get out of here and I wish I had a plan to offer them, but from what I've seen, the security at this villa is tight. My only option is to figure out what makes these men tick and see if there's some way I can use that knowledge to manipulate them. Walls and locks are impenetrable but human hearts are weak. If there's a way out of here, it will be by using these men's weaknesses against them, I'm sure of that.

Even if I can only save the women, and not myself.

"Do you think that screaming and crying will get us anywhere?" I ask. "Did it help the first Number Eleven? Has it helped the five women sitting downstairs? I'm watching. I'm listening. You all need to do the same. When the time comes and you see an opportunity, you have to take your chance." I stare around the group of scared, shivering women. "You're getting out of this alive. I swear it."

They exchange glances, some of them hopeful, but the others too scared and hungry to believe there's life beyond this hateful villa.

"Why should we believe you?" Marija asks, tossing her hair. "Yesterday you were having a good chat with them like you're all old friends."

I point to the judging room door. "Whatever I do in there, whatever I say, it's an act. It's a strategy. Don't believe a word that comes out of my mouth. I'm only Lilia when I'm out here with you all."

Olivia puts her hand on my shoulder and squeezes. "I believe you."

"Thank you," I whisper, giving her a smile. I turn back to the others. "You're all going home to your families, but first you have to be clever. You have to use their code against them."

"Their code?" asks Nicoletta. "This place seems pretty goddamn lawless to me."

I shake my head. "The Bratva code. The mafia is a brotherhood, and a man's word is more binding than any law. If he swears something to one of his brothers, if he says he will do something, he'll never go back on it. There are no empty threats."

"But that tall one said he was going to break your arms and he didn't," Daiyu points out.

"Yet," I reply, and her face falls. "Elyah will finish what he started when I'm eliminated. He has to."

"So? What's the point of knowing this?" Madison snaps.

"It means we're not completely in the dark. We can predict what will happen next and look for opportunities to escape. This pageant will continue until there's one woman left. At the rate we're being eliminated, this will probably happen tomorrow or the day after. A winner will be declared, and you'll all be transported back to wherever Konstantin lives. Probably a large city. On the way, you can look for ways to escape. The three men might fight about something. The guards might get careless. There could be a distraction while you're being transported out of the country."

It's important they understand this because they're going to have to do this without me. My body will be weighted down with stones at the bottom of the lake by the time these women leave the villa.

"How do you know so much about them?" Deja asks.

"Because my father was one of these men. I was married to one of these men." I swallow, my eyes dropping to the floor. "I fell for one of these men."

"The tall one with cold eyes?" Imani asks. She was still waiting for her turn when I was strapped into the lie detector yesterday, but someone must have told her about what happened.

"Yes, Elyah. He worked for my husband, and back then, he was charming and kind. It was a horrible mistake letting him get close to me, and I've regretted it every day of my life since."

Silence stretches in the stuffy room, and I know they're all trying to imagine how the cold, silent, and aggressive Russian could possess even one sliver of charm or kindness.

"We were listening to you and your lover talk yesterday," Madison says, a bitchy expression on her face. "Did you really betray your husband to the cops like Elyah said?"

"He's not my lover and I—"

There's a deafening bang from the other side of the door, so loud that we all jump. Klara clutches my arm and whimpers. "What was that?"

"It sounded like a gunshot," someone hisses.

"They're executing us now?" Celeste wails, rounding on me. "You said we were only going to be eliminated."

"Don't blame Lilia for what's going on in there," Olivia says. "She's trying to help us help ourselves. If Alejandra is..." She stumbles over the word *dead*. "If something has happened to Alejandra, then it's no one's fault but those assholes'."

Celeste dissolves into sobs, and she backs away from us, slides down the wall and falls into a wretched heap. I watch her helplessly, wishing I knew what to say to comfort her.

A few minutes later, Nicoletta is dragged into the judging room. I crane my neck to see around the door, hating the thought that I might see bloodstains on the floor, but I need to know what's going on. I catch sight of Konstantin and his hard gaze meets mine for a moment before the door slams in my face.

Olivia looks pale and clammy like she might faint. I draw her to one side and we sit down on the carpet together.

"Do you really think they're killing us in there?" she whispers.

Anything's possible, but I don't say that. "They want us alive. Konstantin wants to toy with us and turn a profit once he's finished here. Dead women can't make him any money."

She seizes my hand and holds on tight. "I have to get home, Lilia. I *have* to."

"You will. You'll be all right."

Taking a shaky breath, she goes on, "It's not me I'm worried about. Before I came to Italy, Mum was given four months to live. I told her I wouldn't leave her side, but she insisted I keep working. She reasoned it was only for a few days and then I'd be home to tell her all about Milan and show her the photos of me on the catwalk. She wanted to be proud of me in her final days. I can't imagine what she's going through right now."

My stomach plummets through the floor and a lump forms in my throat. Each and every one of these women have friends and family who are worrying themselves sick over their whereabouts.

Tears slip down her cheeks. "The worst thing is, this is not the first time this has happened to Mum. My big sister went missing two years ago. Just disappeared like she vanished into thin air. We never found out what happened to her."

I stare at Olivia in shock. That something like this could happen to both daughters is terrible. Her mother must be distraught. "You're going to get home to your family, I promise you that."

Olivia nods quickly, blinking fast. "Yeah. We're going to do it, Lilia. Screw these men, I believe in you."

I wrap my arms around her and hold her tight.

"What about you?" she asks. "Who's worrying about you, your father?"

"No one. And especially not him."

We watch as the door opens and the next woman is dragged into the room.

"You have to tell me if there's someone you love," Olivia tells me. "They have to know what happened to you if...if..."

If I'm killed. I think about my grandmother. My mother's mom. I even open my mouth to tell her about *Babulya* but it's too dangerous for Olivia. She might go looking for her and that will put her on a crash course with my father. Even though it makes my heart ache that *Babulya* will never know why I disappeared, I shake my head. "There's no one. I have no one."

"I'm sorry, Lilia. That's really sad."

We sit in silence while Daiyu and then Marija are summoned into the judging room, and I can tell we're both wondering which one of us has it worse. That someone's desperately missing Olivia, or that no one's missing me.

There are no more gunshots, but it's agony not knowing what's going on in the judging room. I watch one woman disappear into that room after the next, a sick feeling growing in my belly. Will the men be covered in blood when I enter the room? Will I ever see these women alive again?

Finally, it's my turn, and I walk in with my head held high and my shoulders back, determined to face whatever horrors await me like a *Pakhan's* daughter should. Elyah is standing in the middle of the room holding a gun with a hard, hostile expression in his pale blue eyes. The scent of gunpowder hangs in the air.

Konstantin is settled back in his winged chair, a smile playing around his lips as he watches me search the room with my eyes for any clues about what happened to the other women. There are no bloodstains on the carpet. No blood on the men.

Elyah points to the hard wooden chair beside him. "Sit."

I stay where I am. "What did you do to Alejandra? Did you hurt her?"

The fair-haired man towers over me, his expression cruel and gloating. He pushes the release on the barrel and swings it open, revealing an empty chamber. The bullet that was discharged while Alejandra was in the room. Digging in his pocket, he takes out another bullet and loads it into the cylinder, flips it closed, and spins it.

"I told you to sit. You are answering our questions, not the other way around."

The chair in the middle of the room faces Konstantin. I stalk over to it and sit down, glaring at the man who's responsible for all of us being here. "These women's families will be going out of their minds worrying about them. Did you ever think of that?"

Elyah jabs the barrel of the gun against the side of my head and keeps it there. "No one asked you, Number Eleven."

My heart turns cold hearing Elyah call me by that hateful number. "What are you testing today? Willpower? Our ability not to piss ourselves?"

Konstantin watches me in silence for several minutes. "I'm testing your courage, Number Eleven."

Kirill strides toward me, and my stomach floods with

sensation as I watch his powerful body moving. I shrink away from him, but his T-shirt reveals the dark ink of the tattoos on his strong biceps, and I remember the flex and bunch of his abdominal muscles as he thrust into me in my dream last night.

"A gun to her head? This is too easy for her," Kirill says, stopping directly in front of me. "Number Eleven is used to guns. A few threats aren't going to frighten her."

"You are right, Kirill. We will have to think of something better for Lilia Aranova." The press of the barrel vanishes, and Elyah moves around in front of me. He flicks open the cylinder of the gun and, one by one, removes the bullets. All but one, which he shows me. "Let's play a game of Russian roulette."

Shit.

He closes the cylinder, spins it, and points the gun at my head. With his narrowed gaze on me, he asks the room, "Who would like to place a bet?"

Sweat breaks out over my flesh as I stare down the barrel of the gun. A one in six chance to survive. I don't like those odds. "Elyah. Don't. This isn't you."

"How do you know what is me, Lilia? Were you my best friend? My lover? If I remember right, you are the bitch who betrayed me."

"I already told you that I didn't."

"I do not believe a word out of your lying mouth. We will let fate decide. Trial by chance."

Kirill saunters over to me. "I think we can make this even more interesting. Let's give Number Eleven a sporting chance, and turn this snack..." He cups my chin and draws the pad of his thumb over my lower lip. "Into a meal."

There's a hungry, animalistic expression in his eyes that I don't like.

"What did you have in mind?" Konstantin asks.

"A little game. I've been dying to get my hands on Number Eleven."

"Don't you fucking touch me," I snarl.

He raises one brow, his dark curls falling into his eyes. "Do you forfeit? Would you like Elyah to take you down to the lake and put a bullet in your head right now? Say the word, Number Eleven, and this will all be over." When I don't move, he smirks. "I didn't think so. Take off your panties."

My mouth falls open in shock and there's a guilty, twisting feeling in my guts. Does he know what I imagined in my sleep last night and now he's tormenting me with it? I stare straight ahead, desperately searching for a way to take back control of what's happening in this room. Konstantin's eyes are bright as he witnesses my internal struggle.

"Don't make me ask twice," Kirill warns.

"What are you going to do?" Elyah asks, spinning the revolver once around his forefinger and catching it again.

"I'm going to lick your *solnyshko*, and if she comes, you're going to pull the trigger."

Yesterday, he seemed angry at the thought of Kirill touching me. Today, Elyah laughs, and my heart shrivels at his cruelty. He leans down close to me, his voice dropping into a murmur, a mockery of all those times he whispered sweet, hot things in my ear. "Lilia loves being licked, do you not? So, what is it going to be? Are you going to do as you are told, or do I load all these bullets back into the gun and eliminate you from the competition here and now?"

I tear my gaze away from his. Fuming silently, I reach

beneath my dress, angle my hips up, and slide my thong down my legs. Elyah holds out his hand to take my underwear, but I shove them down the front of my dress. If I give them away, I'll never get the damn things back.

Kirill sinks down between my thighs, cups the backs of my knees, and tugs me sharply toward him.

I grab the seat of my chair. "If I don't come, I can go?" It should be easy. Not coming was the defining feature of my sex life with my husband.

Kirill laughs in a way that tells me he doubts that's even an option. "Sure. Why not."

"You seem very sure of yourself for a creep who can't talk to women."

"I've never been surer of anything, *neordinarnaya*," he says, lovingly drawing one of my legs up until it's resting over his shoulder. "Besides, my tongue can do better things than talking."

Without warning, heat flashes through me.

He pushes my thighs wide, and suddenly I'm spread open before him. My shoulders hit the back of the chair and a vision of Kirill's mouth on my pussy and his fingers thrusting inside me fills my mind. I try to push that thought away, but the sight of his tattooed hands gripping my inner thighs short-circuits my brain.

My gaze darts around the room. We're about to have sex, or something close to it, while two other men are watching. Six more women are behind that glass mirror. I open my mouth to beg for another test, but Elyah jams the barrel of the gun against my head.

I grit my teeth against the oncoming humiliation. I do not beg. There's no way Kirill is going to win, so all I have to do is sit here for ten minutes like nothing is happening. If I keep my eyes averted, I can pretend I'm getting a wax or a doctor's examination. I'm certainly going to enjoy it about as much.

Kirill dips his head, and I inhale sharply at the first swipe of his tongue. I feel nothing. It's awful and I don't like it. I tell myself that, anyway.

The second lick sends a fizzle through me. The third has me breathing harder. Kirill notices and he smiles against my pussy.

Elyah wraps his free hand around the nape of my neck, holding me in place. "She tastes sweet, doesn't she?"

"She tastes like heaven," Kirill murmurs, giving me another loving lick of his tongue. He looks up at me, saying between swipes of his tongue, "You're getting wet, Number Eleven. Your little clit is swelling against my tongue."

I shake my hair back and stare determinedly over their heads. I'm not enjoying this. I'm not even aware of it.

I'm *not*.

Kirill licks me like he already knows exactly how I like it. His practiced tongue coils around my clit, and without realizing I'm doing it, my head falls back, and a moan of pleasure escapes my lips.

"Have you been thinking about me, *neordinarnaya*? Have you been dreaming about me?"

My cheeks flood with heat and my head snaps up. "You wish."

Kirill finds the spot where it feels best and caresses me mercilessly. "You wouldn't tell me lies, would you?"

What kind of demon is he? How does he know? Unless… "Did you come down to the cellar last night?"

Kirill freezes.

"Did you stand outside my cell? If I was saying anything about you in my sleep, it was because I was dreaming about murdering you slowly."

The barrel of the gun digs dangerously into my skull. "You were dreaming about Kirill?"

"Dreaming of killing him."

"That's not what it sounded like to me," Kirill replies, and sucks on my clit.

My toes curl. Jesus fucking Christ. An insane killer is going down on me and I've never known anything so heavenly. Ivan took my virginity on our wedding night, and he didn't bother with foreplay then or any night after. Oral sex was beneath him unless it was me having to perform it on him. Elyah was the first man to touch me like this, and though his mouth and tongue were delicious, we never had time to explore what felt good.

"What did it sound like?" Elyah asks, and there's an edge to his voice.

"Are you jealous of my dream, Elyah?" I say between panting breaths. "For heaven's sake, he's licking me right in front of you."

"What we do to you is one thing. What you dream about on your own…"

"Is my fucking business!" My voice becomes shrill and I gasp in pleasure. Oh, God. *Oh, God.* I'm going to come and Elyah's going to kill me. If I have to die, I don't want it to be at his hands. He doesn't deserve the revenge he craves so much.

I fight for control, my breath hissing through my teeth.

"It is agony, is it not, Lilia?" Elyah murmurs. "Do you feel it, *solnyshko*, the torture of being denied what you crave?"

There's a soft laugh from the other side of the room. I

snap my head up and glare at Konstantin. He's relaxed comfortably to one side in his chair, his head resting against his thumb and forefinger as he watches me. "Do you have a death wish?"

"Of course not."

"Then you're so used to a man making you come that you can't help yourself now? Was your husband so attentive in bed?"

I give a strangled laugh. "You have got to be kidding me."

I make the mistake of catching Elyah's eye, and an exultant expression flashes across his face, like he knew all along that I wasn't getting what I wanted.

Konstantin looks pointedly at what my body is doing, and then back up at me. My leg is squeezing Kirill's shoulder. I can't see my toes, but I can feel that they're curling. I try to unclench but hot sensations are racing through me, and I can barely stop my body from arching into Kirill.

Think about something else, I urge myself, licking my lips. *Math problems. Soggy cornflakes. People walking too slowly on the sidewalk when you're in a hurry. Kirill pushing two of those thick, tattooed fingers inside me and purring, "Good girl," as he thrusts them deep and curls them lovingly into my G-spot.*

"Shit," I mutter under my breath, trying to wriggle away from Kirill.

Kirill slides both hands around my ass and pulls me firmly against his mouth. He's not teasing and playing now, he's found a sweet spot and a rhythm that he's happy with, and he's not going to stop until I come. To my horror, my body is flushing with heat and pleasure, and he's making me lose my goddamn mind.

Elyah lovingly squeezes the nape of my neck and hot

sensations spike through me. He's got a gun to my head with a bullet in the chamber, but apparently my clit doesn't care.

"We are not your husband, *milaya*," Konstantin says. "If we say we are going to make you come, then we will make you come."

"What's this *we* business?"

"You obviously enjoy performing for us."

"It's not like I have a choice," I say through my teeth. Glancing up at Elyah, I see that he's breathing unsteadily as he watches me draw closer and closer to the brink of no return.

You know what? Fuck him.

"Give Kirill the gun," I say through gritted teeth, moving one hand to Kirill's muscular shoulder and holding on for dear life. Literally.

The pressure of the barrel disappears. "What?"

"He's the one doing all the hard work. He should be the one to kill me."

Between my thighs, Kirill laughs and the vibrations course through me. "*Neordinarnaya*, if Elyah hands me that gun, I'm going to fuck you with it."

"Good," I fling back at him. He's not going to get the better of me, this weirdo who watches women sleep. I grip the seat of the chair with both hands. Better a bullet in the guts than the head. I could survive for a while that way. Maybe?

Who fucking knows. I'm not exactly thinking clearly, I just want that gun away from my head.

Kirill's eyes flash and he holds out his hand to his friend. Panic and twisted desire flash through me as Elyah slaps the weapon into his palm. The barrel is thick and ridged, and Kirill shows it to me before lowering it between my legs.

And shoving it inside me.

My head flies back with a gasp, into Elyah's supporting hand. For a moment, our gazes meet as I struggle with the sensation of the strange, hard object inside me.

Kirill pulls it back and then shoves it deeper. "What a fucking beautiful sight. You take that so well, Number Eleven."

He dips his head to resume licking me. I hoped that the weirdness of being fucked with a weapon would obliterate my desire, but the need to come doubles with each thrust of the hard metal.

I can feel Elyah staring at me while he holds me in place. Kirill looks up at me to gauge my reaction. Konstantin is watching me from behind his desk as two of his men play the most twisted game of Russian roulette I've ever heard of. Is this what he was hoping for from his pageant, or am I an unexpected bonus?

Kirill's voice is a husky whisper between my legs. "That's it, *neordinarnaya*, I can feel you getting close."

He urges me on with luxurious swipes of his tongue as my orgasm barrels down on me. My pelvis rocks. My sweaty hand grasps Kirill's shoulder even tighter. I make a strangled sound in the back of my throat and my back arches as I climax. I can feel myself squeezing against the metal of the gun as Kirill groans and thrusts it harder and deeper into me.

As my orgasm tails off, I realize that Kirill is staring at me, and he's breathing hard as well. Watching me come has wiped all other thoughts from his mind, but I want this over with.

"What the fuck are you waiting for?" I snarl, glaring from him to the gun. "Shoot me."

Kirill flinches in anger and pulls the trigger. I brace for the worst because the worst is what I've learned to expect—

There's a muted click, and then nothing. The chamber was empty.

I fall back against the chair as I laugh in relief. My shoulders won't stop shaking and tears leak from my eyes. I'm still not dead? Fate really has a fucked-up plan for me.

"You know what I just realized, Elyah?" I reach out and lazily thread my fingers through Kirill's hair as he draws the wet and shining gun from my pussy. His curls are soft and warm, and I pet him like a cat, still hugging him with my thigh. "You have to go on believing I'm a liar. Otherwise, you'll have to face up to all the cruel things you've done to the woman you love for no good reason."

Elyah's cold blue eyes spark with rage and the muscles of his jaw pulse. "I will have to do no such thing. I know you are liar."

I shrug, pretending that my insides aren't burning with the injustice of never being believed. "If you say so."

Kirill unloads the gun, kisses the bullet, and slips it into his pocket. "I'm keeping this, *neordinarnaya*. A reminder of our time together."

"How touching." I pull my dress down and sit up, turning to Konstantin. "Can I go now?"

My insolent tone seems to amuse him. He wanted a gun held to my head to test my bravery. I played Russian roulette with my pussy. I think he's got his answer.

He gets to his feet, comes around the desk and reaches for my hand, helping me to my feet like a gentleman at a dance.

"You pass again, Number Eleven. I thought for sure you'd be eliminated by now, but you continue to surprise me."

"I aim to please," I say sarcastically.

He gives me a sleek smile and dips his head toward me. Those gray eyes of his sparkle like a frozen lake, and the pitch of his voice is low and rich as he murmurs, "Apparently, you do. Good girl."

Maybe it's my oversensitized nerve endings or that fact that I'm still wet and throbbing from fear and Kirill's tongue, but those two words swan dive down my body and pool in my core. I'm suddenly too aware that I'm naked beneath my dress and Konstantin is holding my hand.

To smother my confusion, I retort, "I'm not doing this for your benefit. I'm trying to stay alive."

Konstantin lazily reaches up and takes hold of my throat. He doesn't squeeze, but I can feel the strength in his fingers should he choose to throttle the life out of me. With his thumb, he slowly but firmly tilts my head to one side and leans down to murmur in my ear, "Whatever the reason, I get to sit back and enjoy you."

Konstantin's smile reveals pointed canines, and suddenly he resembles a scarred alpha wolf.

"Until tomorrow, Number Eleven. I'll be waiting."

I quickly rearrange my features, throw Konstantin a hard, sarcastic smile and allow myself to be escorted from the room.

As I step through the door and it closes behind me, the smile dies on my face. The blood in my veins turns to ice, and terror, true terror, sweeps over me. I fumble for a chair, sit down without a word, and stare straight ahead through the glass.

I can still feel the ghost of the gun between my legs. If I'd lost the game of roulette, would the bullet have killed me quickly, or slowly? I think a gunshot wound to the stomach takes a long time to die from. Plenty of time for Elyah to continue torturing me at his leisure. Kirill would probably have joined in.

"Lilia?"

A tentative hand lands on my shoulder and I turn around and see a woman with dark, silky hair and warm brown eyes.

"Alejandra!" I gasp and throw my arms around her. "We all thought you were—"

"Dead, I know." She grimaces. "He shot at the ceiling, not me."

An awkward silence stretches through the room as everyone stares at me.

"What they did with that gun. Did you really like...?" Klara begins, and then falls silent.

"Of course she didn't like it. She's drawing their heat, remember?" Olivia comes forward and gives me a hug, saying, "I don't know how you do it. One minute they're in charge, and the next you're telling them what to do. It's magnificent. You're the only thing keeping me going."

"Did you really do that for us, Lilia, so they won't touch us?" Daiyu asks.

Several of the women murmur their thanks, but Marija just shrugs. When Olivia glares at her, she says, "What? Lilia's dead anyway. Better her than us."

"Wow. Such gratitude," Olivia says, turning to face the two-way mirror.

Elyah and Konstantin are talking in Russian. I frown. No, from the tone of their voices, they're fighting.

"What do you think they're saying?" Celeste whispers.

"They're fighting about who gets to fuck Lilia next," Madison mutters, and Olivia tells her to shut her mouth.

A moment later, Elyah storms out of the room. Everyone turns and looks at me for an explanation, but I don't know what the hell is going on.

"Maybe these three men aren't such great friends, after all," Imani says hopefully.

"I don't know," Madison replies. "This all seems suspicious to me."

"Suspicious how?" someone asks.

Madison sniffs and stays silent. She seems like she's going to let it go, but then bursts out with, "I'm just saying, we've watched other women get eliminated for daring to scream once, but Lilia can talk back and insult these men and they do *nothing* to her."

I clench my jaw tightly. Like getting fucked with a gun and then the trigger being pulled is nothing.

"What are you getting at?" Olivia asks.

"Maybe Lilia is a spy."

Several women speak at once, their protests angry and defiant.

"Don't get pissy with me for saying what we're all thinking," Madison snaps. "Anything's possible in this crazy place. Maybe she's fucking them at night and laughing at our terror behind our backs." She flicks a disgusted gaze up and down my body.

"Madison, I'm not a spy. Konstantin wants to keep me around because I'm entertaining him. Elyah wants me dead, but he'll put it off until the last second."

"How do you know that?"

"Because he doesn't really want to kill me. He absolutely will," I add hastily. "He's furious with me and he's sworn he'll do it, so that's that. But he has three older sisters he loves dearly, and he's never put a hand on a woman in anger in his life. He once saw my husband beat me and…"

My throat closes up as the worst day of my life flashes through my mind yet again. Why am I even talking about this? Madison can think whatever she likes. I'm a spy. I'm not a spy. Who fucking cares?

"And Kirill?" Marija asks, turning around. "Why is he always sniffing around you?"

Olivia shoves Marija's shoulder until she's facing the mirror again. "Because he's a fucking weirdo. Now leave Lilia alone or I'll smack your goddamn mouth."

12

Elyah

Konstantin stares at the door Lilia just disappeared through, an expression in his eyes like he wants to go after her and find out what her pussy tastes like. Alarm plunges down my spine. I would think that he's had his fill of treacherous women by now.

When I woke up this morning, the first thing I saw out of my bedroom window wasn't the flowers in the garden or the sun glinting on the smooth waters of Lake Como. It was a crow. A huge black crow staring beadily at me from the lawn, its wicked beak glinting. I smacked the glass with my palm and it didn't so much as ruffle its feathers.

When I was in prison, I learned to take these signs seriously. If I saw an inmate who was a friend first thing in the morning, my day would be all right. If I came face to face with an enemy, even if it was just in the line at the canteen, I knew there would be trouble before the sun went down.

I round on Konstantin and growl through my teeth in Russian, "Do you want another bullet in your head?"

I should probably switch the mics off so the women can't hear us in the next room, but none of them speak Russian.

Konstantin turns slowly toward me, his expression neutral as he waits for me to speak my mind. I don't like silence when my head is full of shouting and chaos.

"If I tell you that a woman is a viper, I thought by now you would have learned to believe me."

Kirill loads the revolver with fresh bullets, snaps it closed, and spins the cylinder. "We are bringing that up now when we have just had a lovely time with Number Eleven? You're such a mood killer, Elyah."

I ignore Kirill and keep my eyes trained on Konstantin. I see the way he's started looking at Lilia. He's fascinated by her, and his fascination is growing every day. He wants her. Not to marry her. To fuck her, and if he does that then we're all done for.

I don't know how she'll do it, but if Lilia gets her claws into him then we're screwed.

"Is she going to make you turn on me?" Konstantin asks.

I make a short, angry sound. "Do not be fucking stupid."

I have never dared to talk to my *Pakhan* like this before, but Konstantin is different to the others I've had in the past. He likes us to say what's on our minds. He feels more comfortable that way, knowing we can be honest about any danger and treachery that's lurking about, and that we'll call him out on his bullshit if necessary. After Kirill and I saved his life, the three of us have been more like friends than boss and foot soldiers.

I feel more protective of Konstantin than I am of anyone else on this earth. I would die for him, and I know Kirill would, too.

"He's not thinking of betraying you, Kostya. He's jealous."

"No one asked you," I seethe at Kirill. I have been tied up in jealous knots over Lilia in the past. This is different. There's a sick feeling in my guts that something terrible is going to happen. I'm seeing omens all around me. Spilled salt. Crows at dawn. Dreaming of deep water. I almost feel afraid of Lilia, which is ridiculous because we are the ones holding the guns and the keys to her cage.

Konstantin settles back in his leather chair and spreads his hands. "Just get it out. What is the problem, Elyah?"

I clench my jaw tight. My problem is that he touched her. He called her *good girl*. Lilia Aranova is not a good girl. She is a treacherous little bitch. "This is Valeriya all over again."

Konstantin raises an eyebrow, which scrunches the scar tissue at his temple, and his expression grows colder. "The last time I checked, I'm not going to marry Lilia. You are going to kill her."

Panic shoots up my body and ricochets through my skull. He called her by her name, not by her number. I point a finger at him. "You need to be careful. The things she does in here, the things she says. She is up to something, I know it."

"How do you know it?"

"Because this is not the Lilia that I saw every day, month after month."

"Maybe that woman was a lie and this is the real Lilia. She betrayed you, and you never saw it coming."

I push both my hands into my hair and growl, squeezing the sides of my skull. I'm not a stupid man, but I'm not as smart as Konstantin, and I am nowhere near as clever as Lilia. I was known as *Pushka*. Gun. Weapon. I have the word tattooed on my ribs to remind me what I am good for. I run on instinct, not brains. Trying to tease apart the real Lilia from the one I knew and the one I see before me every day is giving me a headache.

"What do you think Aran Brazhensky will do to us when he finds out we've killed his daughter?" Kirill muses, spinning the gun around his finger and catching it.

Konstantin gives a lazy shrug of his broad shoulders. "He can shove it up his ass. The same as every *Pakhan* I've crossed. I apologize to no one."

"He will probably send assassins after us," Kirill says, sounding amused by the idea.

"That's why I have the two of you," Konstantin says with a smile. "My wolves with keen noses and keener eyes, who warn me of any danger that slinks in the shadows."

And yet he's ignoring everything I say about Lilia. "My instincts are telling me that Lilia Aranova is dangerous to you."

Konstantin's glittering gaze meets mine. "So kill her. End this now."

I swallow, hard. She needs to die, but not like this. Not when her mockery is still ringing in my ears. I want to hear her begging for her life. I need to know why a *Pakhan's* dutiful daughter sold her husband out to the feds. I thought I would have figured out a way to break her down by now, but even Kirill falls under her spell. She was the one to tell *him* to shoot, for fuck's sake. How does she keep turning things around on us when she's the one locked in a cage?

"I need some air," I seethe, and I unlock and wrench open the door that leads into the villa. Striding through the cool, dark corridors, I take deep breaths, visions of Lilia dancing before my eyes, her cheeks flushed and her bare thigh squeezing Kirill's shoulder. Her pussy filled with the thick barrel of the gun.

I groan under my breath and head for my bedroom as the visions continue. Kirill's hands on her thighs as he dipped his head to lick her. The way her back arched as she moaned in pleasure. I remember exactly how she sounded when I touched her two years ago. The tight grip of her pussy on my fingers. Her slippery wetness coating the head of my cock as I ran it against her velvet pussy. I groan and grasp the windowsill. How many times have I jerked off to Lilia? A hundred times? A thousand? Even when I've hated her, my fantasies about squeezing the life out of her lying throat have turned into rough sex. I have never been able to kill her in my mind. The fantasy always ends with her climaxing around my cock.

I have to go back to the others and get through today's event, but my dick is so fucking hard, and I need a release. I slam my bedroom door closed behind me and fumble for the button on my jeans. With one hand braced against the door, I picture Lilia, just as she was a few minutes ago, while I pump myself furiously up and down in my fist.

In my fantasy, I throw the gun aside, turn her head, and shove my cock in her mouth. She sucks me eagerly, working me up and down with her lips and tongue, moaning around me as Kirill devotes himself to her clit.

Konstantin needs to fuck her, too. He's standing before her, stroking his hard cock while he waits his turn. When Kirill moves aside, he looms over Lilia, grasps her thighs and thrusts into her.

She moans desperately around my cock and holds on to my arm and Konstantin's shoulder while we pound into her. It's so fucking vivid. It's so goddamn *hot*. Lilia should be fucked, hard and often, by men who know how to handle her and make her come.

"You suck me so good, *solnyshko*," I mutter under my breath, and then break off with a groan. My orgasm rolls up my body and my head bows as my cum shoots out in ribbons.

I lean against the door, getting my breath back.

I'm so fucking stupid, beating off to a woman who's going to be nothing but a corpse in a few days. I don't know why I'm delaying the inevitable.

The sooner she dies, the sooner I can be free.

13

Lilia

That night, my dreams are soaked with blood, and I'm stalked through dark streets by a tattooed man with his hoodie up. I try to run but my legs won't obey. Doors with complicated locks block my way. I attempt to call for help, but I keep pressing the wrong numbers on my phone.

Kirill brandishes his knife and forces my legs open while I beg for mercy. Elyah stands behind him with his tattooed arms folded, muscles bulging, and a cruel smile on his lips. "Whores love to be fucked."

"Then she'll enjoy this," Kirill replies, his eyes so black there are no whites at all around his irises. He plunges the blade inside me.

I wake up gasping and drenched in sweat.

"It was just a dream," I whisper over and over, rubbing my belly where I can still feel cold metal. "Just a dream."

After my usual cold-water wash, I select a white sundress from the rack and wait for a guard to hand over the usual cereal bar and water. They're sweet but unsatisfying, and my stomach is still rumbling after I've finished eating mine. My exhausted brain can present me with nothing but images of almond croissants, lattes, and eggs Benedict.

I wonder if I'll be allowed to have a final meal before my execution. My mouth waters at the thought of my favorite sausage and bean soup, loaded with onions and herbs. Elyah told me once that my cooking tasted just like home. Maybe I could make us—

I break off with a shudder. Cook for my executioner? Let's not make this any more twisted than it already is.

Elyah took a long time to come back after his break yesterday, and he was silent while Kirill held the gun to Imani's, Celeste's, and Deja's heads. Poor Celeste didn't pass the test. She was already weeping when she was pulled into the room. She broke down sobbing, huddled in a ball on the floor before the barrel even touched her temple.

And then there were ten.

While I wait to be called into the judging room, I sit on the carpet with my arms wrapped around my knees. I'm on a knife's edge of fear and hunger, alternating between memories of my nightmare and the longing for orange juice and fresh fruit salad. My mind is such a jumble that I wonder if I'm cracking up. The worst part is knowing that my nightmare might actually be waiting for me in the judging room. These men are insane and cruel and they're getting worse every day.

Before I realize anyone has even been called in, a guard yanks me under the arm and drags me into the judging room. I stumble a little on the carpet, feeling three sets of hateful eyes on me.

Elyah is standing at the back of the room in shadows, his arms folded and his gaze heavy-lidded. Kirill perches on the edge of the desk, one of his legs swinging back and forth as he grins at me. Konstantin sits in his winged chair, watching me with that cold, predatory gaze, his fingers steepled like a goddamn movie villain.

Who *is* this man?

Elyah I know intimately. Kirill is a sicko and a pervert. There's nothing to fathom there except that he's a dangerous man who does his *Pakhan's* bidding. Whereas Konstantin reveals nothing. He smiles. Asks questions. Listens. Watches. He's almost gentlemanly in the way he talks to us sometimes. In his tailored suits with an expensive, heavy watch on his wrist and cufflinks gleaming on his shirt, he has an air of old-world charm. Culture. Money.

But that's not the real Konstantin.

I've been trying to understand him as much as I'm sure he's been trying to figure me out. Has this pageant got anything to do with the still-healing scar on his face? I sense bitterness in his soul. Disappointment. Fury. A man doesn't just wake up one morning and decide to kidnap sixteen women and put them through an ordeal this cruel. Someone got the better of him, and he's never going to forget it until the day he dies.

I glance around the room, looking for props, wondering how they're planning to torture us today, but I can't see anything new. With more bravado than I feel, I say, "So, what game are we playing?"

Konstantin smiles, though no warmth reaches his eyes. "Good question, Number Eleven. Today is all about reputation. The other women have so many dirty secrets. Number Three has four sugar daddies old enough to be her father. Number Nine sells amateur porn of her feet on the internet."

If Klara is earning a living with pictures of her feet, it sounds like a great way to make bank. Sugar daddies don't seem like a bad idea, either. Why didn't I think of that?

"I already know a lot about you from Elyah, but I was hoping to find out more from the internet. And yet there's nothing. What secrets are you keeping, Number Eleven?"

"I have ugly feet. If they're online, it's news to me, and I wish I had four rich old men to give me money."

Konstantin reaches inside his shirt pocket and pulls out a small, navy-blue book with gold embossing that reads, *PASSPORT. United States of America*. "I found out so much about every woman in this competition, but you...you are an enigma."

My blood runs cold as Konstantin opens it to the photo page and peruses it. That's my passport, and he's getting his thieving, grasping hands all over it.

"Lilia Kalashnik. Yulia Petrova." He peers over the pages at me. "Lilia Aranova. Lilia Brazhensky. So many names. Which one is the real you?"

I shrug, trying to seem unconcerned, and I stare at my only means of freedom and escape. "Why does it matter when all you call me is Number Eleven?"

"It's simple, this numbering system, isn't it? Removes so

many complications. You can be who I want you to be, not what you pretend to be." His eyes narrow. "That was my plan, anyway. But you've been making a mockery of my plans all week."

My stomach lurches. So, he's figured out that I've been putting on an act in here. Kirill doesn't care what I do or say as long as I play his sick games. Elyah is twisted up in knots, trying to unravel the real me from the woman he wanted me to be.

But Konstantin watches, observes, connects the dots. Alarm bells ring distantly in my head. I can play Elyah, I can play Kirill, but this man might be my undoing.

I regard him warily, wondering what he wants. Control, clearly. I suppose he's like me in that way. You become obsessed with control when you've experienced what it's like to have it ripped away from you.

"Who are you pretending to be, Number Eleven?"

I arch one eyebrow. "Who are you pretending to be?"

Konstantin shakes his head and smiles. "It's not going to work on me, Number Eleven. You can't turn this around. I'm not going to tell you tales about the girls at school being cruel to me or pine for you across a kitchen counter. Either you're honest with me, or you'll be eliminated."

I shrug like I don't know what he's talking about, but my heart is racing and a sick feeling spreads through my belly. I've been cornered and there's nowhere to run.

Kirill leers at me and runs his tongue over his teeth, visions of my imminent demise dancing in his eyes. For a second, they look black. Totally black, like a demon. Just like they were in my dream.

Konstantin riffles through the pages of my passport like they are mildly interesting to him. Where I've been. What

I've seen. He places it casually down on the desk in front of him and smiles at me. "It's time to be honest, Number Eleven."

His smile is as hard as diamonds, and I realize I've underestimated Konstantin. I thought the hardest, cruelest man in my life was my father, the man who always used me and pushed me away. Konstantin is drawing me closer. I can feel that cruel smile tugging at my soul, hungry to consume it and leave me a hollow shell.

What does he like? Pain? Control? Does he want me shivering in fear before him or begging for mercy?

No, he already told me what he craves.

Power.

I swallow thickly, wondering what he has in store for the woman who's run rings around his men and made a mockery of his challenges in front of the other women. What can I offer this monster to appease his hunger? I doubt it's anything I would willingly give because what would be the fun in that?

Doesn't he know, though? Hasn't he realized? Any shred of power I've had in here is an illusion. A few clever words, a haughty look, my willingness to double and triple dare his crazy men.

As I stare into those sharklike eyes, I realize he does know. He's just been waiting for me to realize it, too. I haven't been winning all week. He's been playing me like a fish on a line and slowly reeling me in. Now, I haven't got much fight left. I've worn myself out on his men.

"Were you a good daughter, Lilia Brazhensky?"

My palms are sweaty, but I don't dare wipe them on my dress and reveal any sign of weakness. A good daughter? I wonder what it would have taken for my father to think I was a *good daughter*.

What would Konstantin consider a good daughter? Someone who kept herself pure and chaste and received news of her impending marriage with grace and gratitude?

"I was disobedient and thoughtless," I reply. "I never listened, and I threw whatever he gave me back in his face."

Konstantin smirks, as if he suspected as much. He settles back in his leather chair, arms laid comfortably on the armrests. Silver rings glint on his fingers. "Were you a good wife, Lilia Kalashnik?"

I remember Ivan's complete indifference to me beyond what I did in the bedroom and the kitchen. We barely knew each other, and we were never alone together until our wedding night. Ivan wasn't drunk when he took me to bed, but he'd had enough vodka to be callous to the point of monstrosity toward his inexperienced wife.

Was I what he wanted? I don't know. After, as Ivan snored, I curled into a ball and sobbed on the bloodied hotel room sheets. It was my first experience of sex, and I hated it.

Loathed it.

In the morning, I awoke to find myself alone in the suite. His things were still in the room, but he'd gone elsewhere. To breakfast. To gamble. To be with his men. I don't know, but he didn't want to spend the morning after his wedding with his wife. I wandered around the enormous hotel suite, more lavish than anything I'd ever known. I took a scalding hot shower to try and ease the pain deep in my body, and then I stared at myself in the mirror. The vanity was marble. The taps were sleek and gold. The soap delicately scented. Everything was perfect, and I was going to have to learn to be perfect, too.

Once I'd settled into Ivan's house, I became eaten up by jealousy. Which was strange because I certainly wasn't in love with him. It wasn't because of another woman, either. It was because of his men. Ivan would invite them around to eat the food I cooked and drink the vodka I served, and he would talk and laugh with them. He would hug them and pat their cheeks, telling them that he loved them and they were everything to him. Then he'd snap his fingers at me and point to an empty casserole dish or call for a fresh bottle of vodka. The only time he touched me in public was when he showed me off to other men.

"I hated my husband on sight. He was old and ugly, and he treated me like furniture in his house. I was never allowed to refuse him. He showed more affection to his men than to his wife."

Konstantin regards me coolly. If he feels any sympathy for me, he doesn't show it. "Were you a good lover, Lilia Aranova?"

I can feel Elyah's sharp gaze on the side of my neck and my stomach plummets through the floor. Are we really doing this? But Konstantin's waiting for my answer, and he's not going to let this go. This is my punishment for thinking I'm such a clever woman all week.

I don't know what it means to be a good lover. I don't even know what Elyah saw in me. Eighteen-year-old me was overwhelmed by her new role as Lilia Kalashnik, wife of a *Pakhan*. I put on outfits that I thought Mrs. Kalashnik should wear. I cried when the blinis I cooked accidentally burned. I worried that Ivan would realize how much I hated him pawing at me and screwing me until it dawned on me that he absolutely didn't care. My thoughts and feelings were irrelevant to him.

And then Elyah arrived in my life, and suddenly the most beautiful man I'd ever seen was standing in my kitchen and gazing at me with adoration. Fair-haired, startlingly blue eyes, and a body honed like a weapon, but he made himself gentle for me. He poured sweetness into my heart and smiled at me every day. He smelled like the cold wind from a snow-topped mountain and his voice wrapped around me like velvet.

I was terrified of him.

I was obsessed with him.

Every time he touched me, I was filled with ecstasy and fear. I didn't know what to say to him. I didn't know how to touch him. I was too useless to even betray my husband properly.

"I never gave Elyah anything that he wanted. My affection. My body. My love. He was tormented night and day with nothing to show for his agony."

I force myself to keep staring at Konstantin and not at Elyah. If I look into my former lover's eyes and he's staring at me with hatred, I'll crumble from the pain.

Konstantin lets this silence stretch the longest, sensing that I'm fighting to keep control of myself. Finally, he asks, "Were you a good fugitive, Yulia Petrova?"

There's so much time to think, locked in Konstantin's cages. Waiting for hours outside the judging room. I've replayed the night Kirill took me prisoner over and over, and I made so many mistakes. It wasn't just that I had a gun in my hands and he still managed to overpower me, though that stupidity is salt burning in an open wound. I made my first mistake hours earlier when I spoke up for the Kazakh girl and got us both thrown out of the fashion show. I couldn't afford to lose money or draw attention to myself, but I'd done both of those things. The Lugovskayas would never have found me if I'd just kept my mouth shut. I was fucked before Kirill ever pointed his blade at me.

"I jumped at all the wrong shadows. I never minded my own business when I should have."

Konstantin gets up from his chair and walks around the desk toward me. As he saunters, he takes off his jacket and tie and unbuttons the neck of his shirt. He slips his cufflinks off and rolls the sleeves back, taking his time and staring into my eyes the entire time. His shirt sits perfectly on his broad shoulders, and the cotton smells crisp and fresh.

I stand before him with bare feet and tangles in my hair, wearing an ill-fitting dress. He casts a pitiless gaze over me.

"You're not even a good contestant, Number Eleven. What have you done in your short, sorry life that anyone will remember you for? Will anyone say to themselves after you are dead, *I knew a woman once. Beautiful girl. I miss her.*"

Pain slices through my guts and my breath shudders in my lungs. How can he be so cruel?

"No one will miss me." Not even *Babulya*, because I have brought her too much hardship and too many sleepless nights. Tears spring into my eyes and I blink them away.

Konstantin captures my jaw and angles my face this way and that, examining the wetness beading my lashes as if it's diamonds. He wants my tears. He's feeding off my misery like a soul-sucking demon. "You keep reinventing yourself, and for what? Don't you crave that the world leaves you alone? Don't you wish it would all just...end?"

I blink, and hot tears spill down my cheeks. Konstantin draws closer, his face filled with sympathy but his eyes shining with malice. With reverence, he lowers his head and kisses the wet tracks on my cheeks. It's a gesture that should feel loving or even pitying, but he brands me with his hot lips. *This pain? Mine. Delicious.*

Konstantin's kisses trail down my cheeks as his hand slips around my lower back and draws me against him. I reach up to push him away, but he captures my wrist in an iron grip and I'm trapped. His mouth is just inches from mine as we stare at each other, our breaths mingling. The pulse is racing in my wrist where he holds me.

He lowers his head and covers my lips with his in a slow, heated kiss. He groans in pleasure, as if my defeat is the finest wine. He's totally destroyed me, and now he's drinking in my devastation. Finally, he breaks the kiss with a victorious smile.

I've lost.

He's won.

I struggle in his grasp. "You've made your point. Now let me go."

"Are you so eager to die at Elyah's hands? I'm not done with you, *milaya*." *Precious.* He's making a mockery of me. Hasn't he just pointed out that I'm precious to no one?

He goes back to his seat and settles against the leather, a smile lighting his plush lips that tells me the fun is only just beginning. "I learned nothing just now that I didn't already know or suspect. Tell me a secret, Number Eleven. Something you've never told anyone before."

My mouth is tingling from his kiss. "You've already heard all my secrets."

"There must be something you've held back. Something you've done." He drops his voice to a murmur. "Something you crave."

To get out of here alive. For everyone in the Bratva or connected to it to leave me alone forever. I'm not going to be granted that particular wish, so what's something I could ask for that Konstantin might give me? My eyes land on my passport that's lying on his desk. I open my mouth, and then I hesitate.

No, I won't.

I can't.

What else is there? He might have won this battle, but even though I'm beaten down and exhausted, I'm not ready to concede the war. While there's life in me, I have to go on fighting.

Choosing my words carefully, I start to speak, keeping my eyes lowered respectfully. "It's not really a secret."

"Tell me anyway."

Slowly, I raise my eyes to his. "I've never enjoyed having sex."

"You seemed to enjoy yourself yesterday," he points out.

I wrinkle my nose and shake my head. "That? A cruel game in which I was frightened for my life? I want to experience sex like lovers would do it, not have a gun shoved inside me while I wonder if I'm about to have my insides pulverized."

"Sorry, but I haven't got time to delay this pageant while Lilia Aranova goes out into this world and experiences falling in love."

I give him a meaningful look. "That's not what I meant. I

would like to go to bed with a man once in my life and enjoy it before Elyah kills me."

Konstantin gazes at me for a long time. "You have never liked it, and yet you want it. Why?"

"I think I might like it if I was with the right man."

"You've never met the right man?"

Out of the corner of my eye, I see Elyah shift on his feet. If he had been the right man, it would have happened between us. "I don't want to screw my killer, obviously."

Kirill opens his mouth.

"Or a pervert," I add. With a shrug, I explain, "I want someone...normal."

Konstantin laughs, a genuinely amused laugh. I think this is the first time I've seen a real smile from him. "You think I'm normal?"

"God, no. But you're the closest thing to normal in this room."

Konstantin runs a finger over his lower lip, his gaze speculative. He must know he's handsome. Even that scar can't hide his brutal good looks. The scar even accentuates his attraction, depending on your tastes. I can imagine my fingers brushing over the shiny, gnarled tissue and sweeping back his dark hair. His mouth on mine a moment ago showed me that my body reacts to his kisses and his touch. He seemed to know how to handle me as he held me close to him and refused to let go. That kind of total possession...

It's alluring.

It shouldn't be, but it is.

"I could give you to Kirill to punish you for saying that," Konstantin points out.

"If you were going to, you just would. You wouldn't bother threatening me."

Konstantin chuckles. "Are you too clever for your own good, Number Eleven?"

I return his smile with one of my own. "Of course, or I wouldn't be here right now. I'd be sitting on a beach somewhere with my rich old husband while he snores and I flirt with a hot waiter."

"Somehow I think you would be bored if that was your life, Lilia Aranova." Konstantin spreads his hands. "Not Elyah. Not Kirill. I could call my guards in here and you could have your pick of them. I'm sure they'd be happy to screw you. How does that sound?"

He knows who I want, but he needs to hear me say it.

"You smell good. You look good," I whisper, gazing at him from beneath my lashes. "I liked the way you kissed me. Please don't make me beg. If you're not interested, just say so."

His gaze travels down over my body, and this time he really looks. Not like a man surveying merchandise, but the way a man looks at a woman. This is what he's wanted all along, for Number Eleven to be brought to heel. Well, here I am.

All his.

"Take off your clothes."

Heart pounding, I pull the dress I'm wearing up over my head and lay it on his desk. Then I hook my fingers into my underwear, drag them down my legs, and step out of them. I lay them on top of my dress and stand before Konstantin, naked and vulnerable. My nipples pebble in the cool air. I'm not looking at his men, but I can feel Elyah and Kirill are both staring at me, one cold and stony, the other amused and fascinated.

Konstantin pats the desk in front of him. "Up. Kneel here."

I do as I'm told, climbing up on the desk and settling back on my heels. Konstantin is lounging back in his chair two feet away. Too far for me to reach.

Slowly, he stands up, looming over me. His eyes glitter and his breathing deepens as he traces his forefinger around my lips. I oblige him by parting them, staring up at him like he holds my life in his hands.

Konstantin turns his head. "What do you think, Elyah? Should I fuck Lilia Aranova?"

He pushes two fingers slowly into my mouth, and I suck them.

Elyah breathes in sharply, his eyes pinned to the sight. "I have already told you that you having sex with Lilia is terrible idea." There's a long, crackling pause, and he says in a roughened voice, "So terrible I cannot stop thinking about watching you push her down over that desk and fucking her hard."

A hot pulse shoots through me at the heat and longing in Elyah's voice. Seeing me with his *Pakhan* isn't tripping Elyah's jealousy switch. In fact, it seems to be doing the opposite. I get a sudden mental image of Elyah leaning over me and rubbing my clit while Konstantin thrusts into me, and all the while Elyah is murmuring soft, filthy words in my ear.

Do you love the way he fucks you, solnyshko? *Are you our sweet little slut? We are all going to fuck you, and fill your pretty holes with cum.*

I moan against Konstantin's fingers in my mouth. That

shouldn't be so arousing. He drags his fingers from my lips and cups my jaw, looking deep into my eyes. "If you want this, you have to do something for me."

The word drops from my lips on a breath. "Anything."

His smile widens and becomes pointed, and I'm reminded of a wolf again. "Aren't you a good girl all of a sudden. Who knew you had it in you?"

I didn't know that it felt so good to be obliging, either. Suddenly, all I want to do is whatever this man tells me and hear him whisper words of praise and give me loving touches. It's not going to be nice what he asks of me, but I crave to do it anyway.

Konstantin drops the light, teasing tone and he orders savagely, "Arms behind your back. Hold on to your elbows."

I do as I'm told, thrusting my breasts forward and arching my back so I can grasp my elbows.

His heated gaze runs over my body. "If you drop out of that pose before I say you can, Kirill is going to beat you. Do you understand?"

I glance at Kirill, who is sitting just feet away along the desk, grinning darkly. "Please disobey him, *neordinarnaya*. You and I are so good together."

"We'll see how far I can push her, my friend," Konstantin says, digging in his trouser pocket. "You may get your wish. I've been saving these for someone special."

There are two small metal objects nestled in the palm of his hand on a bed of fine silver chain. They're definitely not his cufflinks. They look like miniature tongs or clamps, and I don't understand what they're for until Konstantin reaches out and plucks one of my nipples between his thumb and forefinger.

While I watch, filled with anticipation and a spice of fear, he attaches a clamp to one nipple, and a second to my other nipple. The chain dangles between them, lightly skimming my flesh.

"How does that feel?" Konstantin murmurs, admiring my pinched flesh, which is white and bloodless in some places and angry red in others.

"Tight," I breathe. Almost painful, and I think the pain might increase the longer I wear these things. But I can endure this. I lift my chin proudly. I've endured far worse.

"Good." Konstantin reaches into his other pocket and pulls out two small square objects. Metal and shiny, and they clink softly together. He hooks one to a clamp and it drags on my flesh, sending a flare of pain through me.

"Wait, I—"

Konstantin hooks the second weight to my other nipple and raises his half-obliterated eyebrow at me. This scarred man is daring me to complain about a little bloodless pain. I grit my teeth together and whimper in the back of my throat, and then close my lips. Pain is meaningless. Pain is nothing but a signal in my brain.

I feel no fear.

When Konstantin sees that I've resolved to endure this torment, he settles back in his chair to watch. I count with each breath, four seconds in, four seconds out. The seconds and minutes drag by. I start to sweat. My teeth clench so tightly that my jaw aches.

Kirill fishes beneath the table and comes up with a bottle of vodka. He twists off the red cap with a crack that breaks the seal and takes a healthy swig.

I watch his muscular throat moving, beads of sweat on my forehead. "Can I have some of that?"

We both glance at Konstantin, who says nothing. Finally, he nods.

Kirill slides along the table and then gets up on his knees and looms over me, his expression full of arrogance and gloating. He takes another swig of vodka, upending the bottle into his mouth. Toying with me. Showing me that he's got something I want, and he's not going to give it to me.

Then he jerks his chin with his mouth full, and I realize what he's telling me to do. I lean my head back and open my lips. Kirill slides a possessive hand around my throat, wrenching my head back even farther, and spits a thin stream of vodka into my mouth. His aim is perfect, like he's practiced his whole damn life for this moment. Warm vodka fills my mouth.

"Swallow," he says roughly, playing with the chain that links my nipples.

I do as I'm told, drinking down the vodka in two long swallows. It burns my throat and sends a glow through my stomach.

"Say thank you."

"*Spacibo*," I whisper.

He shoots a heated glance at Konstantin. "Fuck, how do you do it? This hellcat is now a soft little kitten."

Konstantin spreads his hands and gives his friend a sleek, self-satisfied smile.

"Did you ever get her to behave like this?" Kirill asks, turning to Elyah.

Elyah is staring at me. At my lips. My throat. My breasts. He shifts on his feet and folds his arms the other way, his cheeks stained red. He's filled with restless sexual energy and his eyes are half-lidded. "Maybe. For one moment." He presses his lips together and I think I hear a faint groan from the back of his throat. "But now I think about it, it was me under her spell."

Kirill goes back to where he was sitting, laughing under his breath.

Silence stretches in the room once more and I have nothing to distract me from the pain. My scalp prickles. My arms burn from holding them in such an unnatural position. There are pins and needles in my legs. But most of all, the pain in my nipples is slowly becoming unbearable. Each breath hurts and my flesh feels like it's splitting open.

As tears start to fill my eyes, Konstantin pats his thigh. "Come here."

Slowly, awkwardly, still holding on to my elbows, I get down from the table and slide into his lap. My knees squeeze his hips in a desperate plea. All I can think about is Konstantin releasing me from this torture.

His eyes roam over my body and he slides his hands around my bare hips. Beneath me, his thighs are hard and strong. Still gazing at me, he murmurs, "How are you doing, Elyah? Is this torture for you, seeing what I'm doing to Number Eleven?"

"I thought I would go mad with jealousy watching any man touch Lilia, but watching her with Kirill yesterday..." Elyah trails off with a slow breath. "I have never seen anything sexier in all my life. Perhaps until now."

I remember his tight grip on the nape of my neck and his rough breathing as he watched me moan in pleasure. Either his jealousy was shattered by betrayal, or these men are different somehow.

"So, I can touch her?" Konstantin asks, and I have to bite my tongue not to shout, *He said he doesn't care! Take these clamps off me, I'm begging you.*

"Please," I whimper.

Kirill gets to his feet, undoing his black jeans. "I'll fuck her face, Konstantin."

"*No*," I cry, and Kirill freezes and glares at me. Feeding me vodka is one thing, but I'll suck that man's cock over my dead body.

Konstantin's expression turns chilly, and I soften my tone and implore him with my eyes. "I just want you."

Konstantin cups my cheek and strokes it with his thumb. "Seeing as you ask so nicely." He shakes his head at Kirill. "Sorry, my friend."

The dark-haired man sits heavily on the table, grumbling, "I never get anything I want unless I take it for myself."

Konstantin strokes his thumbs over the undersides of my breasts. He skims so close to the clamps that I nearly dissolve into pained sobs.

"Take them off, please," I pant.

"Not until I'm inside you. You may let go of your elbows."

I release my arms and ride a wave of gratitude as my screaming muscles finally find release. I can feel the hard line of his cock against my bare pussy. With hands shaking from adrenaline and anticipation, I undo his pants and reach inside to draw him out. Konstantin's thick cock is blazing hot in my cold fingers, and I squeeze him in my palm, eliciting a groan from his lips.

Our eyes meet, and a moment passes between us. The

room, the whole world, drops away. He takes my ass in his hands and holds me close.

"Are you wet for me, *milaya*?" he murmurs huskily.

I sit up a little and run the head of him between my folds, and he glistens with my arousal.

"Perfect," he breathes. "Sink down on me. Show me how pretty you look stuffed full of my cock."

I do as he asks, holding tight to his shoulders as I sink slowly down his length. For a moment, my insides clench in protest and fear as my body remembers Ivan's unwelcome, repulsive intrusion. Konstantin keeps still. He's not shoving himself into me. He's murmuring soft words in Russian as he caresses my hips, letting me lovingly draw him into myself. I moan at the vast difference in the sensations. Ivan hurt like hell. Konstantin feels golden. Every inch of him is delicious, the pleasure heightened by the continued throb of my nipples.

As I pause for breath, Konstantin removes one clamp, and then the other, and tosses them onto the desk. Relief and endorphins pour through me, and I collapse against Konstantin's chest, burying my face in his neck with an ecstatic moan. My inner muscles ripple around his thick length that's driving deeper into me as gravity pushes me down. I'm sobbing, but from happiness, not despair. He's not my tormentor.

He's my savior.

Konstantin's strong arms wrap around me as he pulls me more firmly down on his cock. I'm filled to bursting with him and I still crave more.

He puts his lips against my ears and murmurs, "You are perfect, Lilia Aranova. You are my angel. My precious."

His deep, gentle words glow golden in my soul. Tears of gratitude run down my cheeks. Within this tight cocoon of our bodies, everything is pure bliss. I'm perfect? I've never been anyone's perfect anything. I've only ever been a problem. Ungrateful. A disappointment. A temptress and a whore. My past is a wasteland of pain.

I rise up his length and then sink down it again, every movement filled with ecstasy. I've moved beyond all that and I'm something else entirely.

I'm Konstantin's.

14

Konstantin

Lilia's tears are damp against my cheek and her body is strung tight with need and gratitude.

I push her back a little, craving her tears while I fuck her. She's so pretty when she cries, her beautiful face glistening, each tear as precious and as sparkling as diamonds.

"My perfect beauty. Show me how much you love my cock."

Lilia grips my shoulders as she rocks against me. How eager she is to prove herself, riding my length with long, delicious movements of her body. I keep a light hold of her hips, letting her set the pace that feels best for her.

"How does it feel so good?" she pants, running her nails through my hair and down my chest. I kiss each of her breasts, lavishing her nipples with tenderness. Lilia works out all of her fear and frustration on my cock, pushing down harder and harder with every plunge of her pussy. Her cries reach a fever pitch and pleasure shoots up her body as she rides out her orgasm on my cock.

I give her a moment to catch her breath, marveling at the desire painting her delicate features. Still buried deep inside her, I pick her up and place her on my desk. She falls back on her elbows. My turn.

With her knees wrapped around my hips, I pull out of her velvet heat almost all the way and then slam into her. She falls back onto the desk with a moan. I set a hard pace and she seems to enjoy this new angle, surrendering to me and what I'm doing to her.

Lounging next to us on the table, Kirill takes a lazy swig of vodka. Elyah swipes the bottle out of his hand and takes a long drink, not taking his eyes off Lilia. They crave to fuck her. To shove their cocks in her mouth or jerk off onto her tits, but right at this moment she's all mine.

Every thrust jolts her body. Lilia tries to hold on to me, her thighs, anything. She resorts to reaching over her head to cling to the edge of the table. Her eyes are closed and pleasure fills her face. Suddenly, she cries out long and loud, and the sight of her tits thrusting upward with her orgasm and the pulse of her pussy around my cock sends me over the edge.

I slam into her with short, urgent thrusts as my climax rocks through me. After few deep breaths, I draw my cock out of her, glistening with her wetness and my cum.

Elyah groans at the sight. Kirill runs his tongue over his upper lip.

I really fucking needed that.

I tuck myself back into my pants and do them up, before resuming my seat. I suppose we're behind schedule now. How many more women are left today?

Number Eleven sits up, pushes off the desk and slips into my lap, her arms coming around me.

I grip the arms of the chair. "Number Eleven," I growl, angling my head away from her, and she stiffens.

"What?"

What. Not *Pardon, ser* or *I'm sorry, ser.* I grasp her waist and shove her to the floor. Number Eleven falls in a heap at my feet, her expression bewildered and full of hurt.

I grip her jaw in my hand and seethe, "When I'm finished with you, wait for your orders. Don't take fucking liberties."

Number Eleven's eyes widen in shock and fear. "I thought—"

"You thought what? That you're special? That you matter just because I fucked you? I was doing you a favor, not the other way around. Did you think that I set up this whole pageant and sourced pink fucking diamonds for a woman who's been passed around by my men?"

Lilia cringes away from me. She really thought she could dance gleefully over all my plans, tearing them apart one by one and laughing behind my back and still get the better of me? I knew I'd break her in the end. People are so easy to manipulate once you discover what they crave and make them believe you're the only one who can give it to them. Number Eleven wanted to be special and I gave that to her. Now, it's over.

I release her with a shove, and she visibly crumples, her shoulders rounding and her head bowed.

Kirill has his head on one side as he contemplates her, his

expression disappointed. Even Elyah frowns in confusion at seeing his precious Lilia Aranova slumped on her knees. Did they think Number Eleven had supernatural powers? If you behave around a woman like she's a flawless, bewitching goddess, then she's going to start thinking she is one.

Now they know: Lilia Aranova is nothing, and tomorrow she'll be dead.

My cold voice cracks across her flesh. "Get your fucking clothes and get out."

Lilia pulls herself shakily to her feet, scoops up her dress and underwear, and bundles them tightly against her chest.

Kirill punches the intercom. "Let Number Eleven out. Bring in the next woman."

A guard enters, raises his eyebrows at the naked woman with her head bowed, and unlocks the door to the room where the women wait at the end of their task. Lilia disappears inside, as meek and broken as I could hope to see her.

When the guard approaches the other door to drag the next woman in, I call out, "Wait. I've had enough for today. Gather all the women in the cellar so I can talk to them."

"*Da, ser.*"

I stride out of the room with Elyah and Kirill at my back. In the cool, marble entrance hall, I turn to both of them. "You see? She's not special, or bewitching, or clever. She's a needy bitch who had to be put in her place."

"I never thought she was special," Kirill counters.

"You applauded her after that first task, *durak*," I mutter with a smirk. *Idiot.*

Kirill grins at me and shrugs. "Well, that was impressive. But you're right. She's nothing special."

"And you?" I ask, turning to Elyah.

His face is closed and stony, and he shrugs. "Me what?"

But he's not getting out of this so easily. I'm going to hear him say it.

Elyah sighs and passes a hand across his brow. "You are right. Lilia is not special. She is a betraying whore, and I have known that for two years." But he speaks flatly as if he's repeating something he's learned by rote. Some part of him still desperately clings to a version of Lilia that never existed.

No woman should ever break you. The sooner he learns this, the sooner he'll be free.

I clap him on the shoulder. "I don't care how you finish this. Fuck her before you kill her if you have to, but just get it done. Now come downstairs with me. I need to talk to the rest of them."

My men follow me to the cellar where ten women are standing in front of their cages and six women are cowering inside them. Two more women were eliminated today, Numbers Three and Nine. The sugar baby and the amateur foot porn artist.

I survey my eight remaining beauties. Several seem unsettled by the display that Number Eleven and I put on in the judging room, but the rest seem to be eyeing me with interest now that they've witnessed the kind of man I am in the bedroom.

I gaze around at them with a slow, heated smile. "I was cruel there at the end, but I think you all understand why I had to put Number Eleven in her place. Any of you are welcome to ask for the same, humiliation and nipple clamps optional. Show me proper respect afterward and you can have a kiss instead of being shoved to the floor."

Number Six gives me a look that tells me she's thinking about it.

Number Seven opens her mouth and closes it again, wanting to speak but uncertain whether she's going to draw my wrath.

"Do you have a question?" I ask her.

"*Ser*, if you like models so much, why didn't you come to the bars in Milan where we all hang out? It's not like you couldn't have met most of us that way."

A bar, where these women are lavished with attention, drinks, and gifts. Wearing an expensive dress and heels with a glass of champagne in her hand, a beautiful woman is confident to the point of disdain. She likes to play. She loves to act like she's someone she's not. I have had a gutful of that kind of fakery for a lifetime.

"Because I want to know who you really are, not who you pretend to be. This pageant is designed to show your true colors. Who is loyal. Who is strong." My attention turns to Number Eleven. "Who is weak."

Number Eleven has put her dress on and has her eyes fixed on the floor like she wishes she were invisible. This is exactly what I wanted. To see her broken.

Conquered.

And yet, I feel a stab of disappointment. It's not just that she's beautiful and whip-smart. I've never known a woman with such strength of character that she could bewitch three killers at the same time. None of us could tear our eyes away from her. Watching her writhe against Kirill's tongue while he fucked her with a gun and then demanded he pull the trigger... That's going to live rent-free in my head long after Number Eleven is dead.

After, she tossed her hair and walked out of the judging room with her head held high. Intoxicating to witness. Magnificent to behold. Mesmerizing even after the door had closed behind her. Today, after a few questions to shatter her confidence, a little pain, and a few words of praise, she fell apart. I was in charge today. She understood how to play Elyah and Kirill with her sass and her pussy, but I'm a different beast entirely.

"I think we all saw someone's true colors today," I tell my jewels, finally looking away from Number Eleven.

Behind me, Elyah shifts on his feet. I hope to fucking God he's working his darling blonde bitch out of his system. I want the man I know he can be once again. Elyah, when he's focused, is an unstoppable force.

"Numbers One, Five, Six, Seven, Ten, Twelve, and Fifteen, you have all done so well this week that I have a treat for you. Many of you must have already realized that there's something strange about this pageant. Rather than let my precious jewels fight among themselves, I'm going to come clean." I pause for effect. "There's a rat among you. One of you is a spy and she's been reporting back to me everything you say and do."

"Why would you admit that?" Number Ten bursts out angrily. "Why should we believe anything you say?"

I narrow my gaze at her. I haven't beaten her, forced her, starved her. I've shown Number Ten every reasonable kindness under these circumstances, yet she still doesn't trust me. I mentally move Number Ten to the bottom of my list.

"Because I don't need her anymore. She sought to ingratiate herself with me for special favors. I instructed her to encourage you all to obey me without question. I have cut you down from sixteen women to seven, and I'm thrilled with my selection." I glance at Number Ten. "More or less. You are all obedient, loyal, strong women who value yourselves as highly as I hope to value you one day."

The seven women look between each other, pride and pleasure flickering on some of their faces. Others seem sickened, but I shall eliminate them soon enough. The tasks from now on will only grow more demanding.

"I have one final task today before my little jewels are fed and put to bed." I stride over to Number One. "Who is the rat?"

She cringes away from me. "I—I don't know."

"Yes, you do. Isn't there one woman here who's been acting strangely from the beginning? One woman who has been persuading you to obey me without question?"

"I don't know," she says again, but with an uncertain look toward Number Eleven.

"Either say her number, or Kirill will beat you." I hold out my arm toward the dark-haired man, who swaggers forward with a menacing grin lighting his features.

Number One shuts her eyes and whispers, "Number Eleven."

I move onto the next woman. Number Five is prompt with her answer. "Number Eleven."

I regard her with my head on one side. Ever since the lie detector test, she's accepted her fate with her head held high. She could well be the eventual winner. How beautiful the pink diamonds will look crowning her raven hair.

I move on, and Number Six answers before I can even ask my question. "Number Eleven."

"Why do you think it's Number Eleven?"

"She's screwing you all. She says she's helping us but everything she does is weird."

"Correct." But I haven't forgotten that she volunteered to be the rat herself.

I move in front of Number Seven. "And you? Who do you think the rat is?"

She replies right away. "Number Eleven."

"And what makes you so sure?"

Number Seven shoots Number Eleven a look of loathing. "She's been telling us from the start to go along with whatever you say. To obey you. Make you happy. She's obviously on your side."

"You don't want to make me happy?"

Number Seven reddens, her eyes darting around the room. "I mean, of course I do. I just want to do it for my own reasons, not because one of these bitches is trying to manipulate me."

I laugh and move on. Nice save.

When I reach Number Ten, her eyes are glittering with fury. "Who is the rat?"

"There isn't a rat," she seethes. "You're messing with us so we turn on Lilia before you kill her. It's a dirty trick and it's not going to work. Lilia's done nothing but try to help us."

My, my. Another one who's too clever for her own good. I glance from Number Ten to Number Eleven. I doubt it's a coincidence that she's sticking up for the woman in the cell next to her. Number Eleven has probably been pouring poison into her ear night after night.

"It's all right, Olivia," Number Eleven whispers. "Just say it's me."

I push my face close to Number Ten's. "What did Number

Eleven promise you? That she could save you? I hope you didn't pin your hopes on a liar and a slut."

Number Ten clenches her fists. "I'm not going to point the finger at any of these women. Kill me if you like. If I die in here, it's going to be on my terms, not yours."

Rage erupts through me, bursting forth like molten lava. Before I can move, Number Eleven tries to throw herself in front of her friend. Kirill lunges forward, wraps his arms around Number Eleven from behind, and drags her back.

I grab Number Ten by the throat and force her into her cage so fast that her back hits the wall. "Your terms? Your fucking terms? Everything that happens here is on *my* terms."

Behind us, Number Eleven is screaming at me to let her go. I tighten my hand around Number Ten's throat so everyone can hear her struggling for breath. This is what happens to anyone who chooses sides against me.

Just before the dark-haired woman passes out, I turn on my heel and storm out of her cell, slamming and locking it behind me. "Number Ten is eliminated."

When I turn to the others, Numbers Twelve and Fifteen both reply in frightened whispers that the rat is Number Eleven. I stride over to the golden blonde, trapped in Kirill's iron grip. Her eyes are sparkling with panic and fury. She wants to kill me. She wants me dead more than anything she's wanted in her whole life.

"They all think the rat is you, Number Eleven. Anything to say in your defense? Will you point the finger at one of the other women?"

She wrenches herself from side to side in Kirill's arms but doesn't speak.

"No? So, you admit it's you? Thank you for your service, rat. It's not needed anymore."

I take a deep, satisfied breath, enjoying this moment. Number Eleven no longer has anyone who looks up to her. The nagging feeling I've had all week that she's been destabilizing my hard work finally dissipates.

"String her up."

Kirill cackles with delight as he drags Number Eleven over to the chains. Beneath her feet is the bloodstain left by the last Number Eleven. With her wrists bound, Kirill drags on the chains and wrenches them over her head. Number Eleven's body hangs suspended for all to see, the tips of her toes just touching the ground.

I saunter over to her. How I love to see my enemies defeated, especially the ones who were so confident that they could get the better of me. "They all see you for who you really are, Number Eleven. A deceitful, traitorous whore."

Elyah is watching from the doorway. A wall has slammed down behind his eyes.

Number Eleven notices him lurking in the shadows. "You're the one in prison, Elyah. You always will be. You'll be in a cage long after I'm dead."

His jaw tightens, and he turns away and pounds up the stairs. Leaving his former lover to her fate.

"Lilia, we know you're not a rat," Number Ten calls. "They had to say someone so they wouldn't be hurt, that's all. I'm sorry."

Icy silence follows her statement, and fourteen sets of eyes are watching Number Eleven. No one else speaks up to defend her. I wait for Number Eleven to address me. Surely she has something to say to me when I'm the one who bested her.

But Number Eleven's lips are sealed tight. She twists her wrists, trying to free herself, but the chains merely clank against each other and hold her fast.

I move close so that only she can hear me and murmur, "You tried to be these women's savior, but you couldn't even save yourself. You've failed, Number Eleven, as I always knew you would. It was amusing to watch you struggle on the end of my rope for a few days."

Number Eleven stays silent when she should be begging for my mercy. That chain is going to bite into her wrists all night. Her muscles will scream for release, and she won't know a moment's rest unless she passes out.

Hardened bitch. I would have liked to hear her beg but she won't give me the pleasure.

"You're eliminated, and tomorrow, Elyah is going to kill you. Enjoy your last night on this earth, *milaya*."

15

Elyah

The moment I open my eyes in the morning, my stomach heaves. I pull myself over the edge of my mattress and vomit onto the floor. I retch painfully half a dozen more times until my stomach is empty.

I roll onto my back with a groan, realizing I'm covered in sweat. Bile burns the back of my throat. It must have been the cold chicken I ate last night that's made me sick. Halfway through eating, I thought it smelled suspect.

What a fucking night. I dreamed I was in prison back in Russia, only my cell was in the basement of this villa and Lilia was my jailer. She crowned herself with Konstantin's pink diamond tiara, only she didn't realize it was covered in murderous spikes. I shouted at her to stop, but she merely looked at me while she pulled it down on her head with all her strength and drove the spikes into her skull. Blood ran down her face and dripped from her hair, and she whispered with blank, white eyes, "I win."

I head through to the bathroom and rinse my mouth with cold water and then use a towel to clean up the mess I made on the floor. Lilia's words from the other day are ringing in my ears. *You have to go on believing I'm a liar. Otherwise, you'll have to face up to all the cruel things you've done to the woman you love for no good reason.*

I hurl the dirty towel into a corner of the room. Lilia is a liar and a snitch, and it's an insult for her to expect me to believe anything else when I saw the evidence with my own two eyes.

I shower and dress, and I step out into the cool morning air using the door into the garden. There's a breeze coming off the water, and the sun is already high in the sky. We've fallen into the habit of sleeping late, and the time must be edging toward midday. No crows today, thank fuck. I remember what Kirill told me, that I'm an old woman when it comes to superstition. I think he must be right, and I push away the last cloying tendrils of my dream.

I find Kirill sitting at the kitchen table eating cereal and reading on his phone. "Where's Konstantin?"

"Out for a run. He'll be back soon." Kirill pushes the cereal box toward me, but my stomach threatens to rebel at the thought of food.

An hour goes by and Konstantin doesn't come back. Then another hour. I pace restlessly up and down the kitchen, wanting today to be over. I need to be free of the burning anger that's plagued my heart for the past two years.

Lilia's down there in the cells right now, strung up by her wrists. Whatever torment I experienced last night, she suffered tenfold. A thousandfold. I wait for the rush of pleasure at this thought, but nothing happens. My soul feels as empty and as wrung out as my stomach.

I push my hands through my hair and groan. I've never felt so dangerously cast adrift as I do right now. In this life, losing focus can mean death. Whoever Konstantin chooses as his bride, he's going to need me to watch her like a hawk for any signs of treachery and protect them both from his enemies. Right now, I couldn't protect a stray kitten.

I'm on the verge of going out to look for Konstantin when we hear footsteps crunching on the gravel outside. Our *Pakhan* enters the kitchen wearing a tank top and running shorts, his face ruddy from exertion but glowing with happiness.

"I want to talk to you about today," I say right away.

"Sure," Konstantin says, but heads for the refrigerator, pulls out a sports drink, and swallows down half the bottle, clearly parched from his long run. He wipes the back of his wrist over his mouth. "What about it?"

"When you are done with Number Seven, leave the room. I want to be alone with her."

There's no need for me to say who *her* is.

"Can we watch?" Kirill asks, a grin lighting his features.

"Knock yourself out," I say, still gazing at Konstantin, silently willing him to hurry the fuck up so we can get on with today's task. My chest feels like my lungs are going to explode. After eating a bowl of cereal and laughing and chatting with Kirill, Konstantin finally heads upstairs for a shower.

Thirty minutes later, we're in the judging room and Number One is being called in. There are four women ahead of Lilia, and the buzzing in my ears is so loud that I can't follow what anyone says to each other. A few minutes later, Number One is sobbing on the floor. She's been eliminated.

Numbers Five, Six, and Seven make it through the task, and my heart is racing so fast that all I can hear is the blood pounding in my ears. I shoot to my feet as soon as Konstantin presses the intercom, impatient for them all to get the hell out of here. My *Pakhan* gives me a long look before he leaves the room, but I can't meet his gaze. I can feel how much he wants the old Elyah back, the resolute, ruthless wall of muscle who scents danger on the wind and savagely puts down anyone who dares cross the people I care about. I want to be that man again, too.

I *need* to be him. That's my worth. He's all I am and all I will ever be.

Konstantin follows Kirill and Number Seven into the room that contains the two-way mirror and the speaker, and the room is mine.

I roll my shoulders and take a deep breath, flexing my head from side to side. I made the preparations last night, so all I have to do is climb up onto the judging desk and attach what I brought in with me to the ceiling.

I could use the intercom to call her in, but I don't want guards to fetch her. This is personal. I pull open the door and find Lilia standing directly on the other side. There are shadows beneath her eyes but other than that, you wouldn't have guessed that she spent a night filled with suffering. Her hair is combed and cascades down her back, and the white dress she wears clings softly to her slender frame.

She lifts her chin and gazes up at me with those sea-green eyes, and I'm fiercely reminded of all the times that we stood opposite each other in a doorway. My heart thunders just like it used to at the sight of her. Lilia smiles sadly, as if she's remembering the exact thing that I am.

I squeeze my eyes shut, a wave of pain and regret slicing through me. When I open my eyes, I want to be dressed in a pressed black shirt, my jaw freshly shaved, and wearing cologne picked out just for this woman. I'll sit at her kitchen counter, and for those few minutes as she bestows her attention and smiles on me, I'll be truly alive. I should have taken her the day she was discharged from hospital after her miscarriage. It would have been easy enough to claim that Ivan had sent me to collect her, knocked her out with some roofied hot chocolate, and driven away with her. She would have been mine. I could have made her happy—

A door slams in my heart. If she'd wanted that, she would have reached out to me, not the feds. We can never go back, and it's all Lilia's fault.

I open my eyes and snarl, "Do not fucking smile at me. Get inside."

I reach for Lilia, but she brushes past me and steps into the judging room. As she sees what's hanging from the ceiling, she stops dead. Her left ankle starts to tremble and her hands clench and unclench at her sides.

I remember the first time I was tested. I reacted the same way Lilia is now. My insides were in turmoil, my guts spasming so hard that I thought I would lose them all over the floor, but I would rather have slit my own throat than show it. I had just joined my first crew, and I had to kill a man in cold blood. I was only seventeen, and though I had already killed my sister's boyfriend, that was in the heat of the moment. I didn't know my target and it sickened me that I was going to execute him without the consolation of hating him first. But I killed the man, and I came out on the other side stronger and harder than before.

Lilia presses her foot against the floor to stop her ankle from trembling. With effort, she relaxes her shoulders and straightens her spine, ready to face this test and pass through it to the other side.

But there is no other side for Lilia. This isn't a test. This is the end.

She glances around the room as if looking for Konstantin and Kirill, but we're alone. I'm not giving her the chance to play us off against each other like she has been all this week. There's just me and her.

And the hangman's noose hanging from the ceiling.

I point at the judging table, which is a makeshift scaffold today, and she clambers up without a word. I get up there with her and stand beside her. With one smooth movement, I place the noose around her neck.

Lilia stares straight ahead as if I'm not there. I watch her closely, knowing I should give her one strong shove now. End this. Watch her dangle on the end of this rope until I'm finally fucking free of her.

But my hands stay balled into fists by my sides because I still crave to understand. "Do you know what happens to man's skull when he is shot with high-caliber bullet?"

Lilia's brow wrinkles with confusion. "I thought I was being hanged, not shot."

"I told Ivan there were snipers, but he was too pig-headed to listen to me. His head exploded like watermelon right in front of me. You are like him, Lilia. If you had listened to me, we would not be here."

"When should I have listened to you? When did I not listen to you?" she demands.

Hot anger pulses through me. She is cleverer than me. I can't forget that, or she'll have me twisted up in knots and chasing my own tail. "If you wanted to get out of your marriage, you should have trusted me, not the fucking feds."

"What you mean is, I should have waited for you in your wardrobe instead of gathering up my dignity and taking myself home. I'm not sorry I decided to think for myself instead of becoming your fuck toy."

I grab the front of Lilia's dress in my fist and shake her. "It was not about fucking. I loved you and you treated me like dirt. I was lower than worm when I met you. Do you know how hard you have to work to make a man feel even lower than that?"

She still won't look at me. "It wasn't hard. I wasn't even trying."

I could fucking slap her.

She must feel my desire as she lifts her chin and angles her cheek toward me. "Go on. Hit me if it will make you feel more like a man."

I'm not going to fucking hit her. I release her dress with a noise of disgust.

"Do you feel like a man yet, Elyah? Has Konstantin fed your ego by allowing you to bully a bunch of defenseless women?"

"He gave me my pride back when I lost everything, and I will show my gratitude with my loyalty until I am dead. This pageant is what my *Pakhan* wants."

Lilia's lip curls, but I don't expect her to understand what loyalty means.

"Just kill me, Elyah. Get this over with so you can help choose a bride for your precious boss."

"No," I growl. "There is going to be no easy way out of this for you. Tell me why you betrayed me, and I will snap your neck and give you a swift death. Stay silent, and I will push you from this table and you will strangle slowly. There is not enough rope for the fall to break your neck unless I do it for you."

Pain, fear, and fury flash over her beautiful face as she struggles for self-control. "I won't beg for mercy. You already have all the answers you crave. You've had them all along, and if you truly loved me, you would have realized the truth by yourself. I'm finished with my life. All I've done is swallow my pride and tried to appease everyone who has more power than me, only to be pushed into the dirt again and again. I'm at peace with death. I welcome it."

But that's not good enough for me. She claims I have answers, but I have nothing but questions and confusion. "I saw the photos of you sitting in the car with the federal agent. There is not chance in hell that you are innocent."

"I don't know what you're talking about. I never sat in a federal agent's car. I have never spoken to a federal agent in my life."

"But I saw you!" I explode.

She shakes her head. "I don't know what you saw. You can believe me or not, but I'm not going to fight with you about it, Elyah."

Frustration courses through me. But the photographs. What Vasily told me. The fact that she vanished into thin air while Ivan was being shot to death by the cops. Not just her, but her jewelry and clothes, too. She knew that Ivan was going to be arrested before anyone else did, and she fled.

"I can't do this anymore," she says, her voice cracking. "It's too painful to be near you, Elyah. We have to end this now and say goodbye. The day we nearly made love was the second biggest mistake of my life."

Pain stabs me through the heart. It's my deepest, darkest secret, but I relive those precious moments with her every day of my life. I have so few happy memories to sustain me through the lonely nights, and even those are tainted with bitterness.

"And giving Ivan to the police and running away was the biggest," I accuse.

Lilia shakes her head, and tears fill her eyes and run down her face. "You still don't get it. All this time, I thought you were smarter than this. I thought you were the only man who would understand."

"Understand what? Stop talking in riddles, Lilia."

"You think I would give the cops anything after what they did to me? Do I really have to spell it out for you?"

"What are you talking about?"

Her eyes squeeze shut and she screams, "*They killed my baby, Elyah.*"

A wave of ice-cold shock slams into me.

"You think I ran to the cops and gave them anything after they murdered my child? You were there when they invaded my life. Did I fake my distress? Am I such a good fucking liar that I timed my miscarriage just to mess with you?"

I cling to a handful of feeble arguments for dear life. *Ivan hit you. Maybe you wanted revenge. You're a liar, and I can't trust anything you say.*

But other memories are louder. Her chalk white face as we stood together in her living room, hatred and fear filling her eyes as she watched the cops pawing through her belongings. Her ice-cold flesh and the way she trembled in fear. Strangers—enemies—were in her house and had arrested her husband. That home was all she had. That baby was all she wanted.

"I never loved my husband, but that house was mine, and it was where I felt safe. Did you know that when I was a child my own father forced me out of my home? He abandoned me at eleven years old, and I was never so scared in my life. Watching those police in my house, I was reliving the worst day of my life. I thought my child would be safe from the world in Ivan's home and would never suffer like I did, but the police trampled all over that."

I picture Lilia lying in that hospital bed, pale in her hospital gown with dark circles beneath her eyes as she whispered, *Maybe it's better this way. Look at what I was bringing a child into.*

A wave of shame and horror overwhelms me. Why the fuck didn't I realize this at the time? I saw her every day while she was pregnant. She was glowing like she was made from sunshine itself. The cops tore away all her happiness, and yet I was still certain that she had run to them to seek revenge.

Pain fills her eyes as she gazes up at me. "Do you know when I fell in love with you, Elyah?"

I grip her arms, relief pouring through me as she speaks of love. Maybe it's not too late. "Tell me, please."

A smile hooks the corners of her mouth. "It was the day after I told you I was pregnant. You'd been so jealous and angry, but you told me you were sorry. You confessed that you did like children and gazed at me with so much longing that I realized I wanted to be married to you. Not to Ivan."

I cup her cheek, stroking her soft skin with my thumb. "That was the first day you ever touched me. Do you remember? You put your hand on mine. I have never forgotten."

"I've never forgotten either," she whispers.

My heart swells with happiness.

And then crashes back to earth again. Lilia isn't a liar, which means I've tortured the woman I love. And yet she reaches up to cup my cheek, those sea-green eyes filled with soft emotion. Her touch feels like absolution, and she's the only one who can forgive me.

"I love you, Lilia. I do not deserve anything from you. I should rot away alone forever for what I have done to you. But I love only you and I always will."

"I love you, too," she says, her voice cracking and tears spilling over her cheeks. "But it hurts to be loved like this, Elyah. We have to say goodbye."

She's not going anywhere, not now that I have her back and I know the truth. I'll find a way to make up for all my cruelty. I won't rest until I've made this right.

Lilia shifts in my grip. Her foot slips. Or maybe she pushes herself off. She plunges from the table, and something tightens savagely around her neck.

The noose. I forgot the fucking noose was still around her neck. Rope that I put there. Her hair tumbles around her face and she makes a hideous choking sound that's quickly cut off.

"*Lilia!*"

I grab her with both arms and pull her back up onto the desk. I try to stand her back on her feet, but her legs buckle beneath her. I fight to keep her weight off the rope and loosen it with both hands, but she's a dead weight and I can't manage both at once. Every time I let go of her to loosen the rope, she slips in my grasp and the rope tightens further.

"Someone fucking help me," I roar. I can feel Konstantin and Kirill watching me through the glass, but the doors stay closed. They want this over. Lilia has been eliminated, and now she needs to die.

Her eyes are bulging and her lips are turning blue. I grasp the rope above our heads and pull it with all my strength. The muscles in my arms and shoulders burn. I grit my teeth so tightly they could shatter.

With a roar, the hook snaps off the ceiling. Lilia and I tumble onto the carpet and land in a heap of tangled limbs.

I wrench the rope from around her neck and fling it aside, but Lilia's not breathing. I pinch her nose and cover her mouth with mine, forcing air into her lungs. I do it again and then a third time. The taste of panic fills my mouth, bitter and shocking.

My lips are crashing over hers for a fourth time when she suddenly coughs, spluttering weakly as her chest heaves. Relief pours through me as she opens her eyes. I wrap my arms around her waist and haul her against me.

"Lilia. Oh, thank God, Lilia." I pull back and shake her shoulders. "Why did you do that? What the fuck were you thinking?"

There's a vivid red burn around her throat. She wipes her streaming eyes and draws in a struggling breath, and instantly I let go of my anger. Of course she did it. I was furious with her, pushing her to relive the worst moment of her life and she couldn't bear it.

I pull her into my arms and rock her against my chest,

anguish filling my heart. "*Prosti menya.*" *Forgive me.* "*Solnyshko*, I am sorry."

She's alive. Thank all the fucking stars in the sky, she's alive.

"Don't, Elyah. Please. It's over." She pushes against my chest, trying to move away from me, but I won't let her go.

"What do you mean, over? Nothing is over."

"Your honor has been satisfied. You said you would kill me, and you did. You brought me back, so now you have to let me go."

My jaw hardens and my eyes narrow. I have to do no such thing. "You are still in love with me, Lilia Aranova. You would not want to die unless you still loved me."

She starts to laugh, a weak, choking laugh. "That is what your love does to a woman? It drives her over the edge?"

Maybe it does, but she drives me insane with her love, too. "I do not know. I have only ever been in love with you. I will only ever be in love with you until the day I die."

Lilia gazes at me, her eyes welling up. Tears slip down her cheeks as I lower my head toward hers. My lips burn to kiss her, and I capture her face in my hands and press my mouth to hers. The tears make hot, wet tracks on her cheeks, and I brush them away with my thumbs as my tongue caresses hers.

She gives in, her mouth softening against mine. She welcomes the gentle invasion of my tongue. She breathes when I breathe. Her hands tighten on my shoulders.

Then she wrenches her head to one side. "No. I don't want this. You're filled with so much anger and hate it scares me."

I take her hands and press them over my thundering

heart. "It is gone now. All my anger is gone. There is only love in here and it is all for you."

She hesitates, staring from her hands pinned against my muscles to my eyes, her brow knits with uncertainty. It's the same expression she wore when I was coaxing illicit kisses from my *Pakhan's* beautiful young wife.

I shouldn't, that expression says.

We can't.

But I want to...

She's so fucking beautiful and she's in my arms once more, heady desire and forbidden love wrapping themselves around us and binding us together. Her lips part and her eyes dilate with passion. My tongue moves against the roof of my mouth like I'm already lavishing her clit. I'm this fucking close to begging for another taste of her. She's been on Kirill's tongue. She's come on Konstantin's cock. I don't give a fuck that I'm the last of the three of us. Following these two men into anything is my pride, not my shame.

And it's different because she *loves* me.

I slant my head toward hers and drop my voice to a coaxing murmur. "You like it when I am sweet to you. Let me be sweet, *solnyshko*. Only for you."

She almost pulls back, but I slide my hand around the nape of her neck, holding her in place.

"Lick your lips for me, Lilia," I whisper, my mouth a fraction of an inch from hers.

As if she's hypnotized, she draws her lower lip into her mouth and sucks on it. When she releases it, it's shiny and pink. I nip it with my teeth and she breathes unsteadily.

I groan and gather her body closer to mine, laying down on the carpet with her. Her body is tight against my hard cock. I know she can feel me. I undo several buttons on my shirt and reach behind my head to pull it off. Lilia traces shaking fingers over my flesh, following the same paths as she once did across the tattoos on my shoulders and down my chest.

"All I've wanted is to love you, protect you, make you feel good. Does my body please you, Lilia? This is all I have to offer you." Not fourteen million dollars of pink diamonds. Just my muscle. Just my arms. My cock. My heart.

"Elyah, this can't happen. You just tried to kill me."

But she clings to me as her protests grow feeble.

I lower my head and press my mouth against her jaw, her throat. I find the rope burn and plant soft kisses over the injury. "I should have tried harder to find you. I should have known that you would never have done anything to help the people who killed your baby. I am so sorry."

Lilia is nearly sobbing once more. "It doesn't matter anymore. You have to let me go."

My teeth clench and I nearly growl a refusal. I have to do nothing of the fucking kind.

"Will you be free if I do?" I challenge her. "Will you stop thinking about me? Will you stop being in love with me?"

Lilia gives me a desperate look, like she's begging me to stop talking. I've swallowed down my pain and hatred for her for two years, and it's been a bitter feast. Words of love and tenderness are coating my tongue and I want to spill them into her mouth.

"Elyah—"

The sound of my name on her lips is heaven. I groan and slant my mouth over hers, tasting her mouth as she lets my tongue sweep against hers.

I should take Lilia out of here. Konstantin and Kirill must be impatient to finish today's challenge and they and the other women are watching us through the glass. Let them watch. I only care about what Lilia is feeling and thinking, and if I move her, this moment might be broken forever. I have to see this through until she's mine, once and for all.

"Lilia Aranova," I murmur, angling my head the other way and kissing her again. "You have always wanted me." I slide both hands down to her ass and squeeze, pulling her firmly against me. This ass I've coveted since the first night she swayed her hips as she walked in front of me. "I have always wanted you. Let me show you, *solnyshko*."

I lay her back on the carpet and her golden hair spreads out around us like she's an angel.

"But how can we do this?" she whimpers. "What future can there be for us?"

"Our future is whatever we make it." I grasp the straps of her dress and ease them down her shoulders. Her nipples are dark pink and sensitive from Konstantin's clamps, and I suck them gently. Lilia moans and arches up into my mouth. How deliciously she reacts to my touch. Nothing has changed about how much we crave each other.

"The first time I touched you, really touched you, was just like this. Pulling your clothes aside. Tasting you where I could." I push her dress up her thighs, grasp her thong, and move it aside. My tongue runs over her sweet slipperiness, and I groan.

I raise my head and our eyes meet. "You always get so wet for me, *solnyshko*. Do you remember how to ask me for this?"

16

Lilia

My heart is beating so hard that it feels like it's going to batter itself to pieces and I really will die today. Elyah's touch has set my soul on fire, and every touch, every press of his lips, every swipe of his tongue is burning me up. This is madness. I need to tell him to release me. He's my killer, not my lover, but those are not the words that come to my lips.

"*Pozhaluysta...*" I breathe. *Please.* That's all I can remember. That's all that I can feel.

Please, Elyah. I'm begging you.

"*Trakhni menya pozhaluysta,* Elyah," he murmurs, and his voice is husky with desire. "Say it, Lilia. I am going to hear you say it."

He dips his head back between my thighs and licks straight up the core of me. The noose lays on the floor next to us like an evil omen. I picture myself suspended off the ground, fingers scrabbling at the rope. Legs kicking uselessly back and forth while Elyah impassively watches the life slowly crushed out of me.

His tongue swirls slowly against my clit. My body wants so desperately to live, and he's making me feel more alive than I have ever been in my life. My head falls back with a moan. "*Trakhni menya pozhaluysta,* Elyah."

"Do you know what you are asking for, Lilia?" He spreads me open with his fingers and torments me even more with his tongue. "Once I possess you, I am never letting you go. I will pursue you to the ends of the earth if you ever run from me again."

I take his head between my hands, and there's a sob in my voice as I say, "You're the only man I've ever wanted. I'm yours, Elyah. Love me. Kill me. I don't care. Just never let me go."

He groans and slides up my body, wrenching his pants open and pushing them and his underwear down his thighs. I tear off my own clothes and wriggle beneath him, capturing his hips with my thighs.

We both look down at the sight of his cock jutting between us. We're here again. Everyone and everything is against us, but we're drawn back together and burning so hard for each other that nothing else matters.

"Lilia," he breathes, and leans down to kiss me. "The world could end right now and I would still make you mine."

His kiss is slow and thorough, a man determined to savor every moment of this.

"You're tempting fate," I whisper, squeezing his muscular body with my thighs. "We could be stopped even without the world ending. I could be ripped from your arms again."

"If anyone tries to take you from me, I will kill them." His tongue swipes my lower lip. "After I am done making you mine."

He takes himself in his hand and strokes his length slowly up my sex. Teasing me with the sight and sensation of him so close to my core. Teasing both of us.

"Elyah, you're driving me crazy." I flex my fingers on his shoulders, digging my nails in, clenching and unclenching.

A smile touches his lips. "I have been dreaming of this forever. Let me drink in the way you are looking at me."

"What look?" I ask, reaching down between us to drag my middle finger up through my pussy. Elyah watches, fascinated, as my finger swirls slowly on my clit. This is what I used to do late at night, imagining I was in his arms. In his bed. Wishing that he were my husband and that I belonged to him.

He makes a delicious noise in the back of his throat as he watches me. "That you might die if you do not get what you need."

"I will. I'll die. Please, you have to—"

Elyah pushes his cock down and surges forward with one determined thrust. I breathe in sharply and clutch him tighter as his thick cock thrusts deep inside me. As he pulls back and drives into me again, I feel like I could shatter already.

The room dims around me. I feel like no time has passed. I'm back in his bedroom, and the man who I've obsessively dreamed about for months is making me his.

Elyah sets a slow, thorough pace, the muscles of his

chest and stomach bunching and flexing. His lips brush over mine. His fingertips skim my breasts. My throat. His touch is gentle even as his thrusts grow more demanding. I scratch my nails in needy lines across the backs of his shoulders. My neck aches from the burn of the rope. Just a few minutes ago he was choking the life out of me, and now he's pounding into me like I'm his queen and he's just returned from a war. Elyah fucks me like he's got something to prove.

"*Solnyshko*, I need more," he growls into my throat.

I roll my head to the side and glance around the room. "The chair."

Konstantin's chair. Loathing for the man spills through me as I remember how he humiliated me yesterday, but it's swiftly replaced by exhilaration as Elyah scoops me up in his arms and carries me over to it.

I kneel on the chair and spread my knees, gazing over my shoulder at Elyah. His fine blond hair is falling into his eyes and his chest is glowing with perspiration. My nails have left red crescents and scratches in his shoulders.

He's never looked more magnificent.

The reflective mirror shows me he has his cock in his hand as he plants the other on the small of my back. I arch my spine and thrust my ass toward him in an invitation more blatant than I've ever made before, begging him to claim me. The swift invasion of his cock has me grabbing for the chair's leather back and crying out.

He slides one large hand around my throat and bends my head back until he can kiss me. "I am always going to fuck you like this, like it is the first time and the last."

The ache inside me builds and builds. I can see the two-way mirror out of the corner of my eyes. *Are you watching this, Konstantin? I'm taking your man from you.*

But then, he was never yours. Elyah was always mine.

"Lilia. My Lilia." Elyah is groaning my name with every thrust of his cock. His hands are burning hot as he grips me desperately. "Come for me, *solnyshko*. I want to feel you squeezing me."

The ache inside reaches a crescendo, and I grasp his hand on my waist as I come, twining my fingers through his. Elyah's thrusts grow haphazard and urgent and then he snatches me up in his arms with a shout, clutching me against his muscled body and forcing me down on his cock. The violent waves of his climax pulse through both of us.

We both breathe hard in the stillness and silence that follows. Elyah groans and buries his face in my neck. Half laughing, half moaning in pleasure, he pulls me off the chair and rolls us beneath the desk. I'm tight against his side, my hand on his chest, and it feels like the two of us are in a safe little cocoon.

"Two years," he says, kissing me woozily. "I have waited two years to make you mine. Never torture me like that again."

Neither of us can predict what's going to happen next, but Elyah is determined that I shall be by his side. He plants soft kisses on the burn around my throat.

"We should try and make our love more boring. I do not think I can take any more heartache."

I laugh. "You're probably right about that. If our love becomes any more interesting, it's going to have a body count."

Elyah sits up a little and turns to me, his fist pressing

against his temple. "The day Ivan died, where did you run? How did you know?"

I trace the tattoos on his chest. That was a terrible day. Not the worst day of my life, but up there. My lips press together at the bitter memory. "My father came and got me. He wouldn't explain anything or answer my questions. He forced me into his car while his men packed up my things and followed behind us as we drove away. I didn't know what happened to Ivan until I switched on the news that night in my father's house."

I don't know what happened to Ivan's children. I presume his sister or mother picked them up from school and broke the terrible news to them about their father. Alexei and Inessa never warmed to me, or I to them, but my heart went out to them the day their father was killed.

"But how did your father know that Ivan was going to be arrested?"

I shake my head helplessly. "I don't know. He said he'd been concerned since Ivan was arrested a few weeks earlier. Maybe he had a cop in his pocket who tipped him off. What about you? You were with Ivan when he was shot. How did you get away?"

Elyah puffs out his cheeks and widens his eyes. "I do not fucking know. I was on autopilot and my only thought was to get to you. I went to the house and you were not there, and..."

He trails off with a wince. He thought the worst. He thought I had betrayed him.

"I tried to find you," I whisper, stroking the tattoo on the side of his neck. "When I escaped my father's house a few days later, I went to your apartment, but you were gone. I went to my house looking for answers. The master bedroom had been destroyed."

I slumped to the floor and cried, shards of broken mirror digging into my legs and cutting them to ribbons. I wasn't crying for Ivan. I knew who had smashed everything to pieces. Elyah's hatred for me was palpable in that room.

He gently cups the nape of my neck. "I am sorry. That was me. I was furious with you and blind with the shock of everything that had happened. I got into car and drove out of the city, and I just kept driving."

It was probably for the best, in hindsight. If he hadn't, he would have been arrested. "You did what you had to do. You're a survivor, Elyah. That's why all these powerful men want you around."

He captures my cheek in his large hand, his expression urgent. "Do you trust me to protect you, *solnyshko*? Do you know that I will do it, no matter what? You are my everything until my dying breath."

I'm no longer a married woman, but I'm still far from free. A short while ago, I was marked for death. I can't see how it's possible that I will leave this villa alive.

There's a click, and a deep voice says, "Please remove Number Eleven and take her to the cellar."

Elyah and I both sit up and see Konstantin standing with his finger on the intercom, his cold, gray eyes fixed on me. A thrill of apprehension goes through me.

Back to the cellar.

Back to being a contestant in his pageant.

Kirill is behind him, leaning against the wall with a hungry look in his dark eyes. "You fuck so beautifully, Number Eleven. I'll never get tired of watching you come."

I give him the finger and turn to find our clothes, scooping up Elyah's pants from the floor.

He steps toward Konstantin, butt naked, the muscles of his back rippling. "She is not Number Eleven. She is Lilia Aranova, and she belongs to me. You already eliminated her from this pageant."

Konstantin's gaze sweeps from him to me, and ice dances down my spine. There's a covetous curve to his lips, as if he's laid eyes on a delectable morsel for the first time.

"So I did," he says to Elyah, but still looking at me. "But circumstances have changed."

"Nothing has changed. We agreed she was mine," Elyah growls.

"Yours to kill. If Number Eleven isn't going to die, then this changes everything."

Konstantin and I gaze at each other past Elyah's naked body. He stripped me bare and humiliated me in front of everyone, proving to himself that I'm useless. Even if I'm not the betraying bitch they thought I was, that doesn't make me the right contestant to be his bride.

"I'm not the woman you're looking for," I tell him.

A smile hooks the corner of his lips, and I can't tell if he's truly reevaluating me or if he wishes to destroy me because I'm taking away one of his most loyal allies.

I push Elyah's pants at him and get quickly into my clothes, then step around my bristling lover to face his *Pakhan*. "Just because you hate me doesn't mean you should hurt Elyah. What happened to the loyalty you spoke about? It works both ways."

Konstantin's expression turns lethal as he addresses Elyah. "We agreed Lilia Aranova would be yours based on the assumption that she betrayed you and her husband and was working with the feds. If that's not true..." An indomitable gleam fills his eyes. "Then she's not eliminated."

Elyah's jaw bunches.

"No!" I cry. "That's not fair."

But in my heart, I know that fair or not, Konstantin rules this pageant with an iron fist. He has the power to demand whatever he likes.

I gaze at the scarred, gray-eyed man, hatred filling my heart. I'm so tired of this perilous game of chess. I'm a dead woman. I'm not a dead woman. I'm free. I'm not free. Now I have no choice but to plead with a man who has a heart of ice. "Please let me be with Elyah. You can see how much we love each other."

Surely he values his man's loyalty and gratitude even if he doesn't give a damn about me.

After a long silence, Konstantin turns to Elyah. "We need to talk about this. The women will go back to their cells. Number Eleven, that includes you."

My shoulders slump and I hang my head, disappointment pouring through me. He sounded just like my father. Just like Ivan, too. There's no point in arguing with a *Pakhan* who has made up his mind. I start toward the door, but Elyah reaches out and grabs my wrist.

"No. Stay." He turns back to Konstantin and snarls, "Lilia is not going back in that cage."

"If you were to leave Number Eleven in your bedroom while we talked, do you suppose that she'd still be there when we were finished? How trusting you are, Elyah."

A muscle in Elyah's jaw tics. "Lilia and I need each other. She is not going anywhere."

Konstantin laughs, looking at me as if we're sharing an inside joke, and what's funny is that Elyah is a fool. "Maybe she wants you, but she's a long way from needing you. Lilia Aranova only needs herself. Don't you, Lilia?"

A prickle runs down the nape of my neck as he talks like he can see right through me. I fight to keep a straight face and say nothing. Konstantin wants to fuck with me, but mostly Konstantin just doesn't trust me.

I turn to Elyah and put my hand on his chest, gazing up at him and speaking softly. "Your *Pakhan* gave you an order, Elyah. I need to go back in that cage, but I'll be waiting for you. I'm not going anywhere."

Elyah's expression melts from anger to love, and he brushes his knuckles over my cheek. I smile and lean into his touch.

"I hate the thought of you being locked up again."

"It's all right. I know there are rules." Everything in this life is about rules, and they can't be broken just because someone changes his mind. Nothing can be resolved until Konstantin and Elyah have talked in private. "When this pageant is over, we can be together."

Konstantin is watching me like a hawk. His sharp gaze pierces the side of my neck. He doesn't trust me, but he can't take his eyes off me either.

Pain fills Elyah's expression. "You are not angry with me, Lilia, that you are going back in that cage? I am angry with myself that this is happening to you."

I shake my head and smile. "Goodbye, but only for now."

"Just for now," he repeats urgently, and covers my mouth with his. I press a hand over his heart, feeling it thunder against my palm.

"I have always loved this sound," I whisper against his lips. "I will always love this sound."

A rough hand lands on my shoulder. It's one of Konstantin's guards, and I'm ripped away from Elyah so fast that I stumble.

Elyah shoves the guard and snarls, "Do not fucking touch her. She is going."

I take one last look behind me and his expression is stricken as if he's terrified that he's never going to lay eyes on me again. Then the door slams, cutting us off from each other.

I grasp the hem of my dress and fiddle with it instead of looking at any of the women, but I can feel their shock and confusion. I was marked for death, and now I'm a competitor again. A real opponent this time, though little do I want it.

Down in the cellar, the guards lock us into our cages and leave us alone. I huddle on my bed and wrap my arms around myself, freezing cold after Elyah's scorching embrace.

"Is this all part of your big plan to help us, Number Eleven?" Marija calls. "What lies are you going to tell us next?"

"She didn't even beg for our lives," Madison says. "Only her own. Do you hear that, Olivia? She just fucked the blond one to try and get out of here, and it nearly worked. But she didn't lift a finger to help us. Not even you. Some friend she is."

"That's not true!" Olivia cries. "Lilia wouldn't leave us behind."

"You're so fucking naïve! Go on, Number Eleven. Tell her the truth. Tell her how you were going to skip off into the sunset with your boyfriend and leave us all behind."

I lock my arms around my knees and grit my teeth. There's nothing I can tell them, and my silence damns me more than anything I could have said.

In the next cell, Olivia starts to sob. "We're all going to die because of these men, Lilia. Would you really have walked away and left us behind?"

I put my head in my hands and rock back and forth. I want to stuff my fingers in my ears to block out her despair, but I can't.

"Lilia? Lilia, how could you do this to us?" Alejandra's voice grows shrill and hysterical as she beats on the bars of her cage. "Lilia! *Answer me.*"

Over her screams, Marija shouts, "They trusted you, you treacherous bitch. Have you got nothing so say to them?"

Alejandra goes on crying and screaming, her broken sobs echoing around the cellar. The other women call out to her and tell her she needs to be quiet, afraid that she's going to draw Konstantin's wrath down on us.

Gradually, miserable silence falls in the cellar.

Madison whispers viciously in the darkness, "It doesn't matter whether you sold out your husband or not, or what your precious Elyah believes. We see who you are for ourselves, Number Eleven. You really are a betraying whore."

17

Lilia

Nine years earlier

"Yeah, yeah, do we rock? Yeah, yeah, take it to the top!"

The chant we learned at cheerleading practice circles through my brain, and I sing it as I walk. The September sunshine spills gloriously across the sidewalk and my ponytail swings from side to side. As I sing, I bounce along, my backpack thumping against my back in time with the tune and my mother's locket jingles on the chain around my neck.

It's not happiness bubbling through my chest and making song burst from my throat. It's defiance. Everyone in this town hates my guts, but am I going to let them see how much that hurts?

Hell goddamn no.

The streets around school have emptied out and there are

just a handful of other students on their way home from glee club, football practice, and cheer squad. I'm only two blocks from home when someone steps out from behind a hedge, pulling me up short. To my dismay, I see it's Seth, the class bully. He's been held back a year so he's bigger than everyone else. I'm the tallest girl in my class, but he still towers over me and he's stocky as well.

I try to pass him but he sidesteps and blocks me.

"What?" I toss at him, going for bravado, though my heart is racing. School has been a nightmare this year. Over the summer, Dad was questioned by the police about a fire at a strip club, and there are articles about him in the news every day. Stolen money. Dead bodies. Missing people from years ago. Everyone's been staring at me like I'm some kind of freak.

Dad didn't do anything wrong. He told me so himself, though he said it in a strange way. *"What do you want to believe? That I didn't do it? Then I didn't do it."*

It felt like he was asking me if I still wanted to believe that Santa Claus and the Tooth Fairy were real, long after I should have outgrown them.

"My dad says your dad beats people up if they don't pay their rent," Seth taunts. "He says he makes his money from whores and he's going to pimp you out when you're old enough."

"He doesn't need me when he's got your mom," I fire back.

Seth's mouth drops open. While his brain is still chugging over my insult like an old laptop, I step smartly around him and keep walking.

"Yeah, yeah, do we rock? Yeah, yeah, take—*hey!*"

Seth has reached out, grabbed hold of my locket, and tugged. The chain snaps and he holds it above my head.

"Give that back," I demand, jumping up and trying to snatch it back. Mom gave me that locket before she died. She pressed it into my hands as she lay sick in a hospital bed, her flesh as transparent as tissue paper and her eyes sunken. *I'll always love you, Lili-bean.*

Seth gives me an evil smirk. "I'll hand it over if you show me your boobs."

My head rears back in shock and disgust. My boobs? I'm eleven and I barely have anything to show. I've inspected myself in my mirror from the front and from the side, and sure I look a little different than I did just a few months ago, but I look weird, and I don't like what my body's doing without my permission. I definitely don't want to go showing myself to the most horrible boy in class.

"Ugh, gross. No way."

He holds out his hand, dangling my locket over a storm drain. "Do it or I'll drop this."

"Don't!" I wail, snatching at the locket as anguish floods my body. Seth just laughs. I know I'm doing entirely the wrong thing by reacting like this. I can hear Dad in my head, scolding me for handing over so much power to my enemy.

Lilia, you must never show your hand until you have to. Wait until you are sure of victory, and then strike.

I desperately search for a way to claim back my power.

"Three," Seth counts menacingly. "Two."

"Wait!" I stare down into the drain. It's deep, and I can just make out water glistening in the darkness far below. If my locket falls in there, I'll never get it back.

I grasp the hem of my T-shirt, stare off to one side, and flip it up and down lightning fast. "There. Are you happy?"

Seth is grinning wider and shakes his head. "Nuh-uh. The bra, too. I want to see *everything*." He leers at me, waggling his eyebrows.

What everything? I barely have anything to show. It's not even a bra. It's a bralette, a crop top with bra straps that you pull over your head, though it was humiliating enough showing that to him.

"If I say *one*, this locket is going in the drain," Seth threatens.

With embarrassment and fury coating my insides, I grasp the bralette along with my T-shirt, yank it up, feeling the cool breeze nipping at my flesh, and then pull everything down again.

A nasty grin splits Seth's face, and I realize it's not because I've shown him something that he wants to see, but because I actually did it.

He throws the locket toward the drain and jogs off, laughing, calling out at the top of his lungs, "Lilia BRA-zhensky! Lilia BRA-zhensky!"

"No!" I lunge for the grate just as the necklace slips through the bars. My fingers touch the fine chain and I grasp it tightly. My heart soars—

And then the locket zips off the end and I'm left holding nothing but the chain. A moment later, I hear the heavy gold oval plop into the water.

Tears fill my eyes as I stare into the inky shadows. I kneel on the sidewalk, head bowed as I sob. Mom died when I was five, and my memories of her are blurred and choppy. That locket was the only thing I had that reminded me that she was once real. That she had loved me.

That *someone* loved me.

Dad talks to me like I'm one of his men. He shouts at me like I'm one of his men, too. Even *Babushka* can't stand to look at me. I'm alive and her daughter's gone, and she hates me for it.

I swipe my hand over my runny nose and get to my feet. Why does everybody in this town hate me so much? Is it just because my family is Russian? Or is it because the rumors are true, and the Brazhensky name is laced with blood and death?

I trudge toward home, to an empty house. It's almost always empty, and I hate being in that big house by myself. I wish Mom were still alive. I wish I had brothers and sisters.

I wish I had anyone.

Predictably, the huge, white house is as silent as a tomb when I let myself in through the front door into the cavernous black-and-white tiled hall. It welcomes Dad and his pristine suits and palpable authority, but it resents my presence, cringing away from my dusty shoes and sticky fingers.

With dried tears on my cheeks, I walk straight through the house to the kitchen to get a glass of water. The locket can't be gone forever. It *just* can't be. My mind whirs over the possibilities. Maybe the city council has some sort of service that you can contact about precious objects that have been lost. Or I could dangle a magnet down there. Is gold magnetic?

I'm picturing half a dozen workmen with orange cones and mechanical diggers excavating the drain when a car roars into the driveway. I recognize the thrum of Dad's Audi, and blink in surprise as he strides through the front door a moment later, slamming it behind him.

The house is delighted to see him, illuminating his tall, strong figure to perfection as he strides down the hall toward me.

"I heard what happened," he says through his teeth, green eyes flashing. There's heavy dark stubble on his jaw. He shaves every morning but it's always back with a vengeance by the afternoon.

My heart leaps with happiness as well as surprise. Somehow he heard what Seth did to me, and he's furious. Dad lifts his hand toward me, grabbing the hair on the top of my head and dragging me from the room. I have no choice but to follow him, my feet stumbling over each other, tears springing into my eyes.

"What's wrong? What did I do?"

He throws me onto the carpet. I sit up and face Dad, realizing that we're in his study. This has to be a mistake or a misunderstanding. He can't be angry with me for losing the locket, can he? Not when Seth was the one to rip it from around my neck and I did everything I could to get it back.

As soon as I'm back on my feet, Dad lifts his huge palm and slaps me across the face. "You disgusting harlot!"

His roar rings in my ears along with the pain, and I'm too shocked to even cry. I suck a heaving breath into my lungs. "I'm sorry. I didn't mean to lose the locket."

"What locket?" he growls.

I blink. Isn't that why he's angry with me?

Dad points toward the front door with a shaking forefinger. "I do not go out to work every day to put a roof over your head, only for you to turn into a cheap little whore. Eleven years old and already you can't keep your clothes on."

Dad starts ranting in Russian and pacing up and down. Then he whirls back to me.

"Showing yourself to a boy on the street where anyone driving past could see you. All my men were laughing at me. When will your daughter be on the pole, Aran?"

"I had to do it because Seth stole Mom's—"

"I do not want your excuses!" he bellows. "My own flesh and blood. I can't even look at you."

Dad turns on his heel and stalks out, throwing over his shoulder, "You can stand there for the rest of the night."

I'm left in cavernous, hostile silence. Dad's austere study seems to be gloating over my disgrace, and I wonder who saw me in the street with Seth. Probably the wife of Dad's second-in-command, a nasty, gossiping woman who takes it upon herself to police everyone's children and tell tales on them to their parents. Girls acting out with boys is her favorite transgression. I suppose it must have looked like I was showing off my chest in the street, but if she'd only looked closer, she would have seen the hatred burning in my eyes.

I stand there for hours as the shadows grow long and the sun dips over the horizon. The lights are switched off and the study is shrouded in darkness. There's an ache in the pit of my belly. Maybe it's fear. Maybe it's loneliness. Maybe I deserve everything that's happened to me. Mom dying. Being rejected by my friends one by one because of the things their parents have told them about my father. Dad's unpredictable cruelty.

When my legs start to throb, I shift from foot to foot, and something warm runs down the inside of my leg. I squeeze my eyes shut in horror. I'm wetting myself? The shame is suffocating, and a fresh fear slices through me. I'm soiling Dad's precious study, and when he comes back, he's probably going to hit me again.

There's the sound of feet in the hall, and then the light snaps on. I'm blinded by the sudden illumination and I'm still squinting with a hand in front of my face when Dad starts to roar.

"Is this how you take revenge on me? By bleeding all over my carpet?"

Bleeding?

I look down at myself and see that there's blood running down the insides of my bare legs. The bottom falls out of my stomach at the grisly sight. Am I dying?

I can barely hear Dad shouting as a high-pitched noise whines in my ear. My legs feel rubbery and my knees buckle, and I sit down hard on the floor.

Dad lunges forward and swipes a kick at me. I try and pull myself out of his reach but his foot smashes into my stomach, and everything turns white behind my eyes.

"Look at this fucking mess. If you act like a cheap and dirty woman, I will treat you like one."

His enormous hand reaches for me, and something inside me breaks. I scramble to my feet and race out of the room, taking the stairs two at a time until I reach my bedroom and slam the door behind me.

Tears are falling down my face as I limp into the bathroom and turn on the shower. I get under the stream of hot water, fully clothed.

As I watch bright red blood pouring down the drain, I don't even feel like me. I think I'm living in a nightmare.

"Up. Get up."

I wake in the morning to Dad shoving things into my school backpack. Clothes. Shoes. He fills it until it's nearly bursting.

I sit up slowly, rubbing my eyes. "Dad?"

But he doesn't even look at me. Instead, he takes my backpack and walks out the door. "Be downstairs in the car in two minutes, or I'll come and get you myself."

That's no idle threat, and I jump out of bed, feeling the uncomfortable crinkle of the toilet paper I shoved in my underwear. I thought the bleeding might have stopped but it seems to be getting worse. With tears burning my eyes, I pretend like it's not happening and pull on a pair of jeans, a T-shirt, and sneakers, and hurry downstairs.

Dad is waiting in the idling car, and when I get in the front seat, he shoves my backpack into my arms. His face is set and closed, and I don't bother asking questions as we drive through the dawn-lit streets.

After a while, I realize we're heading for *Babushka's* house. Mom's mom, a shriveled and mean old woman who comes to our house once a year on my birthday and glares at me with beady eyes like she's a crow and I'm a worm. She never used to be so flinty and bitter. Dad says she became that way after her only daughter passed away. I might feel sorry for *Babushka* if she didn't poke me viciously with her fingers and tell me to stand up straight and wipe "that look" off my face. I don't know what look she means. That's just my face.

I stare at the backpack I'm holding on my lap with a sense of creeping horror. "Dad, why are we going to *Babushka's*?"

Dad takes a left-hand turn in icy silence.

When we pull up outside *Babushka's* bungalow, she's standing on the front step wearing a black dress and a severe expression stamped on her face. Dad stares straight ahead, saying nothing.

"Dad?"

"Get out of the car, Lilia," he says in a flat, angry voice.

I know better than to argue with him when he uses that tone, so I do as I'm told, hoping to placate him. I close the door after me and turn to him, but before I can open my mouth, he guns the engine and roars away.

He's leaving me here.

Panic like I've never known before floods every vein in my body. I drop the backpack at my feet and run screaming after the car, shouting at him to come back, my high-pitched voice rocketing back and forth off the sleepy houses.

"Dad, don't leave me here."

His taillights glow red at the end of the street and I gain on him for a second, my legs pumping hard as I fly down the sidewalk. My heart leaps—

And then crashes through the earth as he takes the turn and the car disappears.

I stand on the corner, paralyzed with terror. No mom, and now no dad. I don't have anyone, and the ache that's been in my belly since last night expands throughout my entire body. What's going to happen to me now?

A sharp voice cracks over me. "Lilia."

Babushka has followed me and is standing behind me. She jerks her head over her shoulder and walks back up the street to her house. With a sinking feeling, I follow her, dragging my feet and not bothering to wipe the tears from my face.

Inside, the dark, somber house is filled with the sound of a ticking clock and the hateful scent of boiled cabbage and vinegar. She pushes me toward the spare bedroom, and I go, but then hesitate.

"Why am I here?"

She shrugs and mutters something in Russian, not meeting my eyes.

"When can I go home?"

Babushka makes a dismissive sounds and turns away.

Fear and desperation lurch through me. "Wait, please. I think there's something wrong with me. My stomach. It won't stop aching and I'm bleeding."

She peers at me, frowning. "Bleeding where?"

"Between my legs," I mutter, cheeks flushing with embarrassment. I wait for the inevitable tirade that everything about me is wrong, annoying, disgusting.

Babushka snaps, "Did no one tell you about periods?"

I frown, recalling an afternoon in health class six months ago when the girls were separated from the boys and the teacher passed around strange cotton objects. That word *period* came up a lot that day, didn't it? I'm not sure because the night before, Dad's brother was shot and we were all at the hospital until two in the morning. I was like a zombie at school the next day.

Babushka tuts at my confused expression, reaches for her handbag, and walks out of the house. I hear her car start and she drives away.

Ten minutes later, she's back and she hands me a purple packet.

"Put them in your underpants," she tells me, watching me open the box and examine the flat, squishy pads wrapped in plastic. "I bought Alyona these things nearly thirty years ago."

For a fleeting moment, *Babushka's* expression is as bleak as midwinter. Then her face hardens and she turns and walks out.

I take a shower in *Babushka's* pastel yellow bathroom that looks like it hasn't been updated in thirty years. The soap is scratchy and smells of tar. She has bought the same cheap-looking soap, shampoo, and conditioner in bulk, and it's all stacked beside the bath.

Her insulin sits on the vanity next to her toothbrush. *Babushka* has always been diabetic, and I have a vague memory of her testing her blood sugar and injecting herself after she eats.

I sit in my room all morning, staring out the window and hoping I'll see Dad's car coming up the street. At midday, *Babushka* calls me into the kitchen for lunch and we eat flavorless stew with stringy meat. I didn't have any dinner the evening before or any breakfast this morning and my stomach is rumbling, so I eat every unpleasant bite.

After I finish, she stares at my empty plate and asks with disdain, "How am I going to afford you?"

I tiptoe around *Babushka's* house whenever I have to leave my bedroom and her disapproving eyes follow me everywhere. She tells me off when I turn the lights on or spend too long in the shower. My shoes are dirty. My hair is tangled. Her criticisms go on and on.

The only place I enjoy being in is the garden. *Babushka* has a beautiful back garden that's filled with flowers and sunshine. All the local birds flock to the trees and shrubs and line up on the birdbath to ruffle and hop in the shallow water. I sit for hours watching them, studying them closely until I think I've learned to tell them apart from each other. How wonderful to be a little wild bird and flit from here to there without anyone caging you in.

Every day, I call Dad and beg him tearfully to let me come home. He listens to me for a moment, and then hangs up without a word. I go to school. I eat dinner in silence with *Babushka* and then sit in silence with her while she watches the news and endless crime dramas. In the evenings, she calls her friends and speaks in Russian, but I can't understand her. She sounds different with them, pleasant and happy. The moment she hangs up her phone and notices me staring, a cold expression descends over her features, and I wonder why she hates me so much.

After I've stayed with her for two weeks, I hear her asking for my dad in English. I'm doing my homework at the kitchen table, and I look across the room to where she is leaning against the sink.

"Tell Aran to come and take her. I do not want her." A long pause. She must be speaking to the housekeeper. "Then put Aran on!"

I cringe and bow my head, pretending to be absorbed in my spelling assignment. I know I'm not welcome here. She could at least wait until I'm in bed so I don't have to have my nose shoved in it.

Dad must get on the phone as *Babushka* switches to rapid, angry Russian. They go back and forth for several minutes, and then *Babushka* curses and hangs up the phone.

Then she does a very strange thing.

The fury melts from her face, and she smiles.

At *me*.

Not a cruel smile, either. A smile filled with warmth and...love?

Babushka comes over to me and draws out the chair beside me with a shaking hand and sits down. Are those tears swimming in her washed-out blue-green eyes?

She pulls a handkerchief out of her sleeve and dabs her cheek, half crying, half laughing. "So many sleepless nights not knowing if it would work. Thank God, Lilia. You can stay."

I stare at her, not understanding anything that's happening, least of all the soft, gentle expression on my hard and bitter *Babushka's* face. I feel like this is how she used to look at me before my mother died, but the memory is hazy.

Babushka gets up and moves around the kitchen, making tea in a pot and getting a biscuit tin from the pantry. She pours black tea into gold and glass *podstakannik*, her beautiful Russian tea glasses, and sets one and a plate of jam tarts in front of me.

"Eat, *kroshka*," she says with a smile.

Sweetie. Isn't that what she used to call me? I haven't heard that word in such a long time. I stare at the jam tarts, filled with gleaming raspberry jam and looking delicious and perfect, but I don't dare reach out for one, fearing my hand will be slapped away.

"Your *papa* told me that you are not allowed home. He is ashamed."

A sob rises in my throat. I struggle to hold it down but my chest convulses. To my surprise, pain fills *Babushka's* eyes.

She reaches out and touches my cheek, and I flinch, waiting for the strike, but she only caresses me softly.

"Thank God," she whispers. "Come here, *kroshka*. Today is a happy day."

She opens her arms to me, but I just stare at her. "But you hate me."

Babushka's smile grows sad. "I have been cruel since your mother died. A horrible, mean old woman."

I wonder if this is a trick question, and I don't answer. *Babushka* takes a sip of her tea.

"Your *papa* never liked his mother-in-law. *Babushka* saw everything he did to Lilia. Made her bruised. Made her cry." Her face transforms in anger at the memory. "I knew he would turn on you one day. He beat poor Alyona—" She stops with a hitch in her voice.

Alyona, my mother. *Babushka* takes a deep, steadying breath, her hand clenched on her tea glass. "I knew you would need to be out from that man's roof one day. I knew it the day you turned six and he sent a little girl to her room without birthday cake."

The memory comes back to me in a blaze of emotion. *Babushka* singing *Happy Birthday* in Russian and me clapping along. I got so excited that I knocked over my glass of red soda and it soaked into the white carpet. Dad leapt to his feet and raised his hand to me. *Babushka* grabbed his wrist, and he growled at her and then shouted at me to go to my room.

The next time I saw *Babushka*, she was cold and mean and criticized everything I did.

"If you were older, I would have told you the day he left you here. You must call your father every day and cry to him that you wanted to go home, I would have said. He needed to believe that you are miserable here."

I stare at *Babushka*. "You wanted me to be miserable here?"

"*Da*."

"And you wanted Dad to know this?"

"*Da*."

"Have you really hated me all these years?"

Her face creases with emotion and she cups my cheek again. "No, *kroshka*. It broke my heart to be cruel to you. Every time I saw you, I came home and cried, begging your mother to forgive me. Do you know why?"

She pushes my glass of tea closer and regards me hopefully.

I think carefully and take a sip of my tea. She always loved me, but for years and years, she pretended to detest me, waiting for the day that Dad would abandon me here as punishment. I compare the warm and smiling woman I remember from years ago to the one sitting before me now, and my heart bursts with happiness as I realize they're the same.

"You wanted me out from under his roof and safely here with you. You needed me to call Dad every day and cry to him that I wanted to come home so he believed he was punishing me?"

"*Da, kroshka*. You are a sweet girl, and I wasn't sure if you could give him tears if I asked you to pretend."

Lie to Dad. Make him believe that I was miserable here so I could stay forever, with someone who really loves me. I picture myself crying down the phone to Dad and begging to come home while *Babushka* smiled and encouraged me. Acting my little heart out for him.

"I could have done that," I whisper, staring into the middle distance. If it meant I could be with someone who loves me instead of someone who hates me, I could have cried him a river.

Babushka gives me an appraising look, and a proud smile breaks over her face. "I think you are right. You are a quick learner, like your mother. Have a jam tart."

A warm feeling spreads through me as I pick up a tart and bite into it. I'm like my mother? No one ever talks to me about Mom or says that I'm like her.

Babushka watches me eat, and then she beams at me. I remember that I haven't said thank you and mumble it quickly around the crumbs.

"Thank you, *Babushka*."

"Call me *Babulya*. You always used to call me *Babulya*."

Granny, not the more formal Grandmother. "Thank you, *Babulya*," I say with a smile.

Babulya takes a sip of her tea and suddenly grows serious. "This is a lesson for you, *kroshka*. You are a clever girl, and I know you will remember what I have to say. There will be times in your life when you will want something so badly that your heart will ache and you will be willing to get down on your knees and beg. You must never do this. There will be moments when someone is standing in your way or holding cruelty over your head to make you do what they want you to do. What must you do instead?"

"I should...I should find a way to get what I want for myself?" I guess.

"*Da*. But how, Lilia?"

Babulya's eyes are sparkling and expectant. There's something she wants me to understand but I don't know what it is.

"Pretend that I don't want it, like you did with me?" I guess.

"That will work sometimes," *Babulya* agrees with a nod. "But other times, it will not be enough. Everyone has weaknesses. Your father. Your future husband. His family. His enemies. Your enemies. Your future will be filled with adversaries because of who your mother married, God rest her soul."

No one's ever talked to me like this, like I have a brain between my ears. *Babulya* is preparing me for unknown battles. I try to imagine what they will be, but I can't fathom anything except a vague sense of dread that it has something to do with what the news is saying about Dad.

"This is not your *babulya* telling you to become a liar. This is survival, *kroshka*. Your life is in danger? You fight like a tigress to be free, but you use your wits as well as your claws."

For years, *Babulya* pretended to hate me, waiting for the day that she could save me from my father's wrath. Years of patience and heartache and she never showed one crack. Could I do that? Desperately want something while pretending I don't, and all the while never know if my plan will work or blow up in my face?

There might come a time when I have no choice. I have no power over my father and men like him. I only have my wits.

"I understand, *Babulya*."

"Good," she says with a sharp nod, and relaxes finally. "Have another jam tart, and then it's time to go to bed."

From that day, everything changes.

When I get up in the mornings, *Babulya* is always there to greet me. After school, she welcomes me home with a smile. She wants to know about my day, and she cares if I'm happy or sad, frustrated or hopeful.

We have no money except for the allowance that Dad grudgingly pays *Babulya,* and he's not giving her more even though she has to pay for all my food and clothes and school supplies as well as her own needs. Insulin is fiendishly expensive, and I worry that she won't be able to buy any because of me.

Money is one thing I've never had to think about. Everything I've ever wanted has been given to me, and I have never had to dread an electricity bill or worry about the unexpected costs of new shoes and school fees. Suddenly my eleven-year-old mind is teeming with information I've never had to know before. The price of bread. Where to buy cheap cuts of meat and on what days. How to make a small portion of leftovers into a meal for two people.

After a few weeks, I notice that *Babulya's* not wearing as many gold rings or necklaces as she used to, and she confessed she sold most of them and put the money in the bank. I cry when I find out because that jewelry belonged to her mother, and she brought it all the way from Russia.

"Don't cry," she tells me sternly. "What is jewelry but something pretty to be sold on a rainy day?"

I nod, still feeling wretched because I know it's not just jewelry to her. "I'd sell Mom's locket to help, but a boy took it from me and threw it down a drain."

Babulya hugs me fiercely, and I remember the lesson she taught me about using my head to get what I want.

"If I called Dad and cried to him that we need money,

maybe we could get your jewel—"

"No," *Babulya* says sharply, holding up a finger. "We do not beg, and we will not poke the bear. We are left in peace, and that is worth more than everything in the world."

~

How right *Babulya* is. Peace truly is everything, but I slowly forgot that as time passed. Every year, my father fades further in my memory until he seems like a bad childhood dream. I never hear from him on my birthday or at Christmas. Occasionally, *Babulya* and I see his car while we are out shopping, and we run into a store or hide behind a pillar. She calls it *hiding from the bear,* and it makes me feel like we're living in a folktale.

When I'm seventeen, *Babulya* and I drive into the city to see a matinee for her birthday. It's a stinking, hot day, and we walk through the park afterward, drinking fresh lemonade. I sit sloppily on a bench, waiting for her to use the public restrooms, when a woman approaches me with a smile and looks me over carefully. I scowl up at her through the sharp sunshine, wondering why she's being so rude. "Can I help you?"

The woman hands me her card and introduces herself. I read the card while fanning myself with my T-shirt.

"Model agent?" I say blankly. "What's a model agent?"

She's in the middle of explaining when *Babulya* marches back to us and demands to know why I'm talking to strangers in the park. The woman introduces herself and hands over another card.

Babulya glares at her suspiciously. "Are you a criminal?"

She doesn't seem offended by the question and explains where she works and what kind of models she represents. Mostly runway models, and I have "the look," whatever that means.

"We will use the email to search for you and check that you are not a criminal," *Babulya* tells her severely.

"You mean the internet," I tell her with a smile.

"Whatever it is, we will use it. We are not stupid. Come, Lilia."

All the way home, I stare at the card and wonder what this means. I'm aware of runway models from pictures in magazines, and I have the vague impression that they live in places like Paris and look serious and intimidating as they march along in rows. I think that they must make good money, though, and I start to get excited.

"Do you think that woman really wants me to be a model?"

Babulya is matter-of-fact, gesturing as she drives. "Of course she wants you. You are a beautiful girl. But she might be a criminal."

"Do you think I should be a model?"

"I think it is good for my Lilia to have a career. Do you want to be a model?"

I don't know. But I'm interested to find out more.

After much searching online and many calls to the scouts' office to try and catch them in a lie, *Babulya* finally lets me go to the woman's office for a meeting. She comes with me, of course, and examines everyone we see in the building with a critical eye, from the security guard to the receptionist and everyone in the waiting room.

As we sit in plush white chairs, I stare at the other women

my age or a year or two older. Are they real models, or are they hopefuls like me? Some of them are glamorous and I'm certain they must get plenty of work. Others seem as ordinary as I feel, wearing old clothes and biting their nails.

"Are you new?" a woman in joggers and a baseball cap asks me with a smile.

"First meeting. What about you?"

"I've been signed for nearly a year." She shows me some pictures on her phone from her last show and I goggle at how striking she looks.

"The makeup. The clothes. The lighting." The woman shrugs. "It transforms you. You'll see."

Excitement thrums through me. Without my father's overbearing presence in my life, I've been free, but I've also struggled to understand who I am. Maybe this is the answer. I'll become a chameleon; someone who is savage and intimidating one day and sweet and benevolent the next. We've never had the money to buy me a lot of clothes and makeup, and I've watched the girls at school apply lipstick and show off their new dresses and designer jeans with envy. Deep down, I know such things are frivolous, but I want my chance to play with pretty things, too. Just for a little while.

When we're called into the model scout's office, *Babulya* marches straight up to her and declares, "My *vnuchka* is the only *vnuchka* I have, and if anyone treats her badly, I will come down here and make them sorry."

"I assure you, your...granddaughter?" she guesses the meaning of *vnuchka*, looking at me, and I nod, "is in safe hands with us. We have years of experience working with young women."

The woman patiently explains what she's offering and

how she can launch my career, and it's dizzying to realize she's offering to represent me. *Me.* I'm valued by someone. I possess something that other people don't. It doesn't matter that I'm poor or that I was abandoned by my father. He took away my pride in myself and my sense of security, but he can't take what this woman is offering me.

The meeting concludes with a photographer taking my headshots and body shots, and then we're free to go. The agent says she'll handle the rest.

Babulya and I leave the office in stunned silence. I sneak sideways looks at her, desperate for her to say something. Hoping that she approves and believes that this could work out for me.

"She reminds me of my aunt Irina. Always making wild plans." *Babulya* sniffs. "But plans that unfold like magic."

Three weeks later, I receive an email about my first booking. A small runway show in Miami. I've never been out of the state before and I envision beautiful, sandy beaches, fruity drinks, and hot sunshine. There's not much time until I'm eighteen and I graduate, which makes everything much less complicated as I don't need to choose between my exams and my new job. I float through the rest of the school year feeling like I'm living someone else's life. Whenever someone asks me what I'm doing after I graduate, I tell them I'm going to try runway modeling. There are lots of raised eyebrows and disbelieving looks. If I hadn't seen the email, I don't think I would have believed it myself.

On the very last day of school, I practically skip home, I'm that excited. I'm my own woman. Every hour of every day now belongs to me and what I want. Golden possibilities unfold before me. Seeing the world. Discovering who I am and what I can do. Making enough money so that *Babulya* can buy the good cuts of meat and never worry about affording insulin ever again.

As I burst through the front door, I shout happily for *Babulya*. "I'm home! Can we drink tea from the *podstakannik*? Today is a special—"

I skid to a halt as I see who is seated at the kitchen table.

"Occasion," I finish in a whisper.

The man occupying one of *Babulya's* wooden chairs seems too big and hard to be allowed in this small, slightly shabby, feminine space. Against the backdrop of the faded wildflower wallpaper, he looks twice as mean as he used to, even though he's smiling at me.

But it's not a pleasant smile.

"Hello, Lilia. Congratulations on your last day of school." Dad speaks these words carelessly as his eyes run over me, examining the young woman I've turned into since the day he abandoned me.

Babulya has her back pressed against the sink and her hands are clenching each other so tightly that they're turning white. She gives me a desperate, frightened look, and I know she's as bewildered as I am.

How dare Dad push his way in here after leaving me.

"Hello," I reply coldly, pleased that my voice sounds so steady even though my insides are quaking. "Thank you for the congratulations. You can go now."

"I want to talk to you, Lilia."

Anger rushes up and bursts forth from my mouth. "I have nothing to say to you! You're not welcome in this house. You're not my father and you haven't been since the day you abandoned me here."

Dad's jaw bunches with fury as he struggles to maintain his temper. "I see *Babushka* has enjoyed poisoning you against me. You always were a spiteful old woman," he flings at her.

"*Babulya* has done nothing but love me and take care of me. Every drop of poison that runs in my veins, you put there yourself when you hit me and screamed at me and called me names."

He slams his fist on the table, and the remains of *Babulya's* last cup of tea and teapot jump and rattle. "I will discipline my own child as I see fit."

There are silver threads in his hair, new lines on his face, and a few more pounds at his midsection, but he is the same man he always was. I don't know why he's come here today, but it's not to offer his only child an olive branch or to apologize for how he treated me in the past.

"I'm not your child anymore. I'm eighteen, and I don't answer to you."

"Sit down so I can talk to you. Stop acting like a brat."

I fold my arms. "No. I mean—"

My heart pounds in my chest and I suddenly feel flustered. I was saying no to sitting down and talking, but now I do sound like a brat. I refuse to think of this man as a father, so why is it he can make me feel like a child?

"This isn't your house. You don't give orders here. We do, and *Babulya* and I want you to get out."

"Are you going to act this way in front of your husband?" Dad asks.

I give a hollow laugh. "Husband? I'm not getting married." Not anytime soon, anyway, and any man I fall in love with is going to be on my side when I'm upset, not Dad's.

Above all, he's going to have nothing whatsoever in common with my father.

"Yes, you are. It's all arranged."

I feel like I've been deluged in icy cold water. He has to be joking. Marriages aren't things that are arranged these day. We aren't living in medieval Russia, and I'm not some privileged daughter of the aristocracy. I'm the dirt-poor and estranged daughter of a mafia asshole.

But as I stare at my father, I remember that he never tells jokes and he's clearly not joking now.

Babulya steps forward, shaking with rage and fear. "You are not doing to Lilia what my husband did to my Alyona. I kept my mouth shut like a good wife back then, but I will not be silent—"

"Shut up, old woman," Dad roars at her, making her flinch. "This is between me and my daughter."

"You want to know what I think of this arrangement?" I challenge him. "I don't want it. I'm going to be a runway model. I've already booked my first job and it's all arranged."

Dad leaps to his feet and his chair hits the wall. "Like hell you are! Put your body on sale? Parade around with nothing on while everyone calls you a cheap little whore?"

"That's not what modeling is, Dad." Tears of rage glitter on my lashes and blur him in my vision. I wish I could wash him away with my tears, but when I blink, he's still there. "Besides, what's wrong with being a whore or a stripper? At least that way I'd be in control of my own destiny."

Dad pounds around the table and grabs hold of my upper arm in a brutal grip. *Babulya* screams and scrabbles in her pocket for her phone. "I am calling the police!"

Dad points a finger at her and roars, "Put that fucking

phone down or I'll kill you, old woman. I swear I will."

Babulya slowly lowers her phone, her hand shaking and her face pale with terror.

Dad is breathing hard and he's red in the face. "Lilia and I are going into the garden for a private chat, and then I'm leaving. No one has to lose their fucking heads, all right? Fucking women," he growls, stalking toward the back door and dragging me with him.

I writhe and struggle every step of the way, finally breaking free when we're standing by the birdbath. I rub my upper arm, which I'm sure is going to bruise from his cruel fingers.

"In three days' time," Dad says through clenched teeth, "you are going to meet with Ivan Kalashnik. You are going to smile at him and act like a polite, humble, and obedient daughter. In three weeks, I will walk you down the aisle and you are going to marry him. This is non-negotiable, Lilia. Ivan and I have a deal."

I stop rubbing my arm and lift my chin. "You are deluded. Screw your deal."

Dad gazes around the garden and then over at the house. "It would be a shame if your *babulya* was thrown out of this house and had no money and nowhere to go. Diabetes is a cruel disease and her medication is expensive. I pay for that shit. Maybe I'll just...stop."

There's a loud buzzing in my ears and I can't feel the tips of my fingers. "You monster."

"You're the one who doesn't love her grandmother." Dad is smiling now, the cruel, twisted smile of a boy pulling wings from butterflies.

"I have a job. I'll make my own money. I'll make sure

Babulya has everything she needs."

Dad pretends to muse on this. "Even if you could, terrible accidents can happen to old women left all on their own. Slips. Falls. Such a pity you won't be around to take care of her."

The world slides out of focus as I imagine one of Dad's thugs coming into *Babulya's* house and breaking her legs the moment I board the plane to Miami. "Even you wouldn't stoop to that."

Dad's eyes glitter with malice and triumph. "I can, Lilia. And I would. I've already promised you to Ivan Kalashnik, and I will lose face if I go back on my word. I never break my word." He pushes his face close to mine and snarls, "But I will break your fucking bones if you don't do as I say. See how many catwalks you can prance down then."

He turns on his heel and marches back into the house. A moment later, I hear the front door slam.

I sink down onto the grass, gripping the birdbath with all my strength to keep from fainting. Just minutes ago, I was the happiest I've ever been in my life. Out of nowhere, iron bars have slammed down around me, caging me in. I'm still sitting on the ground when I feel gentle hands on my shoulders, helping me to my feet. *Babulya* has tears running down her face.

"Did he hurt you, *kroshka?*"

I stare around her beautiful garden, at the flowers and fluttering birds that were my comfort in the days after I first came to live here. I thought this place was my punishment, but it's been my sanctuary away from a cruel and unfeeling world. Am I really going to be forced back into that world, this time as a mafia bride instead of a mafia daughter?

"What am I going to do?"

"I don't know, *kroshka*. But whatever happens, you are not going to marry anyone of your father's choosing. Come inside, and I will make tea and we will find a way out of this."

I follow her back to the kitchen, but each of my steps are leaden with dread.

Three days later, an expensive black car pulls up in front of the house. I watch through the curtains as Dad gets out of the back seat holding a carrier bag and smooths his tie down his chest.

The doorbell rings and *Babulya* clutches my arm, shaking her head at me.

"We are not here," she whispers urgently. "Do not answer that door."

He's not going to just go away. I tug myself free and open it, dread turning the blood in my veins to ice.

Dad shoves the carrier bag at me. "You have one hour, and one chance. If you do not do what I say..." He trails off meaningfully and glances into the house. Then he turns and goes back to his car.

I glare at his back, hating the very sight of him. Fear and anger compete for which emotion can claim my heart. I want to scream and throw things, and I want to cower under my bed in fright.

I've thought of nothing else but my arranged marriage for the last three days. I have no friend I can turn to for help. No powerful person who can make Dad back down. There's only me and *Babulya*, and we have nothing but the threadbare clothes we stand up in. The police will not protect us from mere threats, especially when they hear who is making them.

Brazhensky family? Solve your own problems. You cause us enough.

When it comes to the police, I loathe them as much as they hate my family. I'm trapped. My shoulders slump and I turn around, defeated.

In my bedroom, I pull a flimsy, silky dress from the carrier bag, one that looks and feels expensive. It's probably worth more than my whole wardrobe. The cheap clothes that I've been forced to wear year after year suddenly aren't good enough for Dad.

Anger flares through me as I throw the dress onto my bed and put on a plain black cotton dress from my wardrobe. *Babulya* mended the belt loops when they ripped off. The fabric waist tie was lost long ago, and I've been using a black shoelace instead.

I kiss *Babulya* goodbye and walk quickly out of the house before she can stop me.

Dad glares at me as I come down the front path. "What's wrong with the dress I bought you?"

I give him a flat, angry look. "You said you wanted me humble. I'm humble."

He doesn't argue with that.

We drive in silence to my suitor's house, who I learn is called Ivan Kalashnik. He's shorter than me and almost as old as Dad. He looks at my tits more than he looks in my eyes. Not that I have much to look at, and I'm forcibly reminded of Seth, the boy who tormented me in the street years ago by staring at my chest, because he could, not because he wanted to.

I'm silent.

I'm dull.

I'm *obedient*.

Everything I wanted I can feel slipping away from me as I sit on the expensive sofa in Ivan's living room while he and Dad talk.

Hopelessness smothers me like a blanket, but there's one small consolation. *Babulya* will be taken care of. Even if Dad stops her allowance, I'll surely be able to persuade my husband to allow me to take care of one sick old woman.

But I'll have to be good for my husband if I want anything in return. Cook for him like my mother and *Babulya* taught me. Keep the house clean. Let him fuck me. Have his children. That might be another small consolation my sad future holds. Babies would make *Babulya* smile. They would make me smile, too. If I have to be married, then at least I'll know that my children will be safe in his house and will never want for anything, including my love.

The world closes in around me, feeling smaller and smaller until I'm suffocating and barely able to breathe.

Three weeks later, it's my wedding day.

The church doors open wide, and Dad walks me down the aisle. Hundreds of people I don't know or barely remember turn to stare at me, the eighteen-year-old bride of Ivan Kalashnik.

Standing at the altar is a man I barely know. A man just like my father. A man who will probably treat me just like he did.

I plaster a smile to my face and pretend this is what I want. That my feet are moving of my own free will, and I'm not being dragged down the aisle.

Right into a gilded cage.

18

Lilia

Present day

The women's accusing words sink into my bones. Every time I swallow, my throat throbs and the tattoo of the hangman's noose burns around my neck.

What would *Babulya* have done in my situation? She's a woman who knows how to play the long game so well that she went against every instinct she had and was cruel to her own granddaughter, year after year. How it must have broken her heart to treat her dead daughter's child so coldly. How she must have cried after pinching and prodding me and making sure that I was terrified of her. How much she must have wished to take me in her arms and love me openly. Her heart was steel. She locked it up tight until the day she'd waited so long for finally dawned. And she won. For seven wonderful years, I was loved.

Somewhere up above me, Konstantin, Elyah, and Kirill are discussing what to do with treacherous Number Eleven. Elyah is going to fight for me. He will insist that I am his and I was never part of this twisted beauty pageant.

Kirill will want whichever outcome causes me the most pain and gives him the most malicious pleasure.

Konstantin... I can't predict what Konstantin will do. I'm not sure that even he knows what he wants to do with me.

"But that doesn't matter, does it, *Babulya*?" I whisper in the dark.

I get to my feet and reach beneath my thin foam mattress, feeling around for a split in the fabric. A moment later, I draw out a small, flat object. Konstantin was so eager to prove to everyone that I'm a stupid, needy whore. What fun he had, fucking me and humiliating me. I think that must have been the highlight of his week. Stupid Number Eleven laid her clothes across his desk as she undressed for him, and after, when the *Pakhan* had broken her, she bundled her clothes up in her arms and hurried out.

Taking her passport with her.

I feel around inside the hem of my dress. I carefully unpicked a small section with my fingernails while I was waiting to be called in to be executed. Today was going to be the day that Elyah would kill me. His honor as a man had to be satisfied, and so I satisfied it. I stepped off the table and his rope tightened savagely around my neck. I was seconds away from death.

But he brought me back. He held me close and made love to me. He spilled words of love into my mouth and allowed Lilia Aranova to touch his clothes and slip her treacherous fingers into his pockets.

All the while he argued with Konstantin, I kept my fists tightly closed. Angry, upset Lilia. The moment I left the judging room, I clutched the hem of my dress in despair.

I draw the key out of its hiding place, and it gleams in the dim light. You taught me well, *Babulya*.

She turned her heart cold to get what she wanted, while I made mine daring for Kirill, needy for Konstantin, and fiery hot for Elyah. Every day, I watched those men and learned what I could about them. I discovered what they needed to make them feel like they were getting the better of me. While Number Eleven was getting everything she wanted.

The dress I'm wearing has a belt and I use it to lash my passport against my ribs, out of sight. Reaching through the bars, I slip the key I stole from Elyah's pants into the lock and turn it. I've never appreciated it until this moment, but there's something blissful about the way a key moves in a lock. The resistance of the metal as the catches and springs move against the key. Then the resistance is gone, and the lock pops open.

With the merest press of my fingers, the door swings silently open, and I take my first step outside this cage as a free woman.

The other contestants are still awake, and they see someone moving outside the cells.

"What's going on?"

"Is a guard unlocking a cell?"

"Who's out of their cage?"

I take another step toward freedom, and another, and then turn to face the women. There are half a dozen gasps, and someone cries, "Lilia!"

I put my finger to my lips, warning them to be silent as I

hold up the key for all of them to see. It catches in the light, sparkling and precious. Far more precious than pink diamonds.

"Does anyone still wish to call me a stupid little whore?" I call softly.

Fifteen pairs of eyes stare back at me in shock.

I walk slowly along the row to cages six and seven. Marija and Madison are sitting on their beds, gripping their mattresses as hatred mars their beautiful faces. I'm their jailer now, come to gloat over my victory.

"I told you everything I did up there was to help us down here. I told you that every word I spoke to those men and every look I gave them was a lie, but you wouldn't believe me."

"I suppose you're going to take your revenge by letting us rot in here," Madison snarls.

I glance up the row of cages, at the desperate fingers curled around the bars. Some of the women are sobbing quietly and pleading with me in whispers.

I could do that. I could leave them all behind to be punished for my escape in my stead. But that was never my plan. No matter how many of these women stepped on me and ground me into the dust, they were just trying to survive.

"That's not the revenge I want." I slip the key into the lock on Madison's cage and unlock it. Her face slackens with shock, and she jumps to her feet.

One by one, I unlock every cage in the cellar, holding my finger to my lips as I go to remind the women to stay silent. Every single one of them is able to walk out on her own two feet. Even Hedda, though she accepts Deja's arm around her waist for support. Her broken nose looks painful and she's going to need a doctor.

Marija stares around at everyone, unable to comprehend what's happening. She turns to me and whispers, "You really meant what you said, but I didn't trust you. I was horrible to you." She purses her lips. "I don't know if I would have let you out if our positions were reversed."

"Yes, you would have. Besides, I need you. Someone has to help these women get out of here, and you're the strongest. You're going to lead them."

Her eyebrows fly up. "Me? What about you?"

I glance toward the stairs and back at her. "I have unfinished business with our captors."

Our captors have to pay for what they've done to us. Proud Russian blood runs in my veins, just as it does in theirs. It's not enough that Konstantin loses face tonight, outwitted by the women he locked in cages. He needs to lose everything. Total humiliation.

"You're crazy," she breathes, but there's admiration in her eyes.

The women gather in a semicircle facing me, shivering and afraid, but hopeful for the very first time. They know what's up there. Guards. Dogs. Machine guns. We're going to face them all before dawn comes.

Tears are pouring down Alejandra's face. "I said horrible things about you. I thought—"

"Lilia, how did you get that key?" Nicoletta asks.

I shake my head. "It doesn't matter now and there isn't time to explain. I need all of you to get ready. Wait here."

I motion for the women to press themselves against the

far wall so that anyone peering down the stairs will see only a row of cells. It's dark enough that you can't tell they're empty.

Carefully, I creep to the top of the stairs and look around. There's just one bored-looking guard in the corridor, humming to himself. As I watch, he reaches behind himself and scratches his ass.

Back at the bottom of the stairs, I conceal myself against the wall by the doorway and whisper, "Someone call out for help."

Deja cups her hands around her mouth and screams, "Hedda! Something's wrong with Number Sixteen. I think she's dying. Someone help!"

"What are you going to do?" Olivia whispers at my shoulder.

"Tackle him," I breathe, pressing my back against the wall and listening to the guard coming down the stairs.

The moment he appears, I lunge for him. To my amazement, two more women jump on him as well, and we all fall into a heap. He manages one shout and nearly throws us off, but Olivia and I hold him down and strip him of his weapons while Daiyu uses the belt from her dress to gag him. Upstairs and far away in the garden, a German Shepherd heard the man's shout and starts barking.

Shit.

I hand Elyah's key to Olivia and pick up the assault rifle. "Drag him into a cell, quickly. Everyone else, get back against the wall out of sight."

Olivia and Daiyu lock him in, and Olivia picks up the guard's handgun with a look in her eyes like she means to use it.

I clutch her wrist. "Are you sure?"

She nods, taking up position by the door. There isn't time to argue with her as I can hear the dogs getting closer.

I make my way back up the stairs and listen. The guards are in the garden and they're going to come through the side door. I crouch behind it, both hands gripping the weapon. My upper lip is slick with nervous sweat, and I swipe it away with my tongue.

I don't have to wait long for the sound of footsteps on gravel. The door opens and the guards step inside, one with a German Shepherd on a leash that's barking hysterically.

"Andrei?" a guard calls.

I step out of the shadows and shove the point of my weapon into the man's neck. "Don't move. Drop your weapons."

Over their shoulder, Olivia has appeared at the bottom of the steps, pointing her gun at the men like a goddamn badass. I don't know if the men understand me or can even hear me over the dog, but I make my meaning clear by grabbing the strap of his assault rifle and tugging on it. Both men hesitate, look from me to the other woman, and then do as I say, laying their guns on the ground.

"Do you speak English?"

The guard's eyes widen but he doesn't reply, and I have to jab him viciously with the gun. "I will fucking shoot you. I said, do you understand me?"

He nods quickly.

"Good. Shut that dog up, now. You have two seconds."

He makes placating gestures and utters a few words to the dog, and it calms down.

"Walk. Down the steps."

"You're a dead woman," he seethes.

So I've heard. But I'm still breathing, and now I have a machine gun.

The women tie gags around the men's mouths and force them into separate cells, one with the dog.

I smile at the one who told me I was a dead woman. "Don't worry about me, boys. Worry about your own skins when your *Pakhan* finds out you've been disarmed and locked up by a group of runway models."

That's three guards taken care of, but there are definitely more lurking around. Should we try to run now, or should we wait a few minutes to make sure no one else is coming? If Konstantin, Elyah, or Kirill show up, they're not going to quietly step into a cell just because we're holding a few guns.

"Marija?" I call, and I motion her to follow me up the stairs. We crouch together by the door to the garden. It's dark outside now and the warm evening air washes over us.

"I think the coast is clear, but you'll have to be quick." I point across the shadowy garden. "Head that way down to the water. Everyone is going to follow you. There are cliffs to the left, so head to the right. Wade around the edge of the lake until you reach another house. Ask the residents for help or break in and call the police. Do you think you can do it?"

Marija stares into the darkness for a few seconds, and then she nods. "Yes. We'll do it. But what about you?"

"I'm staying for a little longer. It's not enough that I escape," I reply, and I hear the venom in my voice. Every electric shock they gave us. Every beating. Poor dead Valentina, the first Number Eleven. The terror. The cold. The cages. Their hands on me. Their mouths on me. Their lust. Their cruelty. These men are going to pay.

"I'm getting revenge for all of us."

Marija's expression hardens. "Then I'm coming with you."

I clutch her arm. "These women are scared and I'm sure some of them can't swim. They need you. Link arms in the water and lead them through the shallows. You'll do whatever it takes to save them, I know you will."

"But why do you believe that when I was going to sell you all out?" she blurts.

That's why she needs to be the one to do this. Marija is going to look back on this week and feel so many things, and she needs to remember herself as a hero, not a traitor. Besides, she'll be ruthless in the face of any obstacles and that's what these women need right now. "I know you're a better person than the one thing you said in a moment of terror."

She blinks rapidly like she's trying not to cry. "All right. But you—"

Konstantin could realize at any moment that there are guards missing. "There's no time. Get all the women up here and just go."

Marija's jaw works like she wants to argue with me, and then she shakes her head slowly. Not in defiance, but regret. "Why do I have the horrible feeling you're about to sacrifice yourself for our sakes? After all this, don't you dare die."

I check the safety is off the machine gun I'm holding. "I have no intention of dying. Don't think about me a moment longer and go get those women."

But she still hesitates. "Lilia, the other night, Kirill came down to the cells and—"

"I said go!" Cold sweat has broken out all over me. I don't give a damn what that psycho did this week. Whatever it was,

I'm paying him back for it now by destroying his *Pakhan's* precious pageant.

Marija nods and dashes back down the stairs.

I stay crouched by the door with the gun in my hands as fifteen women crouch-walk up and file silently past me and into the darkness. I whisper encouraging words to each one as they go. "That's right, keep your head down. Everything's going to be okay. You'll be back with your families soon. Follow Marija and do whatever she says. She's going to get you out of here."

As Olivia reaches me, the coppery-eyed young woman looks stricken. "You're coming with us, aren't you?"

"I'll be right behind you, but don't wait for me," I say, telling a little white lie. I don't know where I'm going or what will happen next, but I'll probably never see her again.

As if she knows that, too, Olivia gives me a swift hug, tears in her eyes as she whispers. "You did it, Number Eleven. I knew you would."

I hug Olivia back. Behind her, Celeste is shivering and crying and barely seems to know which way is up, let alone who she's following.

"You guys at the back, Marija will need you to make sure Hedda is able to keep up. Can you do that, Celeste?"

I know she's scared, but she needs to keep it together for just a little longer. Giving her something to do might help her focus.

Deja nods and takes Celeste's and Hedda's hands. "Come on, guys, we can do it."

With my heart beating in my throat, I watch the final three women cross the threshold and follow the others into the darkened garden. Hope is a fierce dagger in my heart, and

I send up a wish to the stars. *Please, all of you get to safety and live long and happy lives.* I watch as Deja, Celeste, and Hedda disappear among the bushes. Silence falls.

And then there was one.

I turn and stare down the corridor toward the villa. Konstantin, Elyah, and Kirill are somewhere in there, and so is the prize that I plan on snatching from under their noses. I'm taking all of Konstantin's jewels from him. Every last one of them.

With the machine gun strap heavy on my shoulder and the grip sweaty in my hands, I edge my way down the corridor and into the villa. There are voices coming from one direction that I suspect might be the kitchen. The voices sound like our captors having a heated discussion.

I head the other way, looking for the bedrooms. The first one I look into has an unmade bed and a discarded T-shirt on the floor. That probably belongs to Kirill. The next one is scrupulously neat with just an empty backpack laying on a chest of drawers. It feels like Elyah's room, and I move on. The last has several suitcases by the door and two neck ties hanging over the back of a chair.

On proud display on his dresser is the fourteen-million-dollar pink diamond tiara.

My mouth falls open when I see it just sitting there. Konstantin is so arrogant, so sure of his power, that he didn't feel the need to lock such a precious object away.

I step into the room and lay the machine gun on the bed. The tiara is more beautiful than I remember, and the diamonds glitter madly. I can't imagine the lengths that Konstantin went through to source them. Did he make the tiara with love, thinking of his future wife, or only with hate? What did he want the woman he crowned with this incredible object to feel after a week of torment at his hands?

I pick the tiara up and turn it in my fingers, dazzled by the sight. If I hadn't just ruined his whole pageant, would I have won? He wanted a woman who was obedient, loyal, and strong.

My lips curve into a smile. I may be strong, I may be loyal to those who deserve it, but I'm also the most disobedient bitch he's ever laid eyes on.

The bedroom door suddenly opens. I whirl around, feeling like a child caught with her hand in the cookie jar. All the air is sucked from the room as I stare into a pair of startled gray eyes. The sight of me standing in his bedroom holding his tiara has short-circuited Konstantin's brain.

"You," he seethes, and lunges for me, his face blazing with fury.

I dive for the open window and leap through it, Konstantin's fingers snatching at empty air.

His bellow follows me into the darkness. "Guards! Where are you? Lilia, don't you fucking run from me."

I race around the side of the villa, my heart thundering loud enough that it might shatter my rib cage. I hear the dual thud of Konstantin's feet hitting the grass behind me, but he's already lost sight of me in the darkness. I keep running, the tiara clutched tight in my hand.

Straight into a broad, hard chest.

The scent of familiar cologne fills my nose. I stare up at the fair-haired man, my voice locked in my throat. His blue eyes burn in the dark and there's a gun in his hand. Just like Konstantin, Elyah stares at me for several frozen seconds before his gaze drops to the tiara in my fist. Hurt and realization starts to bleed into his shock.

An invisible knife twists in my heart as I back away from him. "Don't come after me, please, Elyah."

I turn and run, praying I'm not about to feel a bullet between my shoulder blades. An electric second passes. Then another. He's not going to shoot. He's letting me go.

Elyah's shout rends the night. "Konstantin, Kirill, she is here. She is in the garden."

Disappointment plummets over me. I round another corner of the villa and then press my back against the wall as Elyah shouts in Russian. I listen for several panicked heartbeats. I can't stay here. Any moment now, they're going to regroup and split up. I wanted to head for the main gates and find a way through or over them, but that way is cut off now. If I head for the lake's edge, I'll be leading Konstantin, Elyah, and Kirill straight toward the escaping women.

There's only one choice left. One direction to run to escape. The one place they won't expect me to try for freedom because it means broken bones. Drowning. Death.

I push away from the wall and pump my arms as I run, heading straight for the cliffs with the tiara clutched tightly in my fist. Please let the women make it away safely. Even if I don't and this tiara and I end up at the bottom of the lake, my spirit will rest easily knowing that Konstantin lost his jewels. Every last one of them.

"Lilia!" There's the sound of one set of pounding footsteps behind me and I recognize Konstantin's voice. He seems to realize where I'm going as he snarls, "Don't be fucking stupid."

I skid to a stop at the cliff's edge, so close that I have to wildly circle my arms to stop myself from falling over the edge into the void beyond. The night is so dark that I can't see the water and I don't know how far down it is.

When I glance over my shoulder, Konstantin has slowed his run to a walk, and as he breathes hard to catch his breath, he's smiling. His scarred face is full of triumph. "There's nowhere left for you to run, *milaya*."

I straighten up and turn to face him, the wind catching my hair and the hem of my dress. "I decide what happens next. Not you."

Slowly and deliberately, looking Konstantin in the eyes, I raise the tiara up into the night sky and place it carefully on my head. It has little silver teeth that push into my hair and grip it tight.

"Perfect," Konstantin breathes, gazing at me with naked admiration. "As if it were made for you."

There's just the two of us out here on the cliff's edge, standing in the moonlight. Konstantin's eyes are glittering as he gazes hungrily at me, as if seeing me for the first time. The Number Eleven he knew wasn't real. I haven't been real for a long time. Lilia Brazhensky was a scared, defiant little girl. Lilia Kalashnik tried to force herself to be a living doll, not a person. Lilia Aranova thought she found freedom in the arms of a dangerous man. Yulia Petrova was a terrified fugitive. Now, at long last, I'm me.

Just Lilia.

And Lilia is more than enough.

I lift my chin, feeling the weight of the precious stones atop my head. With my right foot, I carefully feel behind me for the cliff's edge. There's inky darkness below and the sound of waves lapping. The water could be deep and dark, or shallow and crowded with rocks.

As I edge back, Konstantin lets out a burst of derisive laughter. "After all this, are you going to die, Lilia? Don't throw yourself away. A woman like you is worth her weight in diamonds."

"I've ruined your pageant. All the women have escaped."

"You, crowned with that tiara. You're all I want. You're all I've ever needed." He holds out his hand, beckoning me with his fingers like I'm an overexcited child who doesn't want to leave the amusement park at the end of a long day.

I would rather fall into hot lava than take his hand.

He glances past me, down at the darkness below, all the while edging closer. "Do you know what it's like to drown, Lilia? It's pain like no other. Your body is suddenly your worst enemy. The ally you thought you could count on no matter what is desperate to turn on you. One breath. That's all it craves. One deadly breath."

As I continue to edge toward the cliff, the smile drains from his face.

"You're going to die, Lilia. Don't be stupid."

Ever since I awoke locked in a cage in this man's cellar, my only thought has been to escape. Nothing Konstantin could say or do could persuade me to take his hand. I'm leaving, and I'm taking his diamonds with me.

"Don't you get it yet? If I'm going to die, then it's going to be on my terms. Who knows? Maybe I'll live. I've survived crueler men than you."

Over his shoulder, I can see two more figures running toward us in the darkness. Someone is shouting at me to stop.

Someone who sounds like Elyah, more frantic than I've ever heard him before.

I have mere seconds, and I cast one final look at Konstantin. "I will burn like acid in your heart every time you think of me."

Konstantin's face hardens to an expression of pure fury. He lunges for me, but he's too late. I turn, raise my arms above my head with my fingertips touching together, and plunge headlong into darkness. Swan diving into the unknown.

A heartbroken shout reaches my ears and is lost on the rushing wind. My eyes are tightly closed. I'm putting my life into fate's hands, hoping desperately that I can't have survived this long only to be battered to death on rocks.

The past few days flash before my eyes. The huddled, frightened women. Their strength. Their defiance. Their friendship. Kirill gazing up at me with shock as I snarl at him to pull the trigger. Elyah's mouth pressing against mine, whispering words of love as he moves inside me. Konstantin watching me with a new expression in his hungry gray eyes.

Everything rushes faster and faster until I can't hear, can't think, can't breathe. All my senses scream—

I plunge into darkness, and oblivion swallows me up.

19

Konstantin

I barely hear the splash as she enters the water, the blood is roaring that hard in my ears. I rush to the edge of the cliff and peer down into nothingness.

She jumped.

She fucking *jumped*.

I haven't had a clear thought in my head since the moment I walked into my bedroom and saw her standing there holding my tiara. Lilia fucking Aranova, the one I was going to enjoy exploring afresh now that it seemed she wasn't the deceitful bitch Elyah had always claimed. The woman I brought to her knees just the day before.

Or I thought I had. Now I realize what she was really after. Her goddamn passport which was laying on the desk.

As I watched her through the two-way mirror today, I couldn't take my eyes off her. I wanted to know what kind of woman goes to her death so calmly, so magnificently, that she throws herself to her doom rather than beg to be saved.

And now she's done it again.

Kirill and Elyah skid to a halt beside me, both of them breathing hard.

"*Lilia.*" Elyah calls her name at the top of his lungs, frantically pacing up and down and searching for any sign of her. He grabs my shoulders, his eyes wild. "You have to go after her. I cannot swim. *I cannot fucking swim.*"

Kirill scours the darkness. "That crazy bitch. There could be fucking rocks down there."

There are no rocks. I heard her plunge into deep water. Every nerve is screaming at me to turn my back on Lilia and let her die for humiliating me like this. Her arms must be nearly useless after being strung up by her wrists last night. I warned her what it would feel like to drown. Even now, after all these years, I can feel the frantic burn of my lungs as I fight not to take that deadly breath.

Lilia is like me. She won't stop fighting until she's got nothing left. I tear off my shirt and kick off my shoes. Am I going to save her? Or am I going to pull her out of that water only to throttle her with my bare hands? I don't know. I'll make up my mind when I'm looking into those depthless sea-green eyes.

"Get the boat," I order the other two. "Turn on the floodlights and find her."

Without waiting for their reply, I shove my pants down, step out of them, and launch myself off the cliff and into the water.

My dive was perfect, but the water still hits like a motherfucker. I plunge down and down into the darkness. Terror floods my brain as water rushes into my ears and up my nose. I fucking hate the water. It blinds you. It deafens you. It weakens and confuses. The freezing temperature slices into my muscles, and I don't know which way is up and which is down. My lungs start to burn, and I'm a boy of fifteen once more with my brother's hands around my throat, holding me beneath the surface, his savage expression blurred and warped as the water churns above me. Behind him, Mother watches on impassively, keeping her dress carefully out of the way of any splashes.

I'm not a boy. I'm a man. I'm Konstantin fucking Zhukov, *Pakhan* of the London Vanavora Bratva. I force myself to be still and use the only sense on which I can rely. Streams of bubbles rush up my chest.

Up.

That way.

I kick my legs and carve my arms through the water, and a moment later I break the surface with a gasp. Far to my right I can hear the throbbing of the boat's engine and a powerful light sweeps across the lake.

There's only one place Lilia could have swum to for safety and that's straight ahead. I kick my legs and arc my arms through the water in powerful strokes, swimming freestyle. This is how I've kept fit all these years despite my absolute dread of water. Or because of it, to spite my brother and the way he nearly killed me. Lilia is weighed down by a dress with a tiara on her head. Perhaps she swam in her daddy's pool, but she's no match for me.

Every few minutes, I stop and call out for her and listen for any sound in return. My certainty starts to dim as the temperature of my body plummets. Where is she?

Where fucking is she?

The boat's engine cuts out.

"Elyah!" I call across the water.

His shout echoes back, "Have you got her?"

Shit. Maybe she's dead at the bottom of the lake already. The shore isn't far away. I drag myself out of the water and up onto the stones, my chest heaving and my limbs like rubber. I force myself to my feet and gaze across the smooth surface. In the distance, Elyah and Kirill are sweeping the searchlight across the water. Three furious, dangerous men who have survived turf wars, power struggles, and prison, but we can't find one woman.

A bitter taste fills my mouth as I realize I grossly underestimated Lilia Aranova. Is she an innocent woman, or the deceitful bitch Elyah claimed she was all along? A femme fatale who doesn't blink at playing Russian roulette with her pussy, or a woman who's never known pleasure in a man's arms? A fiercely proud woman, or just a good actor?

Is she all those things?

Or none of them?

I feel like I'm in the black water again, not knowing which way is up. Floundering in darkness. Just yesterday, as I cupped her delicate chin as lust and fury pounded through me, she gazed up at me like I was her whole world. Now she's stolen mine from me. In one night, she's ripped everything I built these past eight months right out from beneath me.

I call out to her, my powerful voice rippling across the lake. "I will find you, *milaya*. I will discover who you really are, and you will pay for this. You will regret the day you crossed me."

EPILOGUE

Lilia

BRITISH MODEL SURVIVES TERRIFYING WEEK IN ITALIAN NIGHTMARE ORDEAL.
Runway model Olivia Sparrow survived for six days locked in a cage while armed guards with dogs and machine guns kept her and fifteen other women prisoner.

Sparrow spoke out yesterday about her terrifying ordeal, five weeks after her daring escape from a cage in the cellar of a Lake Como villa. "They wanted us to compete in this twisted game. It was like a reality TV show but one where we were going to die if we were eliminated."

Sparrow appeared emotional but composed as she related how she and fifteen other women were forced to wear a sash and parade around in dresses during pageant-like "events" for three mysterious Russian men. "They claimed it was so one of them could choose a wife, but I think they were sex traffickers and it was some fun for them before we were sold."

The women were tortured with electric shocks and threatened repeatedly with beatings. One sustained injuries to her face. A seventeenth woman was murdered in front of the others.

Sparrow broke down in tears as she described the women's daring escape under the cover of darkness. Forming a human chain, they waded and swam through the waters of Lake Como to safety while another woman created a distraction.

"I could hear a boat engine and the men shouting, but it got farther and farther away from us. It was all because of Lilia. I don't know anything about her. I don't even know if she made it out alive. Number Eleven saved us, and I'll never forget her."

All sixteen women were models abducted from the streets during Milan Fashion Week, where they were walking the runways for some of the world's most prestigious designers.

Italian police made a statement earlier this month that several women were reported missing, but that they found no signs of foul play at the time. They are now working with Interpol to investigate the kidnappings and murder.

This isn't the first time Olivia Sparrow's family has endured the trauma of a missing person. Two years ago, Olivia's sister Beatrix vanished and was never seen again.

The whereabouts of the men who held the women captive are unknown. Seven more women sought help at police stations or at their embassies in Italy and have since returned home. The whereabouts of the other eight women, including the enigmatic Number Eleven, remains a mystery.

. . .

I FIGHT back tears as I slide my burner phone back into my pocket. My hand shakes as I reach for my espresso, the cup rattling against its saucer. I let it go and smooth my sweaty palms over my jeans, relief cascading through me.

Hedda's story was the first one to break while she was still in the hospital in Italy. Then the British tabloids found out about Olivia and have probably been hounding her for a press conference ever since. Deja gave a written statement to the US media but refused to speak on camera. None of the stories told me what I really wanted to know until today, that it wasn't all for nothing, screwing those men, being tortured, being hated and ridiculed.

They made it.

They all made it out alive.

I wish I could see all their beautiful, smiling faces so I could remember them that way and not huddled in cages, scared, and frightened. Some of the women might still be gathering their courage to come forward. Some, I may never hear from again. A pang goes through my heart, but I can understand why they might prefer to just disappear after the ordeal they suffered.

It's a beautiful morning in Trieste, and I adjust my large sunglasses on my face. The sunlight filters through the trees in the piazza as I sit at a café table with an espresso. Five weeks have passed since I dove off the cliff wearing Konstantin's diamond tiara and into the unknown. Trieste is where I've gone to ground. The Italian city is bound by sea on one side and hills on the other. The ancient streets are a warren of Roman arches and medieval cobblestones, red-roofed residences butting up against modern apartment buildings. The

Slovenian border is just a handful of miles away. I could drive to Croatia or Austria in just a few hours. Hopping on a ferry or a train, I could disappear into Hungary, Bosnia and Herzegovina, Albania, or Greece. An airplane could whisk me to London, Frankfurt, or Valencia.

I'm only three hundred miles from Lake Como, but all these international borders are what makes Trieste so appealing. I have a dozen escape routes planned and I'm ready to flee at a moment's notice should I catch sight of a familiar tattooed hand or a pair of cold gray eyes.

But the main thing that's keeping me here isn't the geography. It's the Venetian mafia.

I take out my phone and glance one more time at Olivia's picture from the news conference, wishing there were some way of letting her know I'm alive and in one piece, but it's too dangerous. For her and for me.

Tapping on the screen, I perform the same browser search that I have every day since my escape: "pink diamond." Then I scroll through the results.

Pink diamond buying guide

Shop pink diamonds

Why are pink diamonds more expensive?

Ten things to know about pink diamonds

I breathe a small sigh of relief and take a sip of my espresso. There are no recent hits for stolen pink diamonds or news about the tiara that Konstantin had made for the pageant. I've been braced for stories about the pink diamonds being splashed across the news sites, making the prize I stole from Konstantin both notorious and worthless. I'll never be able to sell the diamonds legitimately, but even criminals won't touch them if they know they're stolen from the Bratva.

After diving into the waters of Lake Como, I struck out blindly in the darkness and swam and swam. My arms burned. My body was exhausted and starving, and I was running on adrenaline and fear. I didn't dare stop until my feet hit the lake bottom and I crawled my way up the bank. A few hundred feet away, a boat with a powerful light was sweeping the water. As I dragged myself into some bushes, Konstantin called out to me.

I will find you, milaya. I will discover who you really are, and you will pay for this. You will regret the day you crossed me.

I couldn't see him in the darkness, but he was close enough that he might have heard me breathing, and I clamped my hands over my mouth and curled into a ball, shaking with exhaustion and fear. I didn't have anything left in me to run, and I abandoned myself to fate.

His fury crackled through the night. Several terrifying minutes passed before his footsteps crunched on stones and faded into the darkness.

I think I must have fallen asleep or passed out, and when I woke it was still dark. The tiara was still on my head, and I tore it from my hair. I stole a backpack, men's clothes, and a bicycle from a nearby villa, prying off the bike's reflectors and only traveling at night. By day, I hid in the bushes on the side of the road. As much as it terrified me to be among people, I knew I had to reach a city.

Three days after the pageant, I hid in an abandoned farm building on the outskirts of Trieste and used a pair of pliers to pull three plain diamonds from Konstantin's hateful crown. I pawned them in Trieste and then hid in a hotel, living off room service.

I would have preferred to stay in hiding. I was safe while I was hidden. The four walls of my room and the heavy curtains protected me from the prying eyes of every Russian man who wishes to get their brutal hands on me. I knew I couldn't stay there forever, that Konstantin might track me here from Lake Como, but what forced me onto the streets wasn't anyone in the Bratva. It was the Mafia Veneta, the Venetian mafia, the dominant criminal organization in northern Italy, similar to the Cosa Nostra, but rumored to be more violent.

I need them. After all, the enemy of my enemy is my friend, and I need cash if I'm going to disappear once and for all.

If I searched Trieste hard enough, I might be able to find a Russian mafia contact who would be interested in pink diamonds, but how long would it be until Konstantin heard about the precious stones hitting the Russian black market? The Mafia Veneta has nothing to do with the Bratva and will —I hope—be interested in sixteen exquisite pink diamonds and a handful of plain ones at a bargain price. It would be nice to get eight million dollars, but I'll settle for six. They'll be able to smell my desperation.

I sit out front of cafés. I watch. I wait. Across the piazza is an Italian restaurant. Tough-looking men walk in and out of a side door every day, including a local jeweler. I've followed him to his shop, and I'm convinced that not every piece that enters his shop is legitimate.

I can't just walk in and ask him if the Venetian mafia would like to buy fourteen million dollars' worth of pink diamonds at a bargain price. I need a plan, so until I have one, all I can do is sit here and drink espresso. Until I think of something, the diamonds are hidden somewhere safe. The tiara's frame I bent out of recognizable shape and threw into a dumpster.

I felt sick as I counted the pink diamonds. Sixteen of them. Sixteen contestants. What a twisted sense of fun Konstantin has. I wonder what gave him the idea for the pageant in the first place. In the world of elite marriages between criminals, arrangements aren't unusual. I had my own arranged marriage, and it was as transactional and loveless as they come. Konstantin probably wanted one of his own, but he wasn't satisfied with the women who were on offer. I imagine him sitting in a deep armchair, swirling a glass of whisky, his head filled with dark, disturbing thoughts of women forced to perform for him.

I remember his hungry expression as he watched me crown myself with his tiara as the wind whipped around us on the cliff's edge.

You wearing that tiara. You're all I want. You're all I've ever needed.

I've been trying to fathom what he meant by that. He had no patience for the contestants who cried and fell apart, or the ones who had no self-control and screamed or froze up. What drives a man to do what Konstantin did to us? He hunted us down like prey, but with mind tricks and games instead of guns through a forest.

If I'd taken his hand and walked into his arms that night, would I be his queen now, or his slave? Memories of the achingly sweet way he kissed the tears from my cheeks haunt my nights. The pain he put me through. The dizzying rush of release. My torturer, and my savior. One hand punishing while the other worships.

You are perfect, Lilia Aranova. You are my angel. My precious.

I blink and give myself a shake. Konstantin's twisted love is even worse than Elyah's violent adoration and Kirill's perversion. Konstantin didn't lift me up. He forced me to submit to him, and once he'd proved his dominance, he shoved me to the ground like a broken doll. I had to make him believe he'd broken me. I had to throw myself from the judging table with the noose around my neck. I needed to let them win. Everything I did in that room was a means to an end, but those men stole a piece of my soul just the same.

And Kirill? I remember his shocked face when I shouted at him to pull the trigger, and I can't help but smile. How delicious it was to ruffle his hair and squeeze his muscular shoulders with my thighs. Whenever I see a shadow moving out of the corner of my eyes, I wonder if it's Kirill that's come to wind a garrote around my throat again and whisper vicious words of hate in my ear as he slowly strangles me. A swift, hot pang goes through me at the thought of him thrusting deep inside me just as I fall into unconsciousness.

"You're fucking crazy, Lilia," I whisper to myself. I need to get a grip before I do something insane like stick my hand down my pants and get myself off to the thought of all of them screwing me. Or become so distracted and careless that I allow them to find me.

Whatever my fantasies might tell me, my head knows that Konstantin, Elyah, and Kirill are hunting me right this moment. Not only did I destroy the pageant and shatter their egos, but I stole fourteen million dollars' worth of pink diamonds from them. If they catch me, they will rip my spine from my living body and beat me to death with it.

I know this, and yet I can't rid myself of one lingering

thought. That I never felt more alive than when I was handing those dangerous men their goddamn asses.

I lock that in my heart and throw away the key. It's my little secret, and I'll take it to the grave.

I check the time on my phone and make my usual call at this time.

An accented voice speaks on the other end. "Hello?"

"It's me. *Ya tebya lyublyu.*" *I love you.*

I never say my name. I never wait for her to reply. *Babulya* knows something happened, that I'm alive and in Trieste. I can't risk telling her anything about what I plan to do next or where I might go. Between my father and Konstantin, it's not safe for me to confide in anyone or ask for help. I'm completely on my own.

Before I can hang up, *Babulya* cries, "Come home, *kroshka*. You will be safe here."

Home. The word echoes with longing through my mind. After so many long and lonely months, I'd give anything to sit at *Babulya's* kitchen table and eat blinis with her.

"You're the one who told me to leave," I remind her. I say it gently, not wanting to accuse her of anything. In the days after Ivan was killed, the rumors spread through the Russian community that I had betrayed him to the feds. She came to see me at Dad's, and she was terrified for my safety.

"I thought you would be better off out in the world, away from your father and the men who wanted you dead. But something terrible happened, didn't it? There's something you're not telling me."

There's so much that I'm not telling her. If I lead Konstantin to *Babulya*, I'll never forgive myself. "I'm sorry. I'll call you tomorrow."

I hang up and press my fingers against my eyes beneath my sunglasses. *Babulya* doesn't know anything that's happened. She thinks I'm merely hiding from Dad, not three more mafia assholes who are capable of cruelty ten times worse than anything my father could dream up. With a lump in my throat, I stand from the café table and reach for my bag.

A wave of nausea and dizziness slams into me, and I stagger into a chair at the next table, grabbing hold of it before I can fall over.

"*Scusa*," I say to the woman sitting at the table who's looked up from her coffee.

She's an older woman, a local, and she rakes me with shrewd eyes. "*Quante settimane?*"

"I'm sorry, I don't speak Italian."

"You are pregnant?"

I look down to where my palm is flattened against my belly and take it away with a laugh. "Oh, no, I'm not…"

The words die on my lips along with my smile, and I feel my face drain of color.

Pregnant.

When was my last period? I've bought myself a toothbrush, toothpaste, sun cream, even some nail clippers, but nothing has sent me to the supermarket for tampons in the past five weeks.

The woman beams at me and nods, as if she's discovered something wonderful. "*Congratulazioni.*"

"I'm not pregnant," I mutter, grabbing my bag and walking quickly away. My feet thud on the sidewalk as my blood roars in my ears. I'm *not*. I refuse. It's absolutely impossible.

Okay, it's technically possible after having sex with both Konstantin and Elyah, but it's not freaking *possible*. I won't even contemplate it's a possibility, even though I haven't had my...the last time I had my period was...

My feet drag on the sidewalk, and I stop dead. My last period was nearly three weeks before I arrived in Milan. I remember, because I was worried that I might be bloated on the catwalk so I double-checked the dates. I'm not a little bit late.

I'm four fucking weeks late.

"No," I moan, clutching my stomach. "Please, God, no. Not now. Not like this. Not *them*."

If I am pregnant, what the hell am I going to do? Do I want the child? I walk mindlessly down the street, my eyes blurry and my head buzzing with white noise. I can't have Elyah's or Konstantin's baby. I *can't*. It's too crazy. I'm on the run and I can barely keep myself safe, let alone a vulnerable little baby. How would I get it a birth certificate? A passport? What if someone takes the child from me and hurts it to get revenge on me? I picture Konstantin and Elyah ripping the baby from my arms. They wouldn't do that, would they, to their own son or daughter?

My throat constricts and my chest feels tight, and I realize I'm about to fall headlong into a full-blown panic attack. I reach out blindly and brace my hand against a stone wall as spots rush and dance in my vision. Breathe, Lilia. First things first. Get a test.

Then panic, in the privacy of your hotel room.

Looking around me, I see I've walked away from the main street, and turn back to find a pharmacy. After a few gestures at my stomach, I make the attendant understand what I need and hand over some folded euros. With the pregnancy test shoved deep in my handbag, I head for my hotel. It's just a handful of blocks away and I keep my sunglasses on until I'm in the elevator heading up to my floor.

It's dark inside my room. I close and lock the door and reach for the slot with my plastic door card that will switch on the lights.

"You really thought you could outrun me, Lilia?"

Fear thrills through me and I whip around. A deep voice with a heavy Russian accent rumbles in the darkness. Someone is sitting in the armchair on the other side of the room, his body in shadows and the outline of his head and long legs just visible.

Alarm bells ring in my head. My chest fills with panic, and I can't feel the tips of my fingers.

With a shaking hand, I shove the door key into the slot and the lights flick on. I see two of the coldest eyes I've ever known staring back at me.

I'm in the presence of a monster.

How did he find me? It should be impossible when I've been so careful. My hand flies protectively to my stomach and splays over something that I don't even know is there. Keeping it safe from *him*.

Two more men step into view, their eyes narrowed with hate. One has his tattooed hands thrust casually into his pants and a proud smirk on his lips.

Every nerve in my body screams at once.

Run.

The Pageant Duet concludes this summer with Crowned – pre-order now

DELETED SCENE

Dear Reader, we hate fade to black, don't we? I'm sure you noticed that there's something missing from the end of Chapter Ten, the scene where Kirill goes down into the cellar and pays a visit to Lilia.

This scene is vital for the events of *Crowned (Pageant, 2)*. It's also a scene that's against the 'Zon's terms of use. There are plenty of books with scenes like it available in the Kindle store, but plenty more books that have been banned for similar content. Authors can never predict which way the axe will fall. I like sleeping at night, and I also like to give proper warnings for you guys, so I cut the scene from the book and I'm making it available as a free download.

This download contains **content of a dark and sexual nature.** I can't spell it out for you here because the words I would need to use are against the terms of use as well. Please read the full content warning if you choose to download the scene.

Download the deleted scene and read the full content warning here: https://BookHip.com/NQLADFK

AUTHOR'S NOTE

I had the idea for *Pageant* several years ago, but as an M/F romance rather than a reverse harem. I was binging the *First Dates* UK reality TV show while doing a deep dive into the JonBenét Ramsey case. I was twelve in 1996 when the child beauty pageant star was killed, and her picture was on the cover of every supermarket magazine. It was one of those moments that crystalized in my innocent brain, and I understood that the world is a lot bigger and scarier than I realized. What is dark romance but our fears poured onto the page where we can confront them without them hurting us?

As I was writing the *Promised in Blood* series, the thought popped into my head that *Pageant* would make a fantastic reverse harem. The initial hero, Konstantin, would remain, but he would have two close friends by his side. Elyah and Kirill would be there to support their *Pakhan*, and they would all become so much more to the heroine than just her captors.

I watched all six seasons of *The Sopranos* while researching *Promised in Blood* and one of the side characters caught my attention. Tony's driver-slash-enforcer, Furio, arrives in America from Italy and efficiently beats people to death. Later in the show, he starts to fall for Tony's wife, Carmela, across her kitchen counter every morning as they drink coffee, and Furio fantasizes about killing his boss and running away with her. They never kiss in the show, so I poured all that unresolved sexual tension into Elyah and Lilia's relationship. I adore a fictional man who can crack skulls one minute and then pine for his true love the next.

Kirill is inspired by Ghostface in *Scream* (something else that's been hanging out in my brain rent-free since 1996) and Toji Fushiguro from the manga *Jujutsu Kaisen*. There is one supremely powerful jujitsu sorcerer, the one and only Satoru Gojo, and yet the infamous assassin Toji hands his ass to him while giving zero fucks. Ghostface also gives no fucks. If you've ever looked at a chaotic asshole killer and thought "a boyfriend!" then Kirill is for you.

I'd written two-thirds of *Pageant* before I found my "inspiration" for Konstantin. I wasn't drawn to any well-dressed, scarred kingpin types in popular media so I thought I would have to do without a muse. Then, up popped crime daddy Silco in Netflix's *Arcane* last November. I hated him for half the show, and then I had to eat my words as more of his character was revealed. Konstantin's past trauma (which you'll learn more about in *Crowned*) and his ideas about power pay homage to Silco.

Thank you to my beta readers Evva, Jesi, Darlene, Claris, and Arabella, and additional thanks to Evva for her music suggestions and Darlene for her deliciously dirty ideas and encouragement. As Elyah would say, Darlene, you are very bad girl.

Thank you, as always, to my wonderful editor Heather Fox for your support and insight.

Thank you to my proofreader and all-round amazing person Rumi Khan.

And thank you to you for reading *Pageant*. If you enjoyed this book, please consider leaving a review on Amazon and Goodreads.

Also by Lilith Vincent – a mafia reverse harem romance trilogy with all the steam, drama, and possessive, dangerous men...

Four ruthless men. A virgin mafia princess to unite them. But first, there will be blood.

On my seventeenth birthday, I learn a terrible secret about my family. My future is in the hands of four brutal men, and what awaits me at their hands is too terrible to imagine.

Four men who desire me. Four men who vow to possess me. Four men who think they can destroy me.

As the only daughter of Coldlake's mayor, I should be kept far, far out of their reach. Instead, I'm being thrown to them as a sacrifice. My father insists only one of them can marry me, but all of them vow to secure my promise.

A promise in blood.

They take. I bleed. Happy birthday to me.

Keep reading for the first two chapters of First Comes Blood.

FIRST COMES BLOOD

Chapter One

Chiara

In one moment, your entire world can shatter.

Irreparable.

Absolute.

Final.

I'm living in a perverse, inverted Cinderella tale of wealth, privilege, and protection. At the stroke of midnight, it's ripped away until I have nothing left. Not even a fairy godmother to pat my cheek and tell me it will be all right.

Nothing will be all right ever again. I belong to them now. My devil princes. Rulers of this city. Harbingers of disaster. Four men who are as dangerous as they are handsome and as brutal as sin. They hold my life in their hands, and I'm their plaything. A pawn to increase their power in this corrupt city.

They'll take what I love and make it bleed.

But none of this has happened yet. It's not quite midnight

on my birthday, and my virginal white dress is clean without even a spot of blood.

My life and heart are in one piece, for a few more hours at least.

Tick tock.

~

Candles light the dining room, and there are fresh flowers along every wall. The table has an elegant centerpiece in black and gold—Dad's signature colors—and gleams with crystal glasses, silver cutlery, and white bone china. The napkins resemble lotus flowers that are spreading their petals on each dinner plate.

Hanging from the ceiling is a baby blue banner that reads, *Seventeen today!*

It's affectionate and kitschy. That will be my mother's touch, and my heart lifts at the sight. Maybe this will be a happy night after all, and over dinner I can ask my father about going to college, and this time he won't walk away or change the subject.

There's no time for my mind to run away with this daydream because the moment I enter the room, I'm called to heel.

"Chiara, come here."

Obediently, I go and stand before my father. He's dressed in a tuxedo, spotlessly neat and groomed. His thick black hair is swept back, and a few silver threads glisten among the strands. He's a powerful man, in all senses. Big and imposing with flashing eyes and broad shoulders, but a powerful man politically, too. He's the Mayor of Coldlake. We're wealthy.

Influential. Untouchable. People like to tell lies about my family, but the rumors never stick. Bad things seem to happen to our enemies, and they just melt away.

Over his shoulder, Mom's hovering, her hands tightly clasping her elbows, her too-thin face even more gaunt than usual. She's wearing a long black evening gown, her blonde hair is coiffed, and she's sparkling with jewels, but her dark eyeshadow makes her face look like a skull.

A specter at the feast.

We studied *Macbeth* in school a few months ago, and the idea that a mournful spirit has come to my birthday party flits across my mind.

I flash Mom a reassuring smile while Dad inspects me from head to toe, from the tiara tucked into my blonde hair to the white chiffon gown that skims my body and pools at my feet. I don't know why he's looking at me like he's never seen this dress before. He chose it for me. I look like a sacrificial virgin on my seventeenth birthday.

I fiddle nervously with the diamond earrings hanging from my earlobes, and he slaps my hand away.

"Stop that. It makes you look nervous, and nerves are for the weak. Do you want to look weak?"

"In front of who?" I peer past him to the table, wondering who's coming to dinner. Dad's been dropping cryptic remarks about an honored guest for weeks but won't tell me anything else. I count the place settings on the oval mahogany table.

Me.

Mom.

Dad.

And...four more places?

Four? "Who's coming to dinner?"

Mom turns even paler, and her throat convulses as if she's going to be sick.

Dad's smile widens. Always that air of mystery. *Father knows best* and *don't ask questions*. Dad's the smartest man I know and there's nothing he won't do for us or the city of Coldlake. When there's a problem or a scandal, he tells us that everything will be fixed, and then it is. According to him, we don't need to know how the problems go away. We're too important for that sort of worry. We're his beautiful girls.

But this isn't politics. This is my birthday party.

"You'll find out." He glances at the clock on the wall. It's two minutes to eight. Two minutes until the mystery guests arrive. The ticking suddenly becomes menacing.

Tick tock.

"Chiara." Mom's voice is shaking. She comes forward to take my hands in hers, and they're cold and bony—like death.

"Please try to eat a little more, Mom," I whisper, gazing into her huge eyes. Lately, she seems to be fading away in front of me. "I worry that you're getting sick."

She squeezes my fingers. "Don't worry about me. You're seventeen today. It's time you learned the truth about—"

The doorbell rings, interrupting her. Dad gives Mom a warning look, and she backs off.

"The truth about what?" I look between my parents, but Dad won't answer, and Mom can't. She's always been in awe of Dad, but lately, she's been downright afraid.

Dad inspects the table, and his face transforms in disgust. He strides over and, with one sharp tug, rips the baby blue birthday banner down and crumples it in his fists.

Mom whimpers, and tears fill her eyes. I grab her hand

and hold it tightly, glaring at Dad's back as he throws the banner into a side room. Now nothing in the dining room is ours. It's all Dad's.

I've seen him like this on the eve of an election or a big rally, feverish with the ambition to win at all costs. His charisma means that everyone around him is swept up in his determination. Mom and I become the perfect, smiling wife and daughter. Mom will give speeches and I'll hold Dad's hand and wave to the crowds. As the longest serving mayor of Coldlake, Dad knows just what to say, just how to smile to convince the people that he's who they want. He's who they *need*.

And he is good for Coldlake. The city is thriving and the people are prospering. You only have to attend the parades or stand on Main Street on a Saturday and see all the happy people shopping and eating to know that this city is something special. Dad's something special.

But tonight, Dad's brought his ambition to my birthday party. As he gazes at me, I feel the full weight of his expectation.

All the hairs stand up on the back of my neck as I hear footsteps coming down the hall toward us, heavy and masculine. Not one set of feet. Many feet.

Before I can take another breath, four men enter the room—big, dangerous-looking men with forceful gazes and intent focus. They line up in a silent row, their expressions hostile. And yet, their faces are familiar. I realize with a shock that I know them. They're famous.

Or rather, infamous.

Standing on the left in a tuxedo like Dad's is Salvatore Fiore, chin lifted with arrogance as he straightens his cuffs, diamond cufflinks gleaming. His rich brown hair is swept back, and his strong jaw is cleanshaven. He owns half a dozen casinos in the city. Those are the legit ones, anyway. I hear that there are a dozen more where bets are placed on more than just blackjack.

Next to him is Vinicius Angeli, hands casually in his pants pockets, but his clever eyes alight with interest. Angeli, like *angel*. He's got a face like an angel, terrible in its golden beauty. He's how I imagine the Archangel Gabriel would look if he appeared before me. Rumors of dirty money swirl around him in the news. *Lots* of dirty money.

The third man is all in black, his shirt tight across his prodigious chest. He wears his black beard short and painstakingly neat. He's got better brows than I do. Black curls just touch the back of his collar, and his eyes are narrowed. Judgmental. His name comes to me after a moment. Cassius Ferragamo, nightclub owner. Strip club owner, too, it's rumored, ones that are filled with the most corrupt people in the city, night after night.

Finally, standing a little apart from the others is a pale-eyed, blond man in a suit with a skinny black tie. He has the tousled hair and muscular body of an Australian surfer, but his gaze is so, so cold that I feel the blood in my veins turning to ice. I'd know him anywhere. Lorenzo Scava. No one knows what the hell he does, but it's rumored to be brutal, dangerous, and highly illegal.

Everyone in Coldlake would recognize these men. Their pictures have all been in the news. They're criminals. Extortionists. Mobsters.

Killers.

And they've all come to my birthday party.

Vinicius' mouth quirks in a smile. "Hey, birthday girl," he purrs in a voice like black velvet. Then he winks.

My face reacts on its own, heat stealing over my cheeks. I attend Coldlake Girl's Catholic High School. The only males I come into contact with are family and the old priests. Now, four seethingly good-looking men are all eyeing me like they're wondering how I taste. I feel like I'm completely naked in front of them.

Salvatore finishes straightening his cuffs and steps confidently forward. "Happy birthday, Miss Romano."

As he places his hands on my shoulders, a hot spark that Vinicius kindled bursts into flame within my chest. Salvatore dips his head to kiss my cheeks, brisk at first, but after the first kiss, he slows right down. I'm out of my father's view thanks to Salvatore's massive back, and his fingers trail across my jaw as a devilish smile spreads over his face. My lips part in surprise, and his hand on my wrist suddenly tightens as his mouth descends on mine.

The seconds his lips are pressed against mine are eons long. Heat flows from him into me. Fire licks up my body. I shouldn't allow this to happen. Before I can put my hand against his chest and push him away, he breaks the kiss. His mouth leaves mine, but I can still feel it.

His eyebrows rise, teasing me. "Pretty girls need a birthday kiss."

"Fiore!" Dad barks.

But Salvatore doesn't move. He stays right where he is, his face inches from mine, his goading expression daring me to call for help. I close my lips and turn my face away, my insides churning.

What the hell is going on?

Salvatore stays where he is a few seconds longer, proving to Dad that he follows no one's orders, I suppose, and then steps aside.

I stay where I am as Dad greets the men, standing between them and me. For a moment, I wonder if he's outraged on my behalf that one of his guests kissed me within seconds of meeting me. He only looks mollified when they all greet him respectfully as Mayor Romano and shake his hand.

It's his reputation he's worried about, not mine.

The men are formally introduced to Mom and me in turn. Only Vinicius smiles at me. Salvatore looks amused, but not in a friendly way. Cassius and Lorenzo both regard me with glacial silence, the former as if I'm massively disappointing him and he's itching to correct me, and the latter like he's wondering whether to sever my limbs above the joint or below. Instead of dousing the heat inside me, their attention makes it burn harder. Every sensibility is telling me to fear these men, and on many levels, I do. Something deeper inside me, something more primal, wants to draw closer.

Dad calls them all businessmen. Important friends and colleagues. I might not know much about people and the world, but I can read. I hear what people say. "I think there's been some mistake."

Dad slips his hands into his trouser pockets, and his hooded gaze flashes with warning. "There's no mistake. They're your dinner guests. Be nice to your guests, Chiara."

"But they're all criminals!" I burst out.

Dad's jaw tightens. He exchanges glances with each of the four men, and then he smiles.

He *smiles*.

They smile too. Four treacherous smiles, all teeth and threat.

"And so?" Dad asks.

"And...we're not." My voice goes up at the end. We're not? Are we? People whisper about the Romano family, that Dad's got irons in many fires and fingers in many pies. Vague things. Nothing that makes the news. Not like these men who seem to be evading a new accusation every week.

There's a dark chuckle from Salvatore. "She's more innocent than I thought." His eyes travel over my lips, my breasts, my hips, as if he's dismantling my chiffon dress with his gaze. My lips are still burning from that kiss.

"Chiara, these are my dearest friends. Show some respect."

Dearest friends? These men? I've heard the accusations about my father, that he's got links to the underworld and friends in low places. Of course, I've had my suspicions...but Dad's always denied the rumors and called them ridiculous. He's my father, and I believe him. He's not the loving, affectionate man that some fathers are, and he expects a lot of Mom and me, but I've always believed he's an honest person. If you can't trust your own father, who can you trust?

Across the room, four men in suits watch me like hungry wolves.

"Sit." It's an order for Mom and me. Mom has her eyes on the floor as she walks quickly toward her chair. I know what she'd tell me if she could find her voice.

Just obey, Chiara. You know it's easier to do what he wants. It will all be over soon.

But I don't dare take my seat. If I sit down, then I'm going to hear terrible things. I know I am. There can be no innocent reason that these four men—these four notorious, dangerous men—are in our house tonight. I look desperately at my father. Dad, what have you done?

What did you promise them?

What do these men *want*?

Mom and Dad are at either end of the oval dining table. The four men stand along one side, and my solitary setting is opposite. They wait behind their chairs for the birthday girl to take her seat.

"Eleonora," Dad says lazily, not even looking at his wife. Mom hurries over to me and tries to push me into my chair, but I resist.

"Sit," she breathes in my ear. "Please, darling. Just get through this night. You're not of age, and nothing can happen to you." Her final unspoken word hangs between us as our terrified gazes meet.

Yet.

But something *will* happen to me. Something to do with me and these men. Not tonight, but soon.

"You don't need to be afraid. I'll find a way to help you before it's time, I promise," she whispers.

My knees weaken, and Mom steers me into my seat before going back to hers. In front of me, the men all sit down. Salvatore. Vinicius. Cassius. Lorenzo. They stare back at me. I feel like I'm being interviewed for a dangerous job I don't want.

Dad rings a bell, signaling the staff to come in with wine and starters. I sip from my sparkling water, trying to make sense of Mom's cryptic words. *I'll find a way to help you before it's time.* Time for what?

Dad and the men talk as Mom and I pick at our smoked

salmon slices. Real estate prices. The industrial developments down at the docks. The new nightclub that Cassius has opened. Dad congratulates them about their latest business ventures, and they smirk as they thank him for deals that have gone through. It sends a shiver down my spine to listen to them.

"Speaking of deals..." He glances at the four guests. "Which of you thinks you should be the one? We can discuss the details in private, but a lady likes to be courted." Dad indicates me with his wine glass and takes a large mouthful.

"Of course she does," Salvatore says, leaning back in his chair and regarding me. His arrogant smile snares my attention. "It should be me, obviously. I'm the richest—and the strongest."

It should be him who gets what? And why does money and strength matter? Salvatore has an aura of impeccable grooming and wealth about him, but I don't know if he means physically strongest or something else. Cassius, who looks like he could bench press a whole lot more, glances at Salvatore and makes a dismissive, "*Tch*," sound.

"Obviously you? Obviously nothing," cuts in Vinicius, and as he glances at me, I'm dazzled again by his good looks. "It will be me because I'm the handsomest and the cleverest."

At the far end of the table, Lorenzo has produced a knife from somewhere and is twirling it in his fingers. The point is wickedly sharp. Mom, who's closest to him, shrinks back in her seat, her shaking hand covering her throat.

I wish they'd all leave, but most of all, I wish Lorenzo Scava would disappear. His face doesn't betray anything, but I have the impression he's enjoying her fear.

"I'm the toughest. I'm unswerving in my duty to others,

and the duty they have to me." This is Cassius. His voice is accented as if he's spent several years or more in Italy. He addresses Dad, but then his attention turns to me as he lets his final words hang ominously in the air. A shiver goes through me. I hope he never has any expectations of me.

Salvatore looks down the table. "And you, Lorenzo?"

Lorenzo Scava acts as if he hasn't heard a word of what's been going on. He's still twisting that knife and flipping it across his knuckles while Mom looks more and more afraid.

My hands grip the napkin in my lap until I can't take it anymore. "Stop that!"

Lorenzo snatches the knife out of the air and pins me with a predatory look. I'm trapped in that pale gaze, and I can't move a muscle, even though every nerve is screaming at me, *run*. "It's simple. If I'm not the one, then you'll all regret it."

"*Cane pazzo*," Cassius mutters. *Mad dog*.

"The one what? What is going on?" I look desperately at Dad. If this is a business deal, then it's the strangest one I've ever heard.

At the head of the table, Dad rests his fists on the wood and smiles broadly at me. Anyone would think it's his birthday he's beaming so much. "Chiara. Tonight, you'll be promised to one of these men. On your eighteenth birthday, you'll become engaged, and when you're eighteen and one week, you'll marry, and the Romanos will be joined with one of the most important families in Coldlake."

Around the table, no one moves. Not even Mom. The room is so silent that I can hear the ticking of the clock. I'm the only one with her mouth open and her eyes wide. Everyone knew about this except me.

My four potential fiancés are drinking in my shock like it's the finest wine. Dad's put me on display before them and they're delighted with the goods.

My palms turn clammy and my breathing quickens. This is the future Dad planned for me all along. He's never been interested in discussing with me what I want because he's been envisioning me as the bride of one of these vicious men. He's always liked to brag that he makes the best business deals. Finds the best leverage. Dangles the juiciest incentives. Only this time, the deal isn't for real estate, or a redevelopment, or a trade deal.

The deal is me.

Tick tock.

FIRST COMES BLOOD

Chapter Two

Salvatore

"You want me to marry one of *these* men?"

Chiara Romano's beautiful face drains of color. I'm glad we're here when she first hears what her father wants. You can tell a lot from a person from how they handle a surprise.

Or in her case, a shock.

Her hands are clenched in her lap and her eyes are round. She's petite, almost doll-like with her long lashes and honey-gold hair. The diamonds in her ears and the tiara in her hair set off her fresh-faced beauty. Those lips of hers, though, they're something else. Lush and sweet and receptive to kisses. I wonder what else that mouth can do.

I glance at the others, and realize they're wondering the same thing. How much fun will Miss Romano be on her wedding night? We like a girl who will fight back.

Mayor Romano glowers at his daughter. "Yes, Chiara. Did

I not just spell it out for you? One of these men will be your husband. After tonight, you can consider yourself promised. When you marry in a year and a week, you'll leave this house and start a new life with your husband."

I gaze at my future bride over my wine glass, expecting the flood of tears to begin. I can't have a woman who's going to fall apart when she gets a fright. Cassius and Lorenzo enjoy a woman's tears, but if my wife cries, I'll have to beat it out of her.

Chiara's eyes are dry. "But why? This is like something out of the dark ages."

I put my wine glass down and lean forward. "It was kind of your parents to spare you from the truth for so long. Kind, but misguided. You were never going to have a choice, Chiara. People like us don't marry for love. We marry for power."

She turns her baby blue eyes on me, and her expression flickers with fear. Chiara Romano needs a better poker face. But that's all right. I'll teach her.

"People like us? But my family isn't like yours. We're not criminals."

On my left, Vinicius pretends to wince at her choice of words. "Please. We prefer the term *entrepreneur*."

"Speak for yourself," Cassius raps out. "I'm a businessman. These are my associates. I don't like your attitude, young lady."

Chiara breathes in sharply, as if Cassius' words have hit her like a whip. If she's already afraid, she won't like what he'll do to her as her husband.

Mayor Romano seems to feel like he's losing control of the conversation and raises his voice. "Where do you think the money comes from to put this roof over your head? Pay for that expensive school of yours? All your pretty clothes?"

"Your job as mayor."

Vinicius laughs. Cassius shakes his head with his brow furrowed. Lorenzo stares at Chiara with cold, hooded eyes. Opposite her husband, Mrs. Romano seems to have fled into the far reaches of her mind. I wonder if Chiara is like that. Weak and fragile.

We'll know by midnight. Each of us has a little present prepared for Miss Romano. If she breaks, then we walk away. Our world isn't for the weak.

"No, sweetheart." Mayor Romano's voice drips with condescension. "It's from the deals I make. The deals that keep this city thriving—with the help of these men, of course."

Lorenzo turns to gaze at the mayor and starts flipping his knife again. No one likes to be talked about like they're an afterthought, especially not us.

"You're going to be an important part of a deal with one of these men."

Vinicius touches the tip of his tongue to one of his pointed canines. "Just one of us? Can't we all have her?"

Cassius' eyes flare with interest. Lorenzo draws his thumbnail over his lower lip and gazes at Chiara like he's imagining something dark and dirty.

My smile widens. "Yes. Why don't we share her?"

Chiara's eyes couldn't hold any more confusion. Poor little lamb. I don't think she's ever been kissed before tonight, let alone imagined what four men at once could do with her. Only one of us can marry her, but we'll all share her, and show her what our world is really about.

The four of us. Brothers, in every way but blood.

The Mayor's lip curls. "I only have one daughter. I can only have one son-in-law."

I swirl my wine lazily in my glass and address my future wife. "One thing you should know. You won't ever come between the four of us. Nothing can alter our bond."

The tiniest of smirks flits across Romano's face and is gone. The mayor thinks he can use his daughter to drive a wedge between us. United, the four of us are stronger than he is. Divided, he can play us off against each other.

Chiara noticed her father's smirk. She regards me, and then all four of us, her gaze finally coming to rest on Lorenzo.

Her expression asks, *Your bond? Even with him?*

"Yes. Even this crazy asshole," Cassius growls, jerking his head at the blond man next to him.

Mrs. Romano sits up and clears her throat. "That's all very interesting, gentlemen. But I think you're forgetting one thing. This is Chiara's choice."

The mayor opens his mouth to contradict her, but I'm tired of hearing his voice. I want to speak to my bride. "All right, then. Who among us would you choose, Chiara? Which of us is your future husband?"

Vinicius casts me a smile and smooths his tie. He knows that for any sane girl the choice is between him and me, and he's better looking.

But looks are the least of what's important. I'm the smart choice. The *only* choice. I'll have her no matter who gets her in the end, but I want my name on that dotted line.

I wait, eyebrows raised.

"What? You want me to choose now?"

I want to hear who she *would* choose. It won't be up to

her, but I'd like to hear her say my name before the inevitable happens. It will make the whole business of marrying her less tearful and irritating if she doesn't need to be forced.

The silence around the table stretches. The ticking of the clock on the wall fills the room.

"I won't." Chiara whispers so softly that her lips barely move. She's staring straight ahead at us.

She dares defy *us*.

"Answer the question, Chiara," says Mayor Romano.

My eyes narrow. The only place a woman should put up a fight is in the bedroom. When she's ordered to do something, she needs to obey without question.

Chiara stands up, her chair scraping on the floor. Her face is flickering with powerful emotions. Without another word, she hurries from the room, her head down.

Mayor Romano starts to get to his feet, but I stand up first, buttoning my jacket. "I'll talk to her. She just needs some persuading."

I catch Vinicius' amused expression and Cassius' smirk. What? I can seem nice. Of the four of us, I'm the most convincing in that department, assuming the charade doesn't get dragged out and my patience worn through. Lorenzo twists his knife over his tattooed knuckles, and his eyes burn in the candlelight. His intent is clear. If I don't bring her to heel, he will.

The house is built around a central courtyard with a huge swimming pool lit up in the darkness. It's a mansion fit for a Hollywood movie star or Wall Street financier. A mayor shouldn't be able to afford this. It's almost as palatial as my own house, which should send alarm bells ringing among

Mayor Romano's constituents, considering my fortune has been built on spilled blood.

I find Chiara in a sitting room, the doors pulled back to let in the warm evening air. The room is dark, but she's luminous in her white dress. She has her back to me, head down, small fists clenched.

Silently, I come up behind her and stroke my fingers across her bare shoulders. Her skin is warm and smooth and feels electric against my own. "You ran out on your dinner guests, Chiara."

It takes all my self-control not to slide my hand around her throat and squeeze until she understands never to do such a thing again.

She turns to face me with a gasp, her eyes are huge and troubled. "I wish you'd all leave, please. There's been a misunderstanding."

A little child, hiding under her blankets and hoping the monsters will go away. My smile widens. "But I've got a present for you."

Chiara closes her mouth and swallows. "If it's another kiss I don't want it."

No? She might fear me, she might fear us, but she responded the moment I kissed her. Fear and desire twined together. It's an intoxicating blend.

I step toward her, enjoying how she steps back. This girl is going to make me fight for every inch of her body. I can't wait.

I take a flat velvet box out of my pocket and open it, revealing the diamond necklace within. It catches the light and sparkles enticingly.

She turns her face away. "No, thank you."

"It's your birthday present. I bought it especially for you."

Bought it. Took it from Vinicius as my cut from his last heist. He posed as the pilot of a billionaire's private plane and held everyone at gunpoint on a remote Venezuelan runway. He needed my international contacts to pay off the airport authorities, and so I got the necklace. I had to wash the blood off, first.

"If I accept your present, I'll be in your debt like my father is. That's it, isn't it? He owes you money and that's why all this is happening."

"If your father owed me money, I'd be coming for his blood, not his daughter, and I'd be brandishing guns, not diamond necklaces."

I move behind Chiara, drape the necklace around her neck and stroke her hair aside. My lips close to her ear, I whisper, "You have a lot to learn about the way the world works. When you marry me, I'll teach you."

I fasten the tiny clasp and admire the way the diamonds sparkle against her skin. Chiara has a beautiful, slender throat, and as I lean over her I want to run my tongue over her delicate skin and feel her pulse beating wildly. I imagine her face down on black sheets, naked except for this diamond necklace and completely at my mercy.

"I don't want anything from you. I don't want to be in your debt. I feel like you'll ask for things I won't want to give you."

"But I ask for so little." *Just your body and soul. Your cries for mercy. Your total obedience and your life in my hands, forever.*

Her fingers reach up to touch the diamonds around her throat. "What is it you do want?"

I put my hands on her shoulders and turn her to face me. "You."

Confusion flickers in those beautiful eyes, and her lower lip softens. I ache to lean down and nip it with my teeth.

"I've heard so many despicable things about you. Who are you really?"

"I'm a businessman. I own hotels. I run casinos." I stand behind her and point at three gleaming skyscrapers, just visible over the roof of her house. "That one's mine, and the two on either side, among many others."

My lips skim the shell of her ear as I talk, and I feel her shiver beneath my fingers.

"That's only part of the truth, isn't it?" she whispers.

"Clever girl. Shall I tell you the truth?"

She nods, still looking up at the glimmering buildings.

I slide my arm around her waist and pull her back against my chest. She stiffens and clutches my arm. "I win, at any cost. What I set my mind on, I get, including you, Chiara."

"I'm not a skyscraper, or my father. I can't be bought with promises and diamonds."

My composure cracks at her defiance. If she were looking into my eyes, she'd be backing away in fear right now. I stroke the diamonds around her neck and keep my voice soft. "No? And yet here you are, in my arms, wearing my diamonds."

"I'll take them off the second you're gone and throw them away."

Heat ripples through my muscles. She's just crossed the line from naïve to disrespectful. My hand drifts higher, stroking her throat. "You think you're not in danger in this house because your father's close by and it's your birthday. I gave you diamonds. I'm being *nice*. You've forgotten your manners, Chiara."

I grip her throat and squeeze. Her eyes fly open and she

grabs my wrist with both hands. Her body flails but I have her clenched tight against me.

Trapped.

Teeth bared, I growl in her ear, "I'll help you remember them. You don't talk back to me. You don't treat what I give you like dirt. I can get to you whenever I want. I can hurt you. I can hurt your mother. I can do whatever the fuck I want in this town, and no one, least of all your father, can stop me."

Chiara gives a strangled whimper, her heels hitting my shins.

"Don't let that pretty mouth of yours put a bullet in your head." I watch her as she struggles, her movements becoming more and more frantic. If she has any sense, she'll only have to hear this once. Finally, I release her and shove her away from me.

Chiara's hand flies to her throat as she doubles over, gasping for breath. I straighten my jacket and smooth my hair. I think she's learned her lesson.

"I can be your friend, or your worst nightmare. Happy birthday, Chiara."

Want to keep reading? The Promised in Blood trilogy is complete and available on Amazon now.

ABOUT THE AUTHOR

Lilith Vincent is a steamy mafia reverse harem author who believes in living on the wild side! Why choose one when you could choose them all.

Follow Lilith Vincent for news, teasers and freebies:

TikTok: https://www.tiktok.com/@lilithvincentauthor

Instagram: https://www.instagram.com/lilithvincentauthor/

Facebook Group: https://www.facebook.com/groups/649473483113116

Goodreads: https://www.goodreads.com/author/show/21460435.Lilith_Vincent

Amazon: https://www.amazon.com/Lilith-Vincent/e/B095M9KHS3

Newsletter: https://www.subscribepage.com/lilithvincent

Printed in Great Britain
by Amazon